He closed  the door partway and led her into the middle of the room.

Pain blazed in his eyes as he turned to her. "I need to apologize to you. I'm sorry I didn't believe you. On some level, I didn't want it to be true for selfish reasons. I don't know how to protect you two from a ghost. Protecting people is my job, and all my training is useless right now."

He was apologizing to *her*? After everything she'd done to him? The realization scraped her insides raw. "It's okay, Brett. I get it. And we'll figure this out, somehow. I just have to keep at it. There has to be more information out there—libraries, historical societies, maybe even some local history buffs. There are tons of cemeteries on Cape Cod. She could be in another town, or a little family plot. There has to be a record of her somewhere." She tipped her head toward the computer. "I just have to search harder."

His gaze followed her gesture, lingering on the desk. "This room brings back some memories." He touched her upper arm, trailing his fingers downward in a slow, agonizing caress. Stepping closer, he moved his other hand to her hip.

What was happening? She struggled to catch up to this sudden shift of reality. Not only was he touching her again, he was referencing their sexual exploits—a previously forbidden topic, according to the unspoken rules.

Her pulse skittered as she gazed up at him, speechless.

He pulled her closer. "I want you. Every…single…second…of the day."

Praise for Kathryn Knight

"*In GULL HARBOR*, [a #1 Kindle Bestseller], the author skillfully weaves the ghost story and romance from separate strands that eventually become entangled. Tension builds as Claire gets closer to learning two painful truths: about the ghost and about Max. There's a perfect blending of clues, hints, and foreshadowing to keep readers informed, but the story never veers into the predictable. Pace, plot, dialogue, and characters combine into a thrilling and thoroughly entertaining page-turner that should delight paranormal romance readers."

~MyShelf Reviews (Top Reviewer Pick)

~*~

DIVINE FALL

won a Best YA Romance Award in 2015

"This delicious YA novel was filled with love, rich in history, suspense, and enough twists to keep the reader turning the pages."

~BTS Reviews

Haunted Souls

by

Kathryn Knight

Haunted Souls

Cover Art by *Debbie Taylor*

The Wild Rose Press, Inc.
PO Box 708
Adams Basin, NY 14410-0708
Visit us at www.thewildrosepress.com

Publishing History
First Fantasy Rose Edition, 2016
Print ISBN 978-1-5092-0841-8
Digital ISBN 978-1-5092-0842-5

Published in the United States of America

Dedication

To my sister Kerry and my brother Alex,
and an amazing childhood filled with shared memories,
crazy antics, and an abundance of laughter and love.

Chapter 1

The car door slammed, the sound echoing through the open windows like a warning shot. This was it. Emily tugged shaking fingers through her blond curls. Drawing in a shuddering breath, she glanced into the framed mirror hanging at the bottom of the staircase. Small beads of perspiration dotted her forehead, and her green eyes glittered with panic.

She shifted her gaze to the small panes of glass framing the front door. Brett strode up the narrow driveway, his tall form leaving a long shadow in the midday spring sun.

Her muscles coiled, begging her to run before it was too late. She shook her head wordlessly. *No.* There would be no running. No more hiding. She couldn't possibly live with the fear and shame any longer. Brett was back—alive—and it was time to come clean. Still, dread pooled in her belly as he approached her front steps.

She'd known he was home for over a month now. Ever since she'd made an emergency stop for juice boxes at the convenience store and glanced at the local newspaper as she waited in line. *Staff Sergeant Brett Leeds Returns to Cape Cod after Two Tours Abroad*, the headline screamed.

Her heart had jumped erratically in her chest as her eyes snagged on the phrase "now stationed at Joint

Base Cape Cod in Massachusetts"; then it had plunged to her feet as she read "suffered blast injuries from an IED." She'd grabbed the paper from the metal shelf and slid it onto the counter with her other purchases, hiding her face from the cashier as if he might pick up on her reaction and put the pieces together.

Since then, she'd skulked around town like a thief, terrified of running into him by accident. She twisted her mouth into a grim line. Maybe she was a thief. She had certainly stolen something from him. Somehow, she'd have to make him understand how it had been back then, when her already precarious world had suddenly crumbled into seemingly hopeless ruins.

She'd never wish those dark days hadn't happened—the outcome was too precious. Maybe she'd do things differently, though, if given a second chance. But there was no going back, and besides, hindsight was always twenty-twenty. Steeling herself, she opened the door before his knock could wake Tyler. Planning Brett's visit during naptime had been deliberate.

His hand froze on its way to the door, and he cocked his head at her preemptive move. Uncurling his fingers, he ran his palm over the light brown bristles of his military haircut. "Hey, Em," he said, a smile twitching at his lips. His gaze traveled down her body, lingering a beat too long on her bare legs. "Wow, you look…really great. I've got to admit, I was surprised to hear from you after all this time. But I'm glad," he added quickly.

That old chemistry burned through her, and she fought the urge to fling herself into his arms before he never wanted to touch her again. Instead, she stepped back and motioned him in. Warm, thick air—the product of an unusual April heat wave—followed him inside, settling uncomfortably on her already sticky skin.

"You look great, too," she said truthfully. She studied him surreptitiously for signs of physical trauma, but any scars from the abdominal injuries were hidden by his tight black T-shirt. And a concussion wasn't exactly a visible wound.

His chiseled features were still impossibly handsome, but his face had lost some of the boyish appeal she remembered. Years of combat overseas had sharpened the hard planes of his cheekbones and added lines to his tanned skin. The ridges of muscle rising along his arms gave no indication of a hospital stay. Of course, that had been…what? November. At least five months ago.

He caught her looking at him as they moved into the living room, and his blue eyes darkened. Their gazes locked, the silence spinning out between them.

Oh, God. She knew that look. An answering spark of desire ran through her, quickening her pulse, even as she fought down the panic. Of course he would think she invited him here so they could pick up where they left off. Why wouldn't he? Their relationship had lasted only two weeks, but they'd had a lot of sex during that brief time period. A lot of really intense, amazing sex.

He took a step toward her, pulling his hands out of the pockets of camouflage pants patterned in the dusty shades of the desert. "It's really great to see you," he murmured, his deep voice growing slightly rougher.

She took a corresponding step backward, but he reached for her anyway, and she jumped away as if his hands were on fire.

His brows lifted in surprise, then pulled together in concern. "Are you all right?"

No. I'm not all right. A wave of dizziness crashed over her, turning her vision gray. This was a mistake. She had to get him out of here—there was still time to stop this. Then she would just leave town, move away. She couldn't afford it, but she'd figure something out.

A hollow rushing sound pulsed in her ears. The blood was draining from her head, threatening to drag her consciousness with it. Her knees buckled, and she swayed drunkenly.

Brett darted forward, catching her underneath her arms. "Jesus, Em." He backed her toward the couch. "Sit down."

Her calves connected with the nubby brown fabric of her secondhand couch, and she sank down onto the cushions. She struggled to pull air into her lungs as the tan and beige splotches of Brett's pants melted together in a sickening blur. *Please. I can't pass out.*

His hand slid beneath her mass of curls, and strong, warm fingers wrapped around the back of her neck. Before she could protest, he forced her head down between her knees.

"Keep your head down." His firm tone allowed for no argument.

"Okay." She stared at the frayed hem of her yellow denim skirt as she fought to regain control. Brett's calloused fingertips kneaded the sides of her neck, sending a new set of shivers through her shaking body. He was touching her, and it was just making things harder.

He kept calling her "Em," too—using her nickname with casual ease, as though they hadn't lost

4

contact for four years. Each time he said it, her heart contracted painfully. Very soon he'd be back to calling her "Emily," she realized with despair. Or perhaps something more along the lines of "You selfish bitch." Actually, military life had probably taught him much more original derogatory terms, all of which she deserved.

"Stay put. I'm going to get you a glass of water."

It took her scattered brain a moment to process the words; then a bolt of alarm shot up her spine. *No!* He couldn't go into the kitchen. She'd carefully removed all traces of Tyler's existence from the living room—his toys and blankets were stuffed into bins she'd tugged into the small room she used as an office. She'd even hidden away all the framed pictures that usually sat on the side tables and hung on the pale blue walls. That way, she could start at the beginning of the story, lay out a methodical explanation. Make him understand.

But the kitchen. There were sippy cups, plastic bowls…a dozen preschool creations hanging on the fridge. Evidence which would not escape the notice of a trained Explosive Ordnance Disposal tech. She pushed herself up, but her leg muscles rebelled. It was too late, anyway. She heard the cabinets opening, the clink of ice, and the splatter of the faucet.

He strode back into the room, crouching down to fit his tall frame into her line of vision. "Drink this." His warm hands encircled hers as he passed her the glass.

So he didn't realize. Yet. "Thank you," she whispered, her throat raw. The water sloshed gently as she lifted it to her numb lips.

"Feeling better?"

She nodded, even though it was a lie. Well, that was her specialty, wasn't it? The dizziness had passed, anyway. But now a jagged knife twisted slowly in her gut, waiting for the fatal blow.

"Do you have a kid, Em?" He shifted over to sit beside her on the couch.

There it was. Outside, a bird chirped a warning trill. It was probably aimed at her cat, Terence, but it felt like an ominous sound effect, the toll of some terrible bell.

"Yes. I have a son—Tyler." She swallowed audibly. This was not the plan, yet it was happening. No turning back now.

"Wow. How old?"

"He's three-and-a-half." She set her glass down and waited.

It didn't take long. A dark cloud of understanding crept across his features. "No," he said, his voice dangerously low. A muscle twitched in his jaw. "Tell me that's not why I'm here."

She dropped her head into her icy hands. "I'm sorry. I never meant—"

He shot off the couch, standing over her. "I have a son?" His fists clenched, exposing the tendons along his forearms.

"Please, lower your voice." She pushed herself to her feet. This time her muscles complied, but Brett didn't move back. He loomed over her, their bodies inches apart. Anger rolled off of him in hot, crimson waves. "He's asleep upstairs."

"My son is asleep upstairs?" he shouted, ignoring her pleas.

A door creaked open. "Mommy?"

"Crap," she murmured under her breath. "We actually have plans tonight, and now he's going to be exhausted."

"Plans?" He looked at her incredulously.

It did sound absurd, given the circumstances. But she'd won the tickets after she'd already left the message on Brett's voicemail. And then she'd gone ahead and invited another young mom, Gayle Stevens, to join her. When her college roommate Kaitlyn Winslow—now Kaitlyn Carpenter—moved across the country last year, Emily had lost her one close friend in the area. She needed to make more of an effort. Especially now. She had a feeling she was going to need a support system beyond just Kaitlyn's family in the near future.

"Yes, plans." This was good, actually. She felt her methodical self returning, pushing away the terrified twenty-five-year-old girl who was falling to pieces in the living room. That was not allowed.

She shrugged, pushing her way past Brett. Her bare shoulder brushed against his unyielding arm, and she could almost hear the crackle of tension as their skin connected. Drawing in a deep breath, she hurried to the bottom of the staircase.

"You need to get back in bed, honey."

"Somebody's yelling."

She flicked an accusatory glance at Brett. "I know, baby, and we're sorry. A friend stopped by, and we just…got excited."

"I'll show him my trains." He turned and padded back into his room.

"A friend?" Brett asked, his tone glacial.

He followed her over to the small entryway where the front door and the staircase converged. His presence filled the space, causing Emily to press herself into the wall.

"Please. Just for now. He's a very sensitive boy, and I don't want to spring something this big on him when he's tired." She started to place her hand on his shoulder in a placating gesture before she realized what she was doing. Snatching it away, she pretended to adjust the thin strap of her white tank top.

He exhaled through clenched teeth. "Fine. Just for now. But I want to spend time with him. Meet him." Lifting his arms, he threaded his fingers behind his head. A black and green tattoo bulged on his left bicep. "God. This is…hard to take in."

"I know. I'm so sorry. This isn't how I wanted things to happen."

"No. I don't imagine it is." The words came slowly, as though from a distance.

Tyler emerged from his bedroom again, this time carrying a plastic bucket full of colorful wooden trains. He started down the stairs, one hand on the banister, the other one clutching the bucket to his chest.

"Careful, honey." She turned back to Brett, dipping her head close to his. "I get that it's a lot to take in. Thanks for agreeing to wait to tell him. You can stay and play trains with him for a while—he'd love that. But now is not the time for a big introduction. Trust me, I know him."

He pinned her with an icy blue gaze. "And I don't. But trust *me*—that is going to change."

*****

Brett jammed the key into the ignition, bringing his

silver truck's engine to life with a roar. A dark red haze clouded his vision, turning everything bloody. Flying limbs. Torn flesh. The pretty pink mist.

No. It was essential that he control his temper, no matter what current circumstances dictated. Especially now, after that damn blast. His career depended on the ability to stay calm in stressful situations. Not only did he need to prove he could still do that to his superiors, he also needed to prove it to himself. Blowing out a breath, he leaned his forehead against the steering wheel and willed his muscles to relax.

Somehow, he'd managed to put all the negative emotions aside the minute Tyler looked up at him with his big blue eyes and said, "Hi, Brett," at his mother's prompting. Emily had set them up together in the living room with a bin of toys, and then hovered only occasionally as they'd built a complicated wooden train track across the floor.

He pulled out his phone and opened the picture he'd snapped before he left. It had been less than five minutes since he'd said goodbye, and he already needed to see him again, if only on the screen. Pale blond hair, in a shade seemingly reserved for kids, swept across his forehead in long side bangs. His chubby cheeks bunched in a smile, and his fingers curled around an orange bulldozer with a face that apparently served as the namesake for their cat. He had on a long-sleeved Red Sox shirt and elastic-waist jeans with a turned cuff at the bottom.

His son. How could this have happened?

I think you know how it could have happened. Memories of their exploits between the sheets surged to the front of his mind, filling his veins with heat as he backed out of the driveway. Hell, they'd been so desperate for each other, sheets—or a bed, for that matter—had never been a requirement. So, yeah…he could see how an unplanned pregnancy might have resulted, despite their precautions.

But to not tell him…he ground his molars together until his jaw sent up a warning signal. There was no excuse. And yet, some small part of him searched for a way to absolve her of the betrayal as he drove away from her house.

Thoughts of their past invariably conjured steamy images, however. Their brief relationship had involved more than just sex, but they'd definitely spent a lot of their time trying to get their fill of each other. After all, he'd just returned from nine weeks of Basic Military Training when they'd met, and he'd been headed right back to Lackland Air Force Base to begin his EOD program after the holiday exodus.

But the physical desire had been mutual, as had the decision to part with no expectations. He had months of intense training ahead of him, and she had her senior year of college to finish. They'd be separated physically by half a dozen states and 2,000 miles. He'd known he would only ever be able to give her a fraction of his attention while he was in school, and then he'd be deployed. She deserved more than that.

Maybe they hadn't known each other very long, but there had been something about her he'd found hard to resist. Physically, she was gorgeous, but she also possessed an inner strength combined with a hidden fragility. Confidence mixed with innocence. A wild streak she claimed only he could elicit. And something else—a mysterious sadness he glimpsed on occasion, buried pain she was always eager to chase away by losing herself in his arms.

He couldn't pretend his motivations for cutting ties weren't partially selfish. At the time, he knew he couldn't possibly handle both the demands of the program and a fledgling long-distance relationship. And he sensed she needed someone who could fully commit—someone who could eventually gain her trust and unlock her secrets.

But she'd been entirely willing to let him go, as well. There didn't seem to be the slightest hint she was playing games when she told him the long-distance thing wouldn't work for her either. It may have injured his ego slightly, but he liked that as well—a woman who wanted only what he could give her in the moment. A woman who simply enjoyed being with him enough to spend every waking hour with him for two weeks without expecting more.

Well, she'd gotten more. She'd gotten pregnant, with his son, and kept this news from him for four years. A fresh wave of anger burned through him, mixing with the shock, once again triggering the horrific memories he most associated with those emotions.

Pretty pink mist. He shook his head, trying to dislodge the images seared into his brain. What he needed was a punishing workout. His gaze drifted to the paved trail winding alongside the road. The urge to run was suddenly so overpowering, he was tempted to pull over right now. But he didn't have his running shoes with him—he'd have to go home first.

Home. Technically, he lived on the base. But the term "home" invoked images of the house he'd grown up in nearby Marstons Mills, where his parents still lived most of the year. How would they react to this news?

A sharp pain throbbed between his temples, a nasty reminder of the vicious headaches he'd experienced in the hospital after the concussion. He'd burn it off on his run. After all, he was used to spending hours jogging through the base, pounding the asphalt for mile after mile, until the demons had no chance of catching up.

Chapter 2

What a surreal day. Emily shook her head slightly as she pushed Tyler's stroller down the sidewalk of Barnstable Village. Four hours ago, Brett had been sitting on her living room floor, building a complicated loop of train tracks with Tyler. Now she was trudging around town with a group of strangers, searching for ghosts.

Brett had finally left around five with a clipped promise to be back in the morning to visit Tyler before preschool. She'd shut the door behind him, then turned and slumped against it, wishing fiercely she could just crawl into bed. But mothers of three-year-olds didn't have that kind of luxury. At least she didn't have to work the graveyard shift tonight.

So now here she was, trailing the guide of a ghost tour as he led them along a circuitous path of historical landmarks and old cemeteries. She wasn't even sure how she'd ended up entering the ticket raffle. There'd been an advertisement on the counter of the deli next to the twenty-four-hour animal hospital where she worked, and she had long ago trained herself to consider signing up for anything offered for free. But she had to admit, the history behind her little Cape Cod town was interesting, and they were moving at a quick enough pace to keep Tyler entertained.

"Our last stop will be the Old Jailhouse," the tour

guide called, walking backward to address the trail of people following him dutifully. "Built in 1690, it's the oldest wooden jail in the country."

"Wow. I've lived here my whole life, and I never knew that," whispered Gayle. She flicked a nervous glance at the guide, as though she might be reprimanded for talking out of turn. "Thanks again for inviting us."

"Of course." Emily gave her new friend a reassuring smile. Well, 'friend' might not be quite the right word—this was the first time she and Gayle had done anything social beyond exchanging small talk during preschool drop-off or pick-up. But Emily had felt a certain bond with the only other mother at the preschool close to her age. Neither one of them was part of the established cliques. And Tyler and Gayle's son, Brandon, got along well.

Emily reached for Tyler's juice box, stealing a sip. "So, you grew up here?"

"Well, not in the village here, but in Barnstable. Did you grow up on the Cape?"

"No, I'm a transplant." She mentally chided herself for somehow steering the conversation toward the past. The story of how she ended up here was always something she avoided, if possible—but the scene this afternoon had left her physically and emotionally exhausted. "I spent some time here during summer and winter breaks from college, and I just couldn't imagine living anywhere else." All true, for what it was worth. There'd been no other options; no other place in the world she'd have been able to manage. She'd had to swallow her pride, but it was that or raise a newborn in a shelter of some sort. Draining the rest of the juice box, she gratefully turned her attention to the tour guide as he began speaking again.

"As you can see, it's a small building," he said, gesturing toward the wooden structure standing behind him. "We'll go in a few at a time, in order to give everyone a chance to see without being crowded. Now, overcrowding's not something they worried too much about while the building was in use during colonial times. When you see the little cells, keep in mind they weren't meant to hold individuals—up to twelve people might be locked up in one small cell at a time. Conditions were less than ideal, and many prisoners died. In fact, rumor has it the Old Jailhouse is haunted." He grinned mischievously, ushering the family closest to him through the door.

"Great, I guess we'll be last," Emily murmured, handing Tyler a bag of goldfish crackers and a new juice box. She and Gayle were the only ones with strollers, and they had ended up at the back of the group. Any minute now, Tyler would realize the stroller had stopped, and the demands to get out would begin.

Gayle checked her watch. "Do you think we'll have to wait long? I told my husband I'd be home by eight."

"It's got to be steamy in there." The April evening was still unseasonably warm. "I bet people will be in and out fast. Does it matter if you're a few minutes late?"

Gayle chewed on her lip anxiously. "I did say eight o'clock. I mean, I'm so glad my husband let me come—I'd hate to be late."

Let her come? Emily tried to hide her frown. After all, what did she know about marriage? "I think we'll be okay. Why don't you let me watch Brandon for a sec while you put the stroller in the car? There's no way we'll manage strollers inside the building, and that way you'll be all ready to leave after our turn."

Tucking her thin brown hair behind her ear, she looked at the waiting crowd doubtfully. "I don't know," she said with a shake of her head. "I should probably just get going."

"Oh. Okay." Emily watched a rivulet of sweat trickle down Gayle's face. Was she really that stressed about the time? *Maybe it's just her clothes.* For whatever reason, Gayle had chosen to wear a baggy sweatshirt and jeans on this muggy evening. Emily tugged at the thin strap of her tank top as she turned to follow Gayle to their parked cars.

"Oh, no, you should stay! Please. I'd feel awful if you missed the last part of the tour because of me." Gayle's caramel eyes shone with a hint of moisture.

Emily glanced down at Tyler. Miraculously, he was still content with his goldfish. "Okay. If you're sure."

She nodded forcefully. "You can tell me about it tomorrow. Thanks again, really."

Emily watched her push the stroller across the small jailhouse parking lot. Odd. Shrugging, she turned and pushed her own stroller closer to the rest of the group. Being a single mom was tough, but at least she didn't have to answer to anyone.

Brett's handsome face flashed through her mind, and she realized that was no longer true. Now that he was back in the States, stationed close by at the base, he was going to be around. A lot. He'd made that very clear before he'd left her house today.

Her stomach flipped at the thought of seeing Brett on a regular basis. But there was nothing she could do about that. However mad he might be with her, he deserved to get to know his son. And Tyler deserved to get to know his father.

Just the word "father" made her feel raw and exposed, as though her heart hung suspended outside her chest, for all these people to see. She'd had a lifetime to learn that loving someone was dangerous. Although she'd hoped for a future devoid of that kind of pain, she obviously couldn't help loving her beautiful son with every cell in her body. Now it was her responsibility, as a devoted parent, to fix her mistakes.

She glanced down at his impossibly fragile head, covered in silky white-blond hair. Was it safe for him? Would Brett stay here, now that he'd completed two tours overseas?

Or would he return to the other side of the world, where people waited to try to blow him up on a daily basis?

If he did stay, would he continue to play with bombs anyway?

The answers didn't really matter, she supposed. No one was safe. It was all an illusion designed to allow people to go on with their lives.

"You're up next, little man," the tour guide announced, snapping Emily out of her grim reverie.

She quickly released the buckles on the elaborate three-point harness, taking Tyler's snack bag from him as he pulled his arms from the straps. He looked eager at the prospect of getting out of the stroller, and she scooped him up before he could bolt through the parking lot. "It's our turn next, buddy," she said, moving aside to allow the previous group to exit the small building. "This is where they kept the bad guys a long, long time ago."

She stepped into the gloomy interior, shifting Tyler on her hip in order to push her sunglasses onto her head. The heavy air clung to her skin, warm and thick.

"If you think it's hot in here now," explained the guide to their little group, "imagine what it would feel like in the summer. Obviously, the cells had no windows, only a little slot for waste removal. And the Massachusetts winters were equally brutal."

Tyler squirmed in her arms, and she put him down beside her. It was safe enough in the building—there was only one entrance, here in the front. She scanned a posted list of colonial crimes, her head shaking in disbelief.

"Ma'am, he's not allowed to be in the cells."

Emily spun around, scanning the room for Tyler. The guide pointed around the corner and she rushed past him, mumbling apologies.

Sure enough, there was a rope hanging across the open entrances to each of the three tiny cells. It hadn't been enough to deter Tyler, apparently. He was turned away from her, standing near the shadowy back corner. His head was tilted at an angle, as though he was listening to something intently.

An icy shiver traveled up her spine. "Tyler, you can't be in there. Come on out, honey."

"Coming, Mommy," he called without turning around. He nodded toward the wall, speaking in a low voice.

What on earth was he doing?

Sweat pooled under the heavy ponytail at the base of her neck even as another chill washed over her. She called him again, glancing nervously at the guide. She didn't want to break the rules further by following her son into the restricted area. "Now," she commanded, leaning over the rope. "One. Two…"

Tyler backed toward her, and she caught the words "I'm sure" before he turned around and ran across the long, narrow floor of the cell. Emily bent, thrusting her hands under his arms and yanking him over the rope. She held him tight, cradling him against her heaving chest. It was too hot in here, too claustrophobic. And yet, a ribbon of cold air curled around her ankles as she carried him back toward the front entrance.

"You can stay in the hallway," the guide assured her. "There's a story about the inscription over there." He gestured toward the lone cell on his left, pointing to the crude letters and dates carved into the ancient wood.

"Thank you, but he's tired." *And so am I.* "We'll just get out of everyone's way."

She squeezed past the three other people attempting to crowd into the back room. "We appreciate the great tour," she called over her shoulder before she stumbled out the door and into the parking lot.

After the dimly lit interior of the windowless building, even the dissolving evening sunlight seemed bright. She blinked and drew in a deep breath, cleansing her throat of the stagnant jailhouse air. A chill washed over her, and goose bumps rose in tight ridges along her flesh. Was it finally cooling down?

She slid the back of her arm across her damp forehead and shifted Tyler's weight against her hip.

With a final glance at the old jail, she grasped the stroller with her free hand and pushed it in front of them toward the car.

Chapter 3

"Crap," Emily growled as milk splashed out of Tyler's cereal bowl and onto the kitchen table. *Whoops.* She glanced at him, covering her mouth with her fingers. He didn't seem to notice her language; instead, he grabbed his toddler spoon and dug in.

Usually she caught herself before a word she didn't want imitated slipped out. But as expected, she'd had a rough night. Her sleep schedule was a mess under the best of circumstances, thanks to the nights she pulled at the veterinary hospital. But the anxiety surrounding Brett's morning visit had her tossing and turning until well after midnight. Then a sudden buzzing noise had her leaping out of bed in the predawn hours. She'd scrambled into Tyler's room to find his electric train set chugging around the tracks, its lights flashing eerily in the darkness. Meanwhile, Tyler slumbered on, undisturbed by the activity.

She'd only dozed for the rest of the morning, slipping in and out of consciousness like a piece of driftwood on the tide. She still had no idea how the stupid train had turned itself on. Tossing a sponge into the sink, she poured some milk into her coffee mug. Then she automatically took out a little plastic plate to give their cat Terence his share.

He wasn't in his usual spot in the kitchen, perched impatiently on a chair across from Tyler. *Uh oh.* She

21

glanced around the room, searching for the big orange tabby. Had he stayed out all night? She couldn't remember if he'd come inside with them when they'd returned from the tour. Terence could take care of himself—he was a stray she'd adopted after a kind person had found him injured from a fight and delivered him to the clinic—but there were coyotes on the Cape that survived on house pets.

"Where's Terence?" asked Tyler, somehow picking up on her thoughts.

He seemed to have an uncanny ability to sense people's feelings. Many adults lacked that skill, and Ty wasn't even four years old. Perhaps she was biased, but she was convinced he was a very special child. Her heart swelled with pride, even as she chewed on her fingernail nervously. "Maybe he doesn't want his milk today." She forced a smile.

"Josiah likes milk." He crunched his cereal, swinging his feet under the table.

Emily nodded distractedly. "Hmm." Padding across the warped linoleum floor, she peered out the sliding glass door to the little backyard. Tugging it open, she sang out her "Here, kitty, kitty" call.

An orange shape emerged from the bushes near the back fence. *Oh, thank God.* She exhaled with relief as Terence trotted across the yellow grass toward the wooden deck.

"Here he comes." She leaned her head against the cool glass of the door, waiting for the cat. The dusting of pollen in the air tickled her throat.

"He had a cow."

She turned back toward the table. "Huh? Who had a cow?"

"Josiah." Tyler's blue eyes were wide with excitement.

A shiver ran through her, and she folded her arms over her chest. She was still wearing the tiny boy short underwear and the tank top she'd been in yesterday. It had been all she could do to pull off her skirt and wash her face after she'd finally gotten Tyler to bed.

"Who is Josiah?" She mentally flipped through the kids at preschool, but she couldn't remember anyone with that unusual name. "Is he in your class?"

"No, he's twelve," he said matter-of-factly as he dipped his spoon back into the bowl in an attempt to capture a floating blue marshmallow figure.

What? Emily shook her head in confusion, setting a plastic plate down for Terence. The pool of milk settled into the center of a colorful border of cars and trucks. "Come on," she said to the cat.

The door was open, but Terence continued to sit on the deck railing, his tail swishing. His amber eyes studied the plate, and he finally jumped down with a soft thud. He froze as he reached the door, his orange fur lifting until it looked like he'd been electrocuted. With a menacing hiss, he backed away, turning and disappearing under the deck.

Her eyebrows pulled together. Was she still asleep, on the fringes of some weird dream? "Suit yourself," she mumbled to the empty deck as she slid the door shut.

A knock on the front door made her jump, and she hit the edge of the plate, dousing her bare foot with cold milk. She bit her lip to avoid another curse as her eyes darted to the clock. *Oh, no.* Brett was here. The kitchen was a mess. More importantly, she wasn't wearing clothes.

"Coming," she yelled, swiping at her foot with a dishcloth. Her top was fine; all she needed was a pair of shorts. She dashed out of the kitchen toward the stairs.

The front door opened, and Brett stepped inside.

What the—? She skidded to a stop to avoid crashing into him, her body continuing its forward momentum.

His hands shot out and caught her upper arms.

"What are you doing?" she demanded. God, her voice sounded more breathless than angry. She glared at him with as much indignation as she could manage, given her lack of attire.

"You said 'come in'. And the door was unlocked." His gaze dropped to her lower body before settling back on her face.

Well, crap. She had left the door unlocked, after she'd picked up a local phone book someone had delivered to her front step. A phone book. Who still used those, anyway? Straight to recycling. "I said *'Coming'*."

"Oh." His lips pressed together as he released her arms. "Do you want me to...?" He gestured back toward the door.

"No, it's fine. You've seen it already."

His blue eyes widened, and she rewound her words in her head. Oh, she was on a roll this morning, and it wasn't even 8 a.m. What she'd *meant* was he'd already seen her in her underwear when she came barreling at him two minutes ago. Big deal. She wore less than that to the beach.

But he was clearly thinking she was referring to *before*—four years ago, during those wintery weeks,

24

when their bodies tangled together under the sheets for hours at a time. When they'd seemed to have memorized every inch of each other's flesh.

"I mean...never mind." She blew out a breath, willing the warmth to leave her cheeks. "Ty's in the kitchen. I'll be back in a moment. See if you can get him to eat his fruit."

*****

Brett sipped his coffee, contemplating the antics of the cartoon characters on the television. Tyler certainly seemed engrossed. Their legs touched as they sat on the couch in companionable silence, and Brett's chest tightened. After playing trains for two hours yesterday, he felt they'd established a tentative friendship. But it was a far cry from the father/son relationship he desired.

His gaze drifted from the screen to Tyler's angelic profile. He gripped the coffee mug, searching for any resemblance between this boy's smooth face and his own hardened features. Ty's hair was silvery blond—obviously that came from his mother, since Brett's hair was brown. Or did most little kids have blond hair? Maybe he was thinking of blue eyes.

Tyler had those, too—and so did Brett. But that was the extent of the similarities he could see. It wasn't much. The unwanted thoughts that had plagued him since yesterday resurfaced. He had to know. "I'll be back in a sec, buddy," he said, pushing himself off the sagging couch.

He found Emily in the kitchen, slicing grapes. She was wearing clothes, now—a flowered sundress covered by a short sleeve sweater. Not that it mattered to him one way or another. But he had to talk to her, and it was distracting to have a conversation with someone who was barely dressed.

"More coffee?" she asked with strained politeness, abandoning her grapes and turning to the pot.

He shook his head, setting the mug in his hands down on the table. "Not right now."

"Oh, okay." She returned to her task, sliding the sharp knife through bright green globes before placing them into a plastic container. "It's our turn to bring snack to school," she explained.

"Should I get a paternity test?"

She cringed, her hands freezing in mid-slice. Her mouth worked for a moment before she found some words. "He's your son. I wasn't sleeping around. In fact, I haven't—" She shook her head, blowing at a blond curl hanging in her face. "Do what you want. If you need to put him through a paternity test, that's your right."

Guilt stabbed at him, as sharp and bright as the knife she was holding. But he had no reason to feel bad—certainly not for accusing her of being with multiple partners. While he couldn't imagine she'd have had the time, or energy, to sleep with anyone but him during their time together, he had no idea what she'd been up to at school before or after.

And as for putting Tyler through anything, he was pretty sure the test involved a cheek swab. No pain. Still, the thought of Ty having to go through any medical procedure set off some primal protective instinct.

"Then tell me how this is even possible. We were pretty careful, if I recall correctly."

A furious blush rose on her cheeks. "Ah…there

was that night the...condom broke." She resumed chopping the grapes as if it were a task that required the intense focus of a skilled surgeon. "Do you remember?"

He cleared his throat. "I remember." How could he forget? They'd been going at it pretty hard, even for them. Memories of those nights faded quickly once he was at EOD school, but they had returned to haunt him during the lonely nights in the sandbox. They'd shared a connection physically that he'd never experienced with any other woman, before or after.

"Mommy! Josiah messed up the TV."

"Who?" he asked, raising his eyebrows.

Her skin still glowed neon red. "I have no idea. That's the second time he's mentioned that name this morning." With a shrug, she set down the knife and headed to the living room.

Leaning against the open doorframe, he watched her push buttons on the remote until the static on the screen was replaced by a clear picture.

"Don't play with the remote," she said, setting it back on the scarred coffee table.

"I didn't. Josiah did. He doesn't understand TV."

She frowned. "Well, tell him not to touch the remote." She raised her hands in an "I give up" gesture, but Tyler's attention was back on his show.

Brett stepped back to ensure their bodies wouldn't touch as she returned to the kitchen. "Imaginary friend?" he asked, folding his arms across his chest.

"I guess. But this is the first I'm hearing of it." She chewed on her bottom lip as she placed a cover on her plastic bowl of grapes. "I suppose it's a normal thing, but the timing of this concerns me." Looking up, she gave him a meaningful glance.

Seriously? He fought to control his temper as his muscles tensed. After a loaded pause, he released a breath. "Don't you dare put this on me. *You* created this situation."

"I know," she said, her voice growing shrill. "I just don't know how to help him through it." She set the bowl on the kitchen table, studying it as though it held the answers. Suddenly her body crumpled; her elbows sank to the table, and she cradled her head in her hands. Her long curls trembled as her shoulders shook. "I don't know the right way to handle any of this." The words came out in hitching sobs.

A tiny bit of his aggravation melted away. Overhead, the kitchen lights flickered, and he pulled his gaze away from her slumped form. Was that old electrical wiring, or the start of a migraine? Rubbing his forehead, he grabbed his forgotten mug and carried it over to the coffee pot. This was hell. His job was to protect people, not make them cry.

He helped himself to the last of the coffee, glancing around the kitchen as he waited for her to collect herself. Cream-colored starfish lined the counter backsplash, and glass jars full of green and white sea glass sat on the windowsill above the sink, catching the morning sun. The light yellow walls were covered in Tyler's artwork.

Turning back to her, he took a healthy swig of caffeine. "Maybe we should all go see a counselor?" he suggested.

She sniffled. "I can't afford that." Straightening, she swiped at her reddened eyes.

"I can. It's part of my medical benefits." He'd been forced to get some PTSD counseling after the explosion. This was different, but surely there was some kind of family counselor available to help them through it. The stakes were high—he didn't want to come into his son's life only to mess it up.

"I think that's a great idea." She smiled weakly, combing her fingers through her hair. "Thank you."

He plunged his hands into the deep pockets of his utility uniform. "I don't want your thanks. I want to see Tyler again today. What time should I come back?"

Her body stiffened, and she threw back her shoulders as if to regain some control. Unfortunately, what he noticed was the way the defiant motion pressed her breasts against the light green cotton of her dress. He cut his gaze to the panel of the countertop microwave, studying the red numbers on the clock while he waited for an answer.

"Um, four? We could take him to the park before dinner."

He nodded. His schedule was fairly flexible at the moment. He was currently teaching several classes on explosives safety and hazardous devices to military and law enforcement groups; between classes and curriculum planning, he had to continue his own training and keep his qualifications up to date. The downside, of course, was that he always had to be prepared to leave for temporary duty at a moment's notice. But as far as he knew, he could be free this afternoon. "Give me directions. I'll meet you there."

Chapter 4

They pulled into the parking lot at exactly the same time, and Emily smiled in spite of herself. Punctuality was something they'd had in common from the beginning. When they'd met, Brett had just completed Basic Military Training with the Air Force; she, of course, had been tossed into the role of adult at the age of fourteen. Whenever Brett had come to get her that winter break, she'd been ready and waiting, fidgeting with anticipation in Kaitlyn's parents' foyer. And if Kaitlyn was coming with them, they'd had to sit outside in the car and wait for her to finish getting ready. Not that they'd minded; they'd huddled together in the cold, their breath mingling as they whispered promises of what they'd do to each other later.

Sometimes they hadn't even been able to wait until the night was over and they could ditch their friends to be alone. The memory of a frantic tryst in a bar bathroom floated through her mind as she cut the engine. And then there were the passion-filled days during the second week, when they'd given up on waiting for darkness in a desperate attempt to get their fill of each other before they went back to their individual lives. He'd been living at his parents' house at the time, but his room was in the basement—and at that point, she didn't even care if the Leeds were upstairs. Although she'd had enough modesty to insist on sneaking through the back entrance in order to avoid being seen accompanying their son to his bedroom.

No. She shook her head forcefully, as if the motion might dislodge the steamy memories once and for all. The tie holding her thick curls slipped, and she sighed. "One second, honey," she said, peeking over her shoulder to the backseat.

Tyler squirmed in his car seat as she wrestled with the ponytail holder. How did she end up with this mass of out-of-control blond spirals? She liked things neat and organized. This hair belonged to a girl who was wild and spontaneous. A risk-taker, even. The last time she'd been wild and spontaneous was when she'd been with Brett. Then Tyler was born, and order and routine once again became the cornerstone of her life.

She was doing it again—thinking about the past. With a grimace, she got out of the car and circled around to the back door on the opposite side, where Brett was already waiting. He was still wearing his uniform—a long-sleeved gray and green camouflage shirt, with long matching pants tucked in to heavy olive drab boots. *Wasn't he hot in this weather?* Actually, this was probably nothing compared to the sweltering deserts of the Middle East. Her chest tightened as she pictured him over there, a constant target in a distant land.

Brett pulled the car door open. "I'll get him out," he said, his voice clipped.

"Okay." She stood back and watched him struggle with the complicated car seat latch for a few moments. A tiny smirk tugged at her lips, and she fought to contain it.

"How does this thing come apart?" He

straightened, bracing his arm on the roof of her old beige sedan.

She raised an eyebrow. "Don't you dismantle bombs for a living?"

He gave her a dark look, but a smile twitched at the corner of his mouth. "Watch yourself," he warned playfully. His finger shot out to jab at her side, but he caught himself immediately and stopped the motion before he could touch her. Adjusting his hat, he cleared his throat. "Show me."

She nodded, bending inward and explaining the trick. "They make them hard, so a bored toddler can't figure it out on a long car ride. That would be disastrous." She helped Ty unthread his arms from the straps and climb down to the pavement.

"I'm sure," he allowed, but his attention was on his son. "You ready to go play, buddy?" They joined hands and headed for the playground, leaving her standing alone in the parking lot. Settling the diaper bag on her shoulder, she trudged toward an open bench.

Did Tyler already feel a special attachment to Brett? Or would he react to any adult who gave him attention? It was hard to say; there weren't too many adults in his life, aside from herself, his teachers, and Kaitlyn's parents. He referred to the Winslows as "Grammy Ruth" and "Grampa Stan" by their request, which was fine—no one else was around to fill the role.

Except for Brett's parents, now. Her stomach clenched as she collapsed onto the warm wooden bench. When they found out, they would hate her as much as Brett did—maybe even more.

She knew they lived on Cape almost year round, with the exception of some winter months spent in

Florida. The risk of running into them had always loomed, but she felt confident they'd never recognize her. After all, she was merely a two-week fling their twenty-three-year-old son had enjoyed before leaving for EOD school. And she'd spent more time sneaking through the back door of their basement than chatting with them upstairs.

Kaitlyn's parents didn't know who Tyler's father was either, and they were kind enough not to ask. Emily sighed, adjusting her sunglasses against the afternoon glare. "Kind" wasn't even the word for it. Stan and Ruth Winslow had literally saved her, giving her a place to live and raise her son. And while the cottage Emily called home usually sat empty for nine months out of the year, it had brought in thousands each summer as tourists descended on Cape Cod. It didn't matter that it wasn't beachfront property; any house available as a weekly rental during the summer generated income. Struggling families sometimes moved *out* of their own houses for the summer, opting to camp at Nickerson State Park during the warm months in order to bring in extra cash from seasonal rentals.

And the Winslows wouldn't take a dime from her, as much as she tried. But they knew as well as she did she really didn't have a dime to spare. Someday, though, she'd make it up to them.

Thoughts of her financial burdens deepened her underlying exhaustion, and she sank further into the bench. Her eyes drifted closed as the sun warmed her skin. Maybe she could just sneak in a few minutes of rest. She'd tried to nap while Ty had been down; extra sleep was imperative on the days when she was scheduled to work the night shift. But once again, she'd been rudely awakened by one of Tyler's battery-operated toys. This time she found a noisy helicopter on top of the toy basket trying to make an unscheduled flight, lights flashing and blades whirring.

What was with his toys turning themselves on these days? *Maybe it's a full moon*, she thought drowsily. She didn't really believe in that sort of thing, but she did live on a peninsula surrounded by water. If the moon could pull the tides of vast oceans in and out, it could probably be blamed for a few other strange things.

"He's playing with some other kids, so I thought I'd leave him to it."

She jumped, startled out of her semi-conscious state. "Huh?" Straightening up, she pulled her sunglasses off and rubbed her eyes. Tyler was running across the wooden rope bridge connecting two structures, shouting gleefully to several boys waiting on the other side.

"I don't really fit on that equipment, anyway."

She glanced pointedly at his long legs as he stretched them out beside her. "Yeah, they don't cater to the over-six-foot crowd when they build them."

He stared off into the distance. "I still can't believe it," he murmured, scrubbing his hand along his jaw.

She started to point out he'd only had a little over twenty-four hours to adjust to a tremendous change. But that would only serve to remind him how she'd kept the existence of his son from him for almost three and a half years. So instead she made an "hmm" sound as she crossed her arms over her chest. It was still warm, but a cool breeze hinted at chillier weather to come. April on the Cape was mercurial; locals jokingly claimed the seasons went directly from winter to summer here, bypassing spring entirely.

"When did you find out?"

"What—that I was pregnant?" Apparently he didn't need a reminder of what she'd done. Guilt stabbed at her chest as she dug her fingernails into her upper arms. Of course, he would have questions—and she owed him truthful answers.

"Yes."

"I found out that February, when I was back at school." The memories flooded her mind: an icy journey to the pharmacy, an anxious wait with Kaitlyn in their tiny dorm room, a surreal plus sign on the pregnancy test.

He cleared his throat. "Why didn't you contact me?"

Here we go, she thought. She quickly checked on Tyler before noting the location of the other adults. A group of mothers shared a picnic bench, and a dad and a grandmother hovered near the equipment. "You had never contacted me. Not once in the two months since you'd left."

"I was in freaking lockdown!" he shouted, his fists clenching on his thighs. One of the moms at the picnic table looked over at them. Exhaling loudly, he flattened his palms and rubbed them against his patterned pants. His lowered voice came out like a growl. "I was up to my eyeballs in study materials and daily exams. There was no time for *anything* that didn't involve school."

"And I knew that, Brett. You told me, over and over again. I knew all about the three-strike rule. Do you think I wanted to send you that kind of e-mail in the midst of the biggest challenge of your life? Besides, there were other things stopping me as well."

"What other things?"

Alarm bells clanged in her head. She owed him truthful answers, but this was not the place or time to discuss the next part of the story. "It doesn't matter now." And it didn't, really. She had wanted to sit down yesterday—had it been only yesterday?—and walk him through the events leading to her decisions in detailed chronological order. But that went out the window when she'd almost fainted. God, she needed to get her act back together, and fast.

She uncrossed her arms quickly and checked her watch. "We'll have to get going soon," she pointed out in an attempt to change the subject. "I have to get him dinner before we go to work."

"You take him to work?" A hint of disapproval sharpened his voice.

"I don't have a lot of choice." Her stomach clenched defensively, and she willed her body to relax. She'd done all right by them so far. "I work two or three night shifts a week at a twenty-four-hour veterinary hospital in Hyannis. He loves visiting the animals, and I bring an inflatable mattress and set him up in an empty office. It's fine," she finished, drawing in a shaky breath after the tumble of words.

He tilted his head, considering. "I remember you wanted to be a vet."

"I'm not a vet, I'm a vet tech," she snapped. He'd achieved *his* dream, while the best she could do was a pale shadow of her lifelong ambition. *Careful*. Her exhaustion was getting the better of her. Yes, she'd made the sacrifice, career-wise, but he'd never been

36

given the chance to make an informed decision. That wasn't his fault.

"Sorry," she added quickly. "I'm really tired. Night shift is hard, but it pays well, and overall I love my job. I also do some of the billing and paperwork during the day from home, so I never have to be away from Tyler."

"But when do you sleep?"

"I try to nap when he does." A stronger gust of wind suddenly lifted her skirt, and she grabbed at the light material. She caught his gaze moving over her legs as she pulled the dress back down, securing it between her thighs. "It's getting colder," she mumbled, studying the pattern of printed flowers in an effort to hide her flushed cheeks.

He ignored her obvious statement. "Maybe he could spend the night with me tonight." An uncharacteristic thread of doubt accompanied the words. He clasped his hands, gazing toward the distant trees beyond the playground.

"What? Like…in the barracks?" Panic rose in her throat, hot and bitter. She'd never spent one night away from Tyler. She wasn't ready.

He snapped back to attention, blowing out a frustrated breath. "No, I have a private room on the base with a shared bathroom and kitchen. I'm sure it's bigger than an empty office. But I was thinking of my parents' house."

Her heart froze as the panic shot into her chest. *No.* She couldn't face the angry grandparents yet. This was all moving too fast.

"Relax. They're not back yet. They stopped in Virginia on their way home to spend some time with my brother Jeff's family. He's stationed at Langley Air Force Base now."

Breathe. I can handle this. "I think…maybe…it's too soon, you know? Nights can be tough."

Something flashed in his eyes before his icy blue gaze became unreadable. "You're right," he agreed, rubbing the back of his neck with his hand. "Overnights are not the best idea."

Was he sleeping with someone? A tiny splinter of jealousy pierced her belly at the thought, and she bit down on the inside of her cheek to hide her reaction. Ridiculous. She had no claim on him; no right to feel anything even remotely resembling jealousy. For some reason, though, the idea of him spending his nights with someone had caught her by surprise.

Why hadn't it occurred to her? He was a hot, twenty-seven-year-old soldier who had spent the last few years overseas, defending his country and his fellow soldiers. He was a member of the elite bomb squad who blew things up on a regular basis. Testosterone seemed to roll off him in dangerous waves, yet he was kind and respectful. Women were probably lining up to have sex with him.

Her jaw clenched as the image of a pouty redhead floated through her mind. What if it was that tramp Miranda? Even if they hadn't stayed together, she could have read about his homecoming in the paper, just as Emily had. She shook her head imperceptibly. No way was she letting her son spend time with that witch.

But that was a battle for another day. Brett had acquiesced, for now. "Okay, well…I'd better give him a five-minute warning. It helps to prepare him when I'm asking him to leave something fun for less exciting things like dinner and work." She gave him a wan smile and pushed herself off the bench. "I'll be right back," she added, even though she was fairly certain he didn't care where she was at any given time.

His next words proved her right. "Even if sleepovers are out, I want to spend time with him alone. Soon."

She nodded, ignoring the pressure behind her eyes. She would not cry in front of him again. What he was asking was hardly unreasonable. If she balked, he might decide to hire a lawyer. Then she was sunk. "He'll like that. And maybe we could set up some of those counseling sessions soon? Just to make sure we have some guidance."

"I'll look into it tomorrow."

"Great," she said, trying to force the tremor from her voice. "I'll go give him that warning." She turned her back on him and made her way toward the slides, pulling her sweater closer against the advancing chill.

Chapter 5

"Will Mickey be okay?" A worried frown pulled at Tyler's pink lips. He slurped some milk from his sippy cup as he waited for an answer.

"I think he'll be just fine." Emily tucked the last sheet corner around the blow-up mattress on the floor. *Thank goodness he stays in this bed willingly.* She'd had to transition him out of the portable crib when he'd turned three, and although he could easily get out of that if he tried, the illusion of barriers gave her peace of mind. Luckily, he was a heavy sleeper who didn't fight bedtime. Since nights at the animal hospital had been part of his routine since he was born, he felt completely comfortable in the darkened office.

"You'll give him a check-up?" he persisted, clutching a stuffed lamb named Larry to his chest.

"Of course I will. Lots of check-ups. That's my job." Mickey, a young lab mix, had needed emergency surgery this evening to remove a sock lodged in his intestines. Although he'd suffered a few days before the cause of his distress was identified, his prognosis was good.

"Now I want you to get some rest," she added, tugging at the waistband of her blue scrub pants. Darker blue paw prints decorated the matching top. "That way, you'll have plenty of time to say hello to Mickey in the morning before we go home."

He nodded, climbing into his makeshift bed. "Josiah's at home. Will he be okay, too?"

She frowned. "I'm sure he will." When would Brett get them in with that therapist? Maybe she needed to do some of her own research—there were plenty of reputable online sites she'd consulted in the past to help guide her through other mysterious phases. Unfortunately, just the thought of making it through the next twelve hours felt overwhelming. Tomorrow, she needed to find a way to get some sleep. Sinking to her knees, she dropped a kiss on Tyler's warm cheek. His arms circled her neck, and she breathed in the scent of him.

"He's afraid to leave our house," Tyler continued as he released her. He curled into a ball on the mattress. "He's ascared of doctors."

"Scared. And you can tell him the doctors here only take care of animals." Should she be pretending this imaginary friend was real? Hopefully she wasn't doing permanent damage. Pasting on a reassuring smile, she settled the top sheet and the baby quilt Kaitlyn's mom had made over Tyler's small form.

Tyler's fingers found the worn pink satin of Larry's ears, and he began to rub the material, his usual bedtime ritual. "Josiah says animals belong in the barn."

"Well, some animals do. But people like to keep cats and dogs and sometimes other small pets inside their home, with their family. Like Terence." A thread of concern tugged at her as she mentioned their cat's name. He had continued his standoff all day, refusing to enter the house. Finally, she'd left his food and water out on the deck before they left for work.

More unexplained weird behavior. She sighed, glancing at the moonlight filtering through the closed blinds of the office. At some point, she needed to check up on that full moon theory. She didn't think she could blame the cat's sudden aversion to their house on Brett.

"Josiah's pony lived in the barn, but he died of lick."

She pulled her attention away from the window. "Lick? There's no such thing, honey. Now, it's time for sweet dreams."

His eyelids fluttered sleepily, but he wasn't deterred. "Lick. It's like a tummy ache, but for ponies."

"Do you mean...colic?" She leaned back on her heels. How on earth would he know such a thing? They certainly didn't treat horses here.

"Yes. His pony died of lick, and he was sad."

An icy shiver tiptoed up her spine. What kind of imaginary friend had this type of detailed past? Her hands twisted on her lap as she tried to come up with an appropriate response.

"Emily?" Dr. Murray's voice drifted in through the slightly opened door.

She straightened up so fast her right knee popped, nearly buckling to send her back down. Years spent practicing and performing with her school dance teams had resulted in patellar tendonitis—a chronic condition also known as "Jumper's Knee" that flared up whenever she engaged in high-impact activities. Usually she was able to moderate her workouts enough to keep the pain at bay. But the impending meeting with Brett had caused her to go a little overboard yesterday morning. She'd quelled her nerves by practicing all her favorite routines from college, forcing herself to start over if she made a single mistake. Then Ty had joined her for an impromptu dance party that had added another thirty minutes to the initial hour of exercise. Now she was paying the price.

"Coming," she called back, bending to rub the sore tendon. Dr. Murray would be ready to go to sleep too, in the small bedroom used by the nightly on-call vet. It would be up to Emily to awaken the doctor if a case warranted her attention.

Although Tyler's fingers still stroked Larry's ear, his eyes were closed, his breathing even. "Night-night, baby." They could address this Josiah thing in the morning. Maybe if tonight was quiet, she could start looking into the best way to handle this new issue. With one last glance at her sleeping child, she crossed the room and shut the door.

*****

Clearing a suspected weapons cache—a routine call in this never-ending war. But no soldier could ever afford to let his guard down here, especially when searching for explosives. You assumed traps had been set, and took the proper precautions against the increasingly sophisticated techniques. Their detectors could pick up metal components in a hidden IED, their jammers could disable a remote command, and their robots could often render a bomb safe from a distance. Still, looking for anything out of the ordinary, remaining constantly vigilant, and listening to your gut instincts—that was the key to staying alive.

He sees it now, in the dream. But there were no telltale signs on that fateful day; the disturbed spot in the scorched earth is just a manifestation of his subconscious.

The relentless sun beats down on their helmets as they approach the cluster of abandoned buildings. Aside from their armored bodies, nothing else moves in the still, heavy air. The silence is almost as thick as the heat.

Sometimes, the simplest devices are the most dangerous. A pressure-plate IED, packed only with explosives and buried in the dirt, could be virtually undetectable if enough time had passed to allow the earth to settle. An indiscriminate killer—no trip wire, no command signal—just lying under the ground, waiting patiently for its victim.

Dream-Brett tries to scream a warning as their Team Leader's foot hovers over the spot, suspended in slow motion. But no sound emerges. Panic fills his throat instead, dread clogging his lungs.

Then Mac takes that fatal step, and beneath the ground, two plates connect under his weight. An explosion shatters the silence. The earth splits open, unleashing the fires of hell.

And the screams finally came, as Brett leapt from the bed, his bare chest dripping with cold sweat.

Chapter 6

It was after 10 a.m. by the time she returned from dropping Tyler off at Mrs. Winslow's. Still plenty of time to sleep the day away, though, and that was her only goal. Ty didn't have preschool on Tuesdays, and a few hours of rest during his naptime wasn't going to cut it. So despite the fact that she hated asking for more favors from Kaitlyn's mom, she'd called to see if he could spend the day over there. And as usual, his honorary grammy agreed enthusiastically. *Thank God.*

Terence slinked out of the bushes and sat on the front step as she trudged toward the house.

"There you are," she murmured, unlocking the door. She stepped aside to let the cat in, but he just stood outside of the doorway, peering into the little foyer and living room suspiciously.

What was with him lately? She scooped him into her arms before he had a chance to react and settled him over her shoulder. "Let's go take a nap," she said in a soothing voice, kicking the door shut behind her and carrying him up the stairs. Once she was in bed, with Terence's solid weight beside her, she'd drift off easily to the sound of his purring.

The big cat's body stiffened as she stepped onto the top stair, and his claws suddenly sank into the soft flesh of her upper back.

"Damn it!" She staggered forward, flinging

Terence toward the right-hand side of the upstairs hallway. He landed with a yowl and shot through the open door of her bedroom.

What the hell? She clamped her hand across her shoulder, her head swiveling as she surveyed the remaining two doorways leading into the little hallway. Their bathroom was almost directly across from the stairs—she'd nearly stumbled into it when Terence flipped out.

Tyler's room was on the left, opposite hers. Was there something up here scaring the cat? She glanced into the bathroom as she tiptoed toward Ty's room, her heart pounding in her ears.

Her gaze searched the dimly lit room; nothing seemed amiss. His toddler bed stood in the far corner, covered by a rumpled yellow and white comforter. A border of starfish marched across the walls—she'd stenciled and painted them various pastel hues in a burst of third trimester energy. Larry the lamb rested with a stack of books on the seat of a wooden rocking chair; behind it, a pair of windows looked out into the small backyard and the morning's gray sky. The electric train set wound its way in wide loops around various toy bins in the other corner. In the center of the room, a secondhand train table she'd found at a yard sale was covered in yet more engines—bright wooden trains with friendly faces and magnetic connections.

She held her breath as her eyes landed on the closet. The door was closed; a hooded towel hung on the back. There'd be no sleep until she checked it. She took a few slow steps into the room, her pulse skittering with the creak of each old floorboard. Her hand trembled slightly as she reached for the doorknob, but then she froze.

What if there *was* someone in there? She had no weapon. Exhaling shakily, she considered her options. Obviously, there weren't a lot of choices available in a toddler's room. But she wasn't about to turn her back and go downstairs. She finally settled on a metal bucket holding more colorful cargo cars and various pieces of wooden tracks. A powerful swing could result in a broken nose, if she aimed well.

She shook her head at the ridiculous thoughts. There was no one in her house. There was nothing of value here to steal, and she'd been out all night if anyone had the inclination to rob her anyway. Unless someone was just hanging around waiting to attack her, she was alone. With a cat who may be having a psychotic break.

Still, she gripped the handle of the bucket tightly as she closed her other hand around the doorknob; the white ceramic felt cold against her damp palm. With a forceful jerk, she yanked the door open and jumped backward.

Empty. Her muscles trembled with relief. There was no one in the house—whatever was going on with the cat had started before this morning. But it wouldn't hurt to check any other possible hiding places up here, just to be on the safe side. She shut the closet door and carried the bucket into the hall bathroom they shared.

After peeking behind the shower curtain, she turned to the mirror to quickly assess the damage from Terence's claws. She frowned at her messy hair and shadowed eyes before gingerly lifting the scrub top she was still wearing. A few tiny holes now dotted the material in the back; luckily, it wasn't bad enough to pronounce her favorite work shirt ruined.

Her skin, however, had fared worse. Twin sets of parallel scratches traveled up to the top of her shoulder like some sort of tribal tattoo. The angry red lines were tender and swollen, but only a few tiny beads of blood rose up through the torn flesh.

After quickly cleaning the wound, she returned the medical supplies to the locked cabinet over the toilet. Her eyes fell on the bottle of ibuprofen. Some pain pills might help her sleep. Or…her gaze shifted to the similar bottle behind the first—that one, marked with the letters "PM," had an added sleep ingredient. Maybe just one, to help make sure she got the rest she needed.

As she pulled out the bottle in the back, her birth control pills fell from the cabinet, clattered on the toilet lid, and hit the floor with a slap. Her heart seized as she jumped, stumbling backward toward the tub. She reached out a hand to steady herself against the wall. *Good Lord.* If that wasn't a sign she needed the PM capsules, she didn't know what was.

Bending, she picked up the pill packet with a wry smile. Totally unnecessary, considering her nonexistent sex life, but she took them religiously anyway. Her obstetrician had prescribed them for her painful periods, and they did help in that regard, but she was pretty sure the doctor viewed her as an irresponsible flake who'd already failed once when it came to protection and needed all the help she could get for the future. Emily had started to explain about the broken condom, but then she'd changed her mind and just accepted the little blue piece of paper, agreeing to start once Tyler was totally weaned. After all, she couldn't afford another pregnancy, emotionally or financially. Might as well follow the old "better safe than sorry" adage.

She popped one pill from the plastic ring and chased it with water, repeating the process with a PM capsule before any guilt could set in. Needing a little help to shut her mind down was really the least of her worries these days. There was still a traumatized cat hiding in her room.

Once her closet had been cleared, she dropped to the floor to check under the bed. No intruders, only a large orange cat. Although exhaustion was setting in rapidly, she had to look him over to ensure it wasn't a hidden injury making him so skittish. Grabbing the nape of his neck, she slid him across the wooden floorboards until he was close enough to capture with two hands. Then she carefully set him on the bed and gave him a hasty examination.

No animal bites, gashes, or puncture wounds that she could see. He didn't show any signs of sensitivity when she pressed her fingers along his body. "Okay, I give up," she mumbled, scratching him under the chin.

She crawled under the covers, expecting him to curl up next to her as usual. Instead, he settled into a sphinx position on the end of the bed, facing the open door. A faint twitch of his tail told her he was still on the alert.

"Whatever." Groaning, she dropped her head onto the pillow. She was too tired to worry about it anymore. At least she had a watch cat keeping guard over her.

Josiah's at home. He's afraid to leave our house. The odd phrases Tyler had uttered last night suddenly floated through her mind, accompanied by a prickle of fear. She shuddered, opening one eye slowly to check the doorway.

With a violent sigh, she sat back up and grabbed the cell phone off her nightstand. This whole thing was really getting to her, obviously. "Don't forget about therapist," she quickly tapped out in a text to Brett. He would probably find the reminder annoying, but what did she care? It wasn't as if he could hate her more than he already did.

He'd liked her well enough once—back when she was a good person. In fact, *he'd* pursued her. But they'd both agreed early on they were just having fun. Neither one of them wanted any emotional attachments. And yet it had happened anyway, at least for her. She couldn't connect with someone on so many levels and not develop feelings, despite her desperate attempt to guard her heart.

Two weeks later, he'd left for EOD school, and even though he had her cell phone number, he'd never used it. At first, she'd reminded herself how challenging his schedule had to be, and then Miranda had cornered her one night in January and told her a different story.

Emily curled herself into a tighter ball. Thinking about Miranda was not the path to a peaceful nap, but she couldn't seem to stop the flood of memories. Brett's old girlfriend had still had designs on him, even six years after their high school relationship ended. If Miranda had been at the bar that night, Emily and Brett probably would never have hooked up in the first place. But she wasn't.

She'd met Brett when she came home with Kaitlyn for Christmas break their senior year of college. Their first night back, Kaitlyn had brought her to Black Sam's, a local bar named after an infamous eighteenth century pirate, where crowds of young people gathered on holidays to catch up and get drunk. Kaitlyn and Brett had attended Barnstable High School together, although Brett was two years older, and Kaitlyn had introduced them.

He'd been among the noisy group congregated in the back of the room, standing with two male friends at the corner of the mahogany bar. Kaitlyn had dragged her toward them once she spotted people she knew in a position to get the bartender's attention.

Kaitlyn had exchanged hugs and greetings with them before pulling Emily closer. "Dylan, Brett, Alex," she said, gesturing to each in turn. "This is my roommate, Emily."

She shifted awkwardly in her tight jeans as three pairs of eyes raked over her. Forcing her lips into a nervous smile, she nodded at them. Her throat suddenly felt too dry for words. *Order those beers*, she silently begged Kaitlyn. She needed to quell the ache opening up in her chest, the one that reminded her that from now on, she would always be a stranger looking for acceptance, a girl without a home of her own.

"Nice," said Dylan, drawing out the word. "If you guys are looking for a third roommate…or a third anything… I'm available."

Brett pinned him with a warning look, and the leering grin disappeared from Dylan's face.

"Kidding," he amended quickly. "Nice to meet you."

"You, too," she replied, nodding in his direction. It was Brett, though, who captured her attention. Clearly, he was the alpha of this group, and she appreciated his courtesy. But she thought she had recognized

51

something more than chivalry flashing in his eyes—something like possessiveness. With one pointed glance, he was saying, "Back off. Mine."

Surely, she was imagining things. This guy was seriously hot. Yet, her blood warmed dangerously, as though some sort of invisible spark had traveled between them.

"What can I order for you ladies?" he asked them both, although his gaze lingered on Emily. "I have a tab going."

"Oh, that's not necessary," Emily replied at the same time Kaitlyn requested two beers. "Well, thanks," she added after a beat, pulling a hand through her curls.

"No worries," said Alex. "Dylan and I are chipping in. So you don't want to go too far, or you'll miss the shots. We're celebrating Brett's return from nine weeks of hell."

"Air Force Basic Military Training," Brett clarified. "And it wasn't that bad."

"Well, that explains the haircut," said Kaitlyn, tipping her chin up toward his shaved head. Her own dark, razor-straight hair swung back from her shoulders with the gesture. "It suits you, though."

It did, Emily decided. Of course, she had no basis for comparison, having just met him, but she couldn't help noticing how the closely cropped hair highlighted the rugged handsomeness of his sharp, angular features. And she needed to *stop* noticing—immediately. Because he'd uttered the one word that could make her heart seize up. The term "military" conjured a whirlwind of competing emotions, along with one overriding thought: *Stay away*.

She tried, but it didn't work. He continued to

pursue her, and their flirtatious banter was addictive. Despite the alarm bells jangling in her head, she gravitated toward him, hopelessly drawn like the proverbial moth to the flame.

At the end of the night, he backed her into a dark corner, pressing her against the wall. He settled one hand lightly on her hip. "Come home with me." The corner of his mouth lifted in a rakish smile.

Her muscles tightened as adrenaline shot through her veins. Throughout the night, the alcohol had done its work, pushing her inhibitions deeper and deeper. A steady progression of drinks had allowed the first casual touches to become increasingly familiar. She could understand the expectation—and the desire—to take things further. But she just couldn't make the leap to sex when they'd only met a few hours ago.

"I'm leaving with Kaitlyn." She tried to inject her tone with conviction. Hopefully the dim lighting and loud music would conceal the tiny part of her that wanted to be swayed. She pressed her lips together as images of the two of them in bed together flooded her mind.

No. As much as her body seemed to crave his, she wasn't about to ditch her best friend to be his one night stand. "We have a cab coming," she added firmly.

Now, he would accuse her of leading him on. She peered up at him, bracing herself against the anger she expected to see on his face. He loomed over her in the secluded shadows, and a ripple of fear scurried up her spine.

But she didn't detect anything malicious in his expression; although a hint of disappointment shone in his eyes, the slight smile remained. *Okay.* She took a deep breath, inhaling the scent of his warm skin.

"Well…what are you doing tomorrow, then?" He moved a little closer.

"Um, tomorrow? Probably sleeping until noon."

His hand drifted down the outside of her thigh until it brushed against her own. He twined their fingers together loosely. "How about lunch, then? Or brunch, I guess, in your case."

"Why?"

"Why?" He chuckled. "That's why—you make me laugh. You're gorgeous. You like the Red Sox."

That part was true, anyway. Her love for the Boston baseball team had been instilled at an early age, thanks to her older brother.

"And," he added, his voice growing husky, "because I can't stop thinking about you dancing."

Her cheeks caught fire. She and Kaitlyn had hit the dance floor more than once with what could only be described as reckless abandon. Dancing made her feel free, and two decades of various classes gave her confidence. She knew she was at least good enough to have earned a coveted spot on her college's dance team four years in a row. So there was no reason to feel self-conscious…and yet, he made it sound so intimate, as if she'd been dancing only for him.

"So…tomorrow?" he asked again, swinging their joined hands gently.

"Oh. Um, I guess." What was the harm in meeting him for lunch? It would be good for her to get out on her own; Kaitlyn shouldn't be expected to entertain her for the entire four-week break.

He laughed again. "You're not doing much for my ego here, Emily."

He bent down and tipped her chin up, brushing his lips against hers. With devastating thoroughness, he explored the curves of her mouth in a series of lingering kisses.

Her joints turned liquid. When he lifted his head, she continued to cling to him, her fingers wrapped around his biceps. She blinked, slightly dazed.

"That's more like it." He ran his knuckle along her cheekbone. "I'll pick you up at Kaitlyn's tomorrow a little after noon." Then he had pressed her against his side and led her back into the boisterous crowd.

The creak of a wooden floorboard in the hallway suddenly brought her back to the present with jarring force. She tensed under the covers, dragging one eye open to peer out her bedroom door. The hall was empty, at least as far as she could see from here. And she wasn't getting out of bed. Old houses made noises, and she had already checked the upstairs closets.

She was just being overly sensitive, reacting to sounds she normally wouldn't even notice. Hardly surprising. After all, she hadn't slept in over twenty-four hours. Her son was talking to invisible people. Their cat was having a breakdown. And Brett was back in her life.

She'd have to learn how to handle the stress of the Brett situation. She did not, however, have to allow herself to revisit their past. Those memories only served as painful reminders of how good it had been between them for one brief period in time.

The house was silent now; only the occasional hum of a car or call of a bird penetrated the windows she'd closed last night against the cooling weather. She focused on relaxing her muscles and clearing her mind.

No more trips down memory lane. Her limbs slowly turned to lead as the pill she'd taken combined with her overwhelming exhaustion. Sleep finally reached up and grabbed her, dragging her down into blissful oblivion.

Chapter 7

The rest had done her a world of good. She felt like a new person as she buckled Tyler into his car seat. She'd awoken at five o'clock last night to her phone alarm and found a series of texts from Brett. But once she'd explained Tyler was visiting Kaitlyn's parents, he had decided he would just see him today. That was fine by her.

She'd been able to have a nice, quiet night alone with Tyler. After dinner, she'd put him in the jogging stroller and gone for a quick run. It wasn't her favorite form of exercise, but it was something. She'd given him a bath before bed, and then allowed him to pick out three books instead of their usual two. He'd insisted she read to Josiah as well, but that didn't seem to entail anything beyond their normal routine. Still, it was worrisome. Chewing on her lip, she glanced at him in the rearview mirror. He was looking out the window, clutching a wooden train in each hand. *He's fine. He's just adjusting to the sudden presence of Brett in our lives.*

Thankfully, Brett had scheduled an appointment for the two of them today. Emily had been forced to ask Mrs. Winslow to come to their rescue again, but Tyler would only be napping over there today. The therapist felt the first few meetings should involve only the adults. Afterward, Tyler would go on his first outing alone with Brett, if the therapist gave his blessing.

"Time for school," she announced, slipping into a parking spot in front of the historic church that housed Tyler's preschool classrooms. She unbuckled him and engaged in a brief struggle over his refusal to part with one of his trains. "You know the rules, Ty. Thomas can't come to school, but he'll be waiting in the car when I pick you up."

She hauled Tyler out of his seat and kicked the door shut with her foot. Turning, she noticed the back of Gayle's slight form hurrying down the sidewalk toward her parked car. Emily hesitated as she shifted Tyler to her other hip. She could easily get away with avoiding a conversation—and Gayle's rigid posture, hunched against the wind, did not appear to invite social contact. But Emily was trying to nurture this fledgling friendship, and they hadn't spoken since Sunday night. Brandon had been absent on Monday; she should at least ask if he was all right.

"Gayle!" she called out, struggling to catch up while carrying a thirty-five-pound child in her arms.

Gayle slowed, turning around with a mumbled, "Hey, Emily." She lifted her gaze, revealing a bloodied and swollen lower lip.

Whoa. Emily's breath caught in an audible gasp. "Oh my goodness, what happened?" She stared at the dark red scabs, wincing. *Poor Gayle.* Purple blotches spread from the corner of her mouth like a fading ink stain.

Gayle's cheeks flushed, infusing her face with more color. "I'm such a klutz," she said, shaking her head. "I ran into a door. It's my fault for always rushing around." She stared down at her feet as she touched the bruised skin with her fingertips.

"Oh, Gayle, I can totally relate. I'm always trying to do a million things at once. I hope it doesn't hurt too badly."

"No, it's fine." She took a step back in the direction of her car. "It looks worse than it is. But I'd better get going...always in a rush, like I said." Twisting her keys in her hands, she dropped her gaze back down to the sidewalk.

Emily nodded, even though Gayle wasn't looking at her. But she was probably feeling self-conscious about her appearance. *And why wouldn't she be? I can't stop gaping at it.* The marks reminded her of one of those Rorschach tests psychiatric patients were asked to interpret. Clearly, she was more worried about the therapy appointment than she'd realized.

She tore her eyes away from Gayle's jutting lip and focused on setting Tyler down on the sidewalk. "Oh, okay. I just wanted to make sure Brandon was all right...we didn't see you all on Monday morning."

"No, no...he's fine. After this happened," she added, gesturing toward her face, "I decided I needed a quiet day at home."

"That sounds like something I need as well." At least she'd had some time to recharge her batteries yesterday, even if she spent the majority of it sleeping. "Well, I'm glad he wasn't sick or anything. Maybe we can get the boys together later in the week."

"Um, maybe." Gayle tugged at her jacket, wrapping her arms around herself protectively. "I'm pretty busy lately. But...maybe."

"Oh. Okay." She tried to keep the confusion out of her voice. "We can play it by ear." Was she being blown off? She gave Gayle a tight smile and said goodbye, turning back toward the school's entrance.

Had she done something wrong on Sunday night? Before that, Gayle had seemed truly grateful for her attempts at friendship. *How strange*. Maybe she was just reading the situation wrong.

She pulled Tyler along, nodding to another mother on her way out the door. Somehow Skyler's mom was always impeccably dressed, even at nine in the morning. Emily glanced down at the long cuffed jeans shorts she wore under an oversized sweatshirt. Her tangled hair was currently hidden beneath a Red Sox baseball cap. She'd have to make herself presentable before the noon pickup. After that, she wouldn't have much time to get Tyler fed and set up over at Ruth's house before the meeting in Bourne.

"Good morning," sang Mrs. Barrows as they entered the classroom. "They're just starting circle time," she said to Tyler, motioning toward the ring of children sitting on the floor with the assistant teacher.

Emily glanced guiltily at the little circle, complete except for one empty spot where Tyler belonged. Her conversation with Gayle had made them late. *It's preschool*, she reminded herself as she hung Ty's jacket on a low hook near the wall of cubbies. *I probably haven't completely ruined his academic career.*

"Can I speak with you for a moment in private?" murmured Mrs. Barrows, lifting pewter gray eyebrows that were the same beautiful shade as her shoulder-length hair.

Emily stiffened. Maybe she *was* in trouble. Seriously, what now? "Of course." Straightening her baseball cap, she followed the teacher's ample form out into the hallway.

Mrs. Barrows glanced around the empty corridor before pulling the door to the classroom partially shut. Clearing her throat, she turned her concerned gaze on Emily. "I just wanted to ask…is anything going on in Tyler's life at home we should know about?"

Hysterical laughter, tinged with panic, bubbled up in her chest. *Oh, where to begin. It's like this, Mrs. B.,* she thought wildly. *I never told Tyler's father I was pregnant, because I was pretty sure he was going to get blown up in the desert. Now he's back, very much alive, and I've recently introduced them. Of course, Tyler has no idea who he really is, but he's a very intuitive child and I think he might know on a subconscious level. Not to worry, though—he's invented an imaginary friend to help him deal with everything.*

Despite the storm of tangled thoughts crashing through her mind, she managed to keep her composure on the outside. Tyler was currently safe and sound, so she wasn't about to reveal the details of her private life without more information. "Why do you ask?" she countered.

Mrs. Barrows pursed her lips, deepening the lines around her mouth. "Well, it was something he said on Monday… I was planning on catching you at pick-up, but then Brittany had a little…accident," she finished softly, as though she were sharing the deepest of secrets. "Anyway, during story time, we read a book about a little boy who didn't want to go to bed. After the story, I always encourage them to talk about what we read. I asked if any of them didn't like to go to bed—things like that."

Emily nodded to show she was following along so

far. But beads of nervous perspiration were gathering under the brim of her hat. She folded her arms across her chest to keep from waving her hand in a "get on with it" gesture.

Mrs. Barrows hesitated, twining her fingers in the beaded chain holding her eyeglasses around her neck. "Well… Tyler raised his hand and said he had a friend and that someone put his friend to bed under the ground. But his friend didn't want to stay there because he was alone." Her kind hazel eyes widened sympathetically.

The hair on Emily's arms prickled, and she rubbed the sleeves of her turquoise sweatshirt. But she forced a relieved smile onto her face. "Oh, yes. Tyler has recently developed an imaginary friend. From what I've read, it's quite normal at this age." *According to the Internet, anyway.* Hopefully the therapist would confirm this for her later today. She still didn't like the timing, and she certainly didn't like the random facts "Josiah" seemed to know. Or the odd name, for that matter.

Mrs. Barrows nodded so emphatically her entire upper body swayed. "Absolutely. It's very common in children between the ages of three and five. Especially the bright, creative ones," she added with a conspiratorial wink. Her soft features turned serious again. "I suppose it was the context of his comment, really…the way he said his friend was 'underground'. I was afraid maybe you lost someone recently, and Tyler was trying to deal with the confusion of a funeral."

"No, nothing like that." She chewed on her lip, flipping through memories. "Once we buried a dead bird, but that was a long time ago." Suddenly, the image of Cobb's Hill Cemetery, the graveyard they'd toured on Sunday night, flashed through her mind. *Oh, no*. She suppressed a tiny shudder. What had she been thinking? The guide must have scared Tyler with his stories; she hadn't thought he'd been paying attention, but she often forgot how smart and observant he was.

Maybe that's why Gayle was angry with her. Could Brandon be acting out as well? *Crap*. Gayle was probably too nice to mention it. She'd have to find a way to get her alone so they could speak in private. Treating a new friend to a free haunted historical tour of Barnstable Village had been her objective; instead, she'd exposed two little kids to the terrifying finality of death. Maybe she could ask the therapist for a group rate.

She reined herself back in. "Maybe he saw something on TV," she hedged, lifting her shoulders in a dramatic shrug. "If he brings it up again, I'll see if I can get to the bottom of it. Thanks so much for letting me know."

"Of course. I didn't want to alarm you, but his details seemed so...specific. I'm just glad nothing's happened."

I wouldn't go that far, an inner voice responded silently. She hid a dejected sigh behind a fake smile. With a promise to return at noon, she thanked Mrs. Barrows again and trudged up the stairs.

Chapter 8

Brett tried to tamp down his annoyance as he followed Emily's car into the little parking lot by Snake Pond. This was supposed to be his first afternoon alone with his son, but today's therapy appointment had put an end to that idea quickly. Drew, their new family therapist, had been emphatic about taking things slowly. He suggested a "step up plan" of gradually increasing the time Brett spent with Tyler, with time alone off the table until Tyler was "completely comfortable" with Brett. The hour had flown by, and the only other guidance they'd received once they had explained the situation was to maintain Tyler's routines as they progressed with the new relationship. Which basically meant Brett would be forced to spend a whole lot of time with Emily.

And in a final blow, Drew had asked them to do their best to "get along." He'd reminded them that children take their cues from parents, and that any arguments Tyler overheard would lead to more confusion and stress during this transitional period. One big fight could set the whole process back. So, in addition to spending a lot of time with Emily, he was also going to have to be civil to her.

His fingers tightened around the steering wheel as he pulled into an empty spot. Being civil could be a challenge. Since the explosion, his temper flared both hotter and quicker than in the past. The head injury was partly to blame. But even before the blast, each horrific scene he'd witnessed had contributed to a deep, simmering anger that could easily ignite if he wasn't careful. The images of war haunted him. Death. Destruction. Random body parts strewn about the road, cooking in the sun. And every single detail of that last day in Afghanistan was permanently seared into his mind. The memories lurked beneath the surface, waiting to torture him the moment he let his guard down.

He jammed the gearshift forward, cursing under his breath. *Enough.* These types of thoughts would not help his cause. He needed to focus on enjoying his afternoon with his son.

Tyler was already out of the car, bouncing up and down with excitement as he waited. That probably had more to do with the plan to feed the ducks than the joy of seeing Brett, but his heart still swelled at the sight.

Emily stood next to Ty, wearing the same thing she'd worn to their appointment—a cream-colored dress, a denim jacket, and slouchy brown boots that covered her calves. For some reason, the outfit was making him a little crazy. His blood ran hot every time he glimpsed the exposed skin between the ruffled hem of her dress and the tall leather boots.

It was just that he hadn't had much action lately. After November's hospital stay, his priority had been recovering his physical strength. There'd been one woman, Ashley, but he hadn't found her particularly interesting. And she hadn't liked the fact that he refused to spend the night after sex. Since he'd had no intention of allowing her to witness the fallout from his nightmares, that had been that.

He grabbed a bag of bread off the passenger seat and climbed out of his truck. Only two other cars filled spaces in the small dirt lot. From there, a crescent-shaped stretch of sandy beach led down to one of over a thousand lakes and ponds on the Cape. He'd chosen Snake Pond because it was close to the base, and he'd wanted to familiarize Tyler with some of the things near where he lived. Even when Drew had made it clear Emily would be joining them, Brett had seen no reason to change their plans. Eventually, they'd be granted some quality father-son time, and he wanted to introduce Tyler to fun activities he could associate with "Daddy's house."

Emily had apparently never been to Snake Pond, but the directions were easy enough. He'd followed them along Route 130 so she wouldn't feel pressured to keep up if she missed a light. As he slipped on his uniform hat and crossed the lot, he wondered briefly how she'd ended up living here permanently. If he remembered correctly, she had grown up somewhere closer to Boston. Maybe it had been the job. Or Kaitlyn.

"We're here," he announced, stating the obvious for his son's benefit. "I hope the ducks are hungry!"

Tyler immediately positioned himself between the two of them, grabbing both their hands. "One-two-three swing," he insisted as they turned toward the water.

Emily looked at him with her eyebrows raised, waiting to see if he was agreeable to the suggestion.

Somehow he understood what Tyler wanted, but he was momentarily overwhelmed by the first physical contact initiated by his son. The tiny hand was completely swallowed by his own larger one; the connection felt both perfectly natural and wildly discomfiting. He nodded. "I'll let you take the lead."

She snapped off a crisp salute with her free hand. "We gain momentum on the 'one-two-three', then lift on 'swing'," she instructed with mock authority. "Ready?"

Tyler prepared for the game by repeatedly folding his little legs to dangle between them like a pendulum. "Let's do this," Brett replied, returning her smile before he could stop himself. Well, they *were* supposed to get along.

They one-two-three-swung their way down to the water's edge, Tyler squealing with joy as he kicked his feet in the air. Brett adjusted his swing to match Emily's shorter arms, noting the effortless way she lifted her half of the weight. She had always been strong; she had worked out regularly with her college dance team. He remembered that clearly, probably because he'd been so enthralled by her body. In his opinion, she'd had the perfect female figure—not bone thin and frail, but athletic, toned, and fit. He slid a glance at her sculpted legs, which were now almost completely bare, since she'd kicked off her boots and left them up near the cars. It certainly looked like she'd stayed in shape. Another unwanted rush of desire swept over him, sending heat through his veins.

Unacceptable. Even if she was still gorgeous, what she'd done was unforgivable. With steely determination, he pulled his focus back to his son.

Opening the plastic bag, he pulled out a stiff slice of bread and broke off a piece. He tossed it into the pond, then handed one to Tyler. A group of ducks lounging in the shallows by the tall grass immediately perked up and hurried over to investigate. Tyler giggled in delight as the ducks fought for their share of the soggy bread, circling in an enthusiastic swarm. Brett tore off chunks and handed them to Tyler, who improved his throw with each effort.

The feeding frenzy caught the attention of two other children, a boy about Tyler's age accompanied by an older girl. They moved increasingly closer to Ty, until Brett felt to exclude them would be rude. He handed bits of bread to all three children in turn until the bag was empty.

"That's it." He held out his hands as evidence. Damn. How could running out of bread make him feel like such a failure? The children took it in stride, though.

"Chase me!" cried the boy, a fresh grin spreading across his freckled face. He took a few steps back as his sister, judging by the similar freckles, narrowed her eyes. "She's the monster," he told Tyler conspiratorially.

"That's right," she confirmed, hooking her hands into claws.

"Run!" the boy yelled to Tyler as he took off down the beach.

Ty's wide blue eyes slid to Emily for both permission and assurance. She gave him a quick nod, and he turned and ran to catch up with his new friend. The sister gave them a head start before staggering after them with her arms held high.

Brett stuffed the empty bag into his uniform pocket, silently contemplating the ease with which Ty and Emily could communicate, even nonverbally. Would he ever have that type of connection with his son? Perhaps that was something formed during infancy, before a baby's first words were uttered.

He wouldn't have been around for that anyway, he reminded himself. Still, his hands clenched inside his pockets as he fought the urge to say something hurtful. He lost the battle. "I guess I'll have to make arrangements for the paternity test." A trace of guilt shot through him, but he pushed it aside. This *had* to be discussed—the test was another thing the therapist had been adamant about. And it did make sense to know for sure before they moved forward.

She cringed slightly, the small smile disappearing from her lips. "That's fine," she finally said, studying her toes as she trailed them through the sand. "It's just a cheek swab. Drew said as long as we didn't need it for legal reasons, we could do it at home with an online kit. No big deal."

"And you have no doubt?"

"None whatsoever. There's no chance of it coming back anything but positive." Her voice rang with conviction.

He believed her. The knot of tension in his neck loosened slightly. Somehow, he already loved Tyler; a negative paternity test would be devastating. And a small part of him had to acknowledge the other selfish truth; he didn't want to think of Emily with anyone else. He certainly didn't love *her*—it was just some form of primal possessiveness kicking in.

Sighing inwardly, he turned to check on his son. The kids had moved the game up toward the outer edge of the woods that surrounded the kettle pond. Apparently this was now hide-and-seek. The two boys huddled behind the trunk of a large pine tree as the girl searched for them with theatrical difficulty.

He worked his jaw, considering. Despite the paternity question, he and Emily were still managing to get along. He shouldn't stir things up.

The hell with it. He deserved to have some questions answered, and Tyler was out of earshot. "So what made you decide to finally tell me about him?" he asked, adjusting his hat. He could hear the hard edge of accusation cutting into his tone. "Afraid things might get awkward if we were to run into each other?"

She regarded him coolly, her eyes hidden behind sunglasses. "Would you have really thought he was yours? We *were* pretty careful."

"That doesn't exactly answer my question."

Crossing her arms, she turned her gaze back toward the sparkling lake. A trio of ducks still swam nearby, lingering hopefully. "I thought it was safe, now."

"Safe for whom?"

"For all of us. I mean, you've already done two tours overseas. The military has withdrawn from Iraq. Our troops should be out of Afghanistan by the end of this year. It's safe for Tyler to bond with you now…you're here, in one piece, hopefully for the long term. And it's safe for you to focus on your son. I didn't really think worrying about leaving a son fatherless would help your concentration level when dismantling bombs."

Unbelievable. "Don't try to make what you did appear altruistic." A warning throb, hot and blinding, pulsed in his temples.

"Sorry." She caved inward, as if the bright sunshine had suddenly melted her bones. "I really am sorry. It's just…there are things—" Her voice grew thick, and she paused, her head drooping further. Her hair formed a curtain, concealing her face. "Forget it. There's no excuse."

"No, there isn't."

She straightened, tossing her shoulders back. "Well, I'll remind you that you never once e-mailed me from school. I know we agreed no strings, but I felt completely discarded."

There it was. She was attempting to push some of the blame onto him. He exhaled, releasing some of the steam building in his chest. "EOD school takes over every aspect of your life. I *told* you that from the start. Sometimes the tests come daily, and if you don't score an eighty-five, you don't pass. You may get one more shot at it, but if you fail that, you're sent back to the beginning of that section with the next class. And if you don't pass then, it's the third strike, and you're out. Do you know how many of us graduated together, out of an initial class of thirty?"

"Of course I don't."

"Five. Myself and four others."

Her hands plucked at the skirt of her dress, her chunky silver bracelet reflecting the sun's afternoon rays. "Let me ask you this, then. Maybe I don't know the particulars of what you went through in school. But as you just said, you told me how incredibly intense it was going to be. Over and over again. So I knew about the three strikes rule, the unbelievable washout rate. Do you think it would have been helpful for you, during those nine months, to receive an e-mail announcing I was pregnant? Would that have helped you achieve your dream?"

He ground his teeth together. "Probably not," he

admitted reluctantly.

"Believe it or not, I did take that into consideration. I couldn't help feeling a bit abandoned, but I still had feelings for you. I wanted the best for you. Clearly you didn't want anything more from me, and I didn't want you to feel obligated to take care of me for the rest of your life."

"I would have been obligated to take care of *him*. Not you. And I would have been happy to do it."

"I know that now. But at the time, there were so many choices I had to make, so many terrifying decisions. And factors you don't know anything about played into those decisions."

"Such as?"

"It doesn't matter now. And at that point, I wasn't even sure I would keep the baby." The words tumbled out in a rush, ending in a whisper. Her confession hung in the air around them, heavy with guilt and sorrow.

"No." The lake turned bloody as rage boiled up and turned his vision red. How could she have even *considered* that? "No," he repeated, as if he had to deny it over and over again to make sure time didn't reverse and allow her to go through with it. This was *Tyler* they were talking about.

"I know, it sounds horrible," she choked out. Her fingers trembled as she swiped at her cheeks. "It makes me physically ill to think about it now. But it's the truth, and I'm trying to be honest here. I was a college senior. I had no family left. No one. No money. No prospects. I had planned on graduate school, not single motherhood. At the time, it seemed like a reasonable solution."

He fought to clamp down the rising fury. His fists

clenched at his sides, his tendons tight enough to snap. She'd been scared and confused. It was easy for him to say in retrospect that he would have been supportive, but it was hard to imagine how he would have reacted if he'd received that news in the middle of his stressful program.

And she'd just claimed she had no family...did he know that? He seemed to remember the majority of their deep conversations revolving around his future in EOD school. His muscles relaxed by a few degrees as the urge to punch something subsided.

A tiny flicker of shame rose to join the receding anger. Did he ever even ask about her family or her past? He'd been charged up about the challenges that lay in his future; he hadn't given much thought to her life. He'd known she had dreams of becoming a vet—that was about it. And yet, she'd listened patiently to all his passionate monologs about becoming a member of the elite bomb squad. Apparently she'd remembered all his explanations about the difficulty of the program—and understood his veiled attempt at making sure she recognized the reality of the situation: even though he liked her a lot, he wouldn't have time for her when he began his new journey.

Her face was stoic as she awaited his judgment, but the way she clutched her hands across her belly revealed her anxiety. Inhaling deeply, he reminded himself that she made the right choice, at least in that initial situation. And he never would have known if she didn't. It wouldn't kill him to show a little sympathy.

"I'm glad you didn't go through with it," he managed. His gaze slid over to check on Tyler automatically, as if it were an ingrained habit he'd been doing for years. Four days of being a father and he was changed already. "I do appreciate your being honest with me."

"You're welcome," she said quietly.

She appeared so defeated, so vulnerable, that a small part of him wanted to comfort her—to pull her close and shoulder some of her burden. But the dominant part of him shut that thought down immediately. He would never be able to forgive her, so it was best to avoid any physical contact.

Besides, he'd had enough emotional exchanges for one day. First the therapy session, now this. It was enough to drive him to drink. He pulled his cell phone from his uniform pocket to check the time.

While the idea of a few beers was infinitely tempting, that would have to wait. First, he'd need to complete his ritualistic run; then maybe hit the gym to further punish his body with weights. Total physical exhaustion was the only guard against an entirely sleepless night, and even that didn't chase away all the nightmares. He could almost always count on his subconscious interrupting his slumber with at least one replay of his last day in Afghanistan.

He knocked the heel of one heavy boot against the toe of the other, dislodging a shower of tiny rocks. If only a similar technique existed to rid the mind of memories. No, that wouldn't be fair. Mac deserved to be remembered. Brett had made it back home—night terrors were a small price to pay in comparison.

"So...do you have to work tonight?" he asked, breaking the silence.

Her curls caught in the breeze as she shook her head. "No. Thank God. I really need a quiet night at home." She chewed on her lip apologetically, but it was clear what she was saying. You've inserted yourself into our life enough for one day.

"Got it." He tilted his head toward the renewed shouts of the children. "I'm going to go join the fun." Turning his back on her, he strode toward the picnic area nestled among the trees.

Chapter 9

On Thursday evening, Brett announced he was leaving the next day for a long weekend of temporary duty. Other than saying he'd be in Boston, he hadn't provided any other details, so Emily hadn't asked. She tried to stay as far away as possible from him, in fact, as he played with Tyler in the living room. Once Tyler felt comfortable enough around Brett, they could spend time alone, and she wouldn't have to be around Brett so much. That would be the best thing for everyone, so she may as well try to help speed the process along.

Being around him was starting to cause her physical pain. Guilt clawed at her constantly, shredding her insides to ribbons, opening old scars to allow the sadness to seep out. He was such a great guy, and look what she had done to him. Despite the justifiable anger he directed toward her, he was kind and patient with Tyler. Watching them interact made her chest burn with an agonizing mix of regret and gratitude.

And then there was the other problem: he was unbearably hot. His presence had awakened urges she'd pushed into dormancy long ago. Pregnancy and single motherhood left her with neither the time nor the inclination to date. After four years of abstinence, sex had become a distant memory.

Now those memories were flooding back like relentless waves pounding the shoreline. He'd done things to her that she'd never before experienced, and her body wanted more. She couldn't seem to control her raging hormones, and that was frustrating; control was a skill she thought she'd finally honed to perfection. But the force of first love proved a powerful opponent.

First love? She froze in midstride, a laundry basket tucked beneath her arm. What was she thinking? It had been two weeks. Brett had been her "first" in a lot of things...but not love. They were *lovers*, yes. They'd even danced around the suggestion that they *could* fall in love, if circumstances weren't about to separate them so completely and ruthlessly. But those three little words were never exchanged.

She shook her head with disgust as she stomped toward the downstairs bathroom. Thank God he'd finally left—now she was free to move about the house to get a few things done before work.

Yanking open the dryer door with excessive force, she tumbled a load of clothes into her basket. The warm, fresh scent floated upward like a reassuring embrace. She leaned forward to breathe it in, finally exhaling with a sigh. No more thinking about Brett. Nothing could ever develop between them anyway, physically or romantically, since he loathed the sight of her. Besides, she had enough on her plate already. Like locating a clean pair of scrubs before six-thirty.

Resolved, she carried her basket back through the living room. The television was still on, despite the fact that Ty was now up in his room. Brett must have flipped the stations, because now a local news reporter covered the preparations for the upcoming Boston Marathon, which always took place on the Monday in April known as Patriots' Day. Last year, two homemade bombs had exploded near the finish line, causing death and carnage amongst both the runners and the spectators. As a result, heightened security measures would be implemented this year to hopefully prevent similar attacks.

A horrible realization suddenly flared in her mind, and she doubled over as if a battering ram had connected with her abdomen. *That* was Brett's mysterious temporary duty—working with bomb disposal at the marathon. *Oh, no*. Images buried deep in the remote corners of her mind quickly blazed against the backs of her eyes: an overcast sky on a raw winter day, a casket draped in a red, white, and blue flag. She couldn't go through it again. Another cramp seized her as she leaned against the wall for support.

Deep breaths. He'd survived two tours…he was good at his job. The increased security would probably thwart any attempts to plant a bomb in the first place. Maybe she was completely off the mark, anyway, and his trip to Boston this weekend was just a coincidence.

She pushed herself away from the wall, continuing up the stairs with shaky steps. *Please, keep him safe*. They couldn't lose him now. Tyler needed his father.

Their son's lilting voice drifted from his bedroom; he was talking to himself. She glanced through the doorway as she reached the upstairs hallway. Tyler stood at his train table, maneuvering an engine over a bridge while imitating a chugging noise. Beside him, a gauzy figure watched intently, perched on its knees.

She whirled, almost stumbling as her feet changed direction from their path toward her own room. The laundry basket flew from her hands, landing with a loud thump on the floor. Tyler's head snapped up, and the other boy faded like a wisp of smoke. A scream stuck in her throat as she blinked her eyes.

The image was gone. It had disappeared as quickly as the shapes that linger after a camera flash. She swallowed back her hysteria, staring at Tyler's surprised expression. Her pulse pounded in her ears, thick and heady.

"Mommy?"

"Sorry, baby. I...tripped." She glanced at the spilled clothes before quickly looking back at Tyler. His blond head bent forward as he fiddled with his trains. No one else was there. Her exhausted mind had simply manifested some random vision, because she was worried about Brett, and Ty had been talking to himself. Or...*the friend*?

"Who were you talking to, Ty?"

"Josiah."

Her skin prickled, tightening with goose bumps. She wobbled slightly as she fought a wave of dizziness.

He glanced up to select another colorful car from his train bucket. "He doesn't know about trains."

Or televisions, she thought wildly. Maybe explaining things to this imaginary friend helped Ty to make sense of his own changing world. "He must, ah, like that," she managed.

"Yes. He likes it here." Tyler inserted the new wooden car in front of a battered red caboose. The magnets connected with a crisp click. He dug back into the bucket and pulled out two tiny toy logs.

Great. So glad their guest didn't find their hospitality lacking. "Um...how long do you think he'll stay?"

He tilted his head intently, as if listening to an

unseen voice. "He misses his mamma," he finally said in one of those non-sequiturs for which three-year-olds were famous.

She sagged. Maybe she should not be making herself so scarce when Brett was here. Bending all the way down, she started to scoop up the scattered laundry. Her right knee sent up a warning flicker of pain, and she shifted her weight.

"I told him I share."

"Hmm? Share what, honey?"

"My mommy. Sharing's good," he pointed out, looking at her expectantly.

"Yes. You're right." Chewing on her lip, she hesitated for a moment. "You said you'd share me?"

He nodded, returning his attention to the action on the tracks.

The fake smile she'd conjured up slid off her face as she turned away. This was too much. She clutched the rigid basket to her belly as if it were a protective shield and forced her feet to carry her into the master bedroom. Her eyes landed on the bed. All she wanted to do at the moment was crawl under the covers. Although, she decided with a small shudder, a part of her was very glad they wouldn't be spending the night in this house.

Chapter 10

Emily watched the clock on Saturday morning, waiting for the numbers to flip to a reasonable hour so she could call Gayle without worrying about waking anyone up. They'd made tentative plans after school yesterday, and Emily desperately needed to get out of her house. But when she finally dialed the number, Gayle's voice came through the phone as a thready whisper, begging forgiveness.

"I'm so sorry. It just came on so suddenly." She coughed and sniffled. "I feel terrible. Not just from the cold, but because I'm letting you down."

"Oh, well, don't worry about that," Emily insisted, trying to mask her disappointment. "You just take care of yourself. Hopefully you'll feel better tomorrow, since the Easter Bunny can't take the day off." Sinking into a kitchen chair, she drummed her fingers against the tabletop. What could she do to help her friend? She was pretty sure Gayle had mentioned her husband worked as a security guard someplace, a job which required some weekend and night hours. If Gayle was alone, she'd have to forgo rest in order to watch her toddler. "Do you want me to come and pick up Brandon? I could take the boys to the playground myself so you can get some sleep."

"Oh." Her tone suggested she was surprised by the gesture. An awkward pause stretched out, punctuated with a few jagged breaths. Clearing her throat, she finally continued. "No, no, but thank you anyway. I think Brandon might be coming down with it too. I wouldn't want to get you sick. Besides, Joe is home today."

"Oh, good, I'm glad he's home. He can take care of both of you." She nibbled at a fingernail as she waited for a response. None came. Outside, a reluctant lawn mower engine roared to life in her neighbor's yard. "Well, hopefully we can reschedule soon."

"You're so sweet. Thank you. And I'm so, so sorry I messed things up."

She lifted her shoulders in a "what can you do" gesture that Gayle couldn't actually see. "No big deal. Feel better and I'll talk to you soon."

Setting the phone down, she slid it away and folded her arms across the table. Her head descended slowly, suddenly too heavy for her neck, until her forehead rested on the backs of her hands. Now what? Brett was away, and she couldn't sit around worrying about his safety. The Winslows were in San Diego, visiting Kaitlyn for the next few weeks. They'd invited Emily and Tyler to join them for the Easter weekend, and even offered to pay for their tickets, but Emily had politely declined. As much as she would have loved to go, she couldn't take any more charity from them. She was already in their debt for more things than she cared to count. Then of course there was work; taking time off meant forgoing that money. If she did that, she'd be in even more financial trouble. She was barely staying afloat as it was.

All her office paperwork had been completed this morning; she'd awoken early when the cat had flipped out yet again. Sometime before dawn, a plaintive yowl had wrenched her from a deep sleep. A second later, a muffled thump was followed by the scrabbling of paws as Terence flew into her room and took refuge under her bed. She'd bolted upright, her heart pounding in her ears, but no other sounds broke into the early morning silence. After that, she'd tossed underneath the covers for a half hour, emitting frustrated sighs no one but the offending cat could hear, until finally giving up. She'd trudged downstairs for coffee as the first rosy streaks of light filtered through the windows.

Tyler was happily watching his shows at the moment, but she needed a new plan for the day. At least something to keep them busy until naptime. She gazed around the kitchen, searching her mind for a suitable distraction.

Soup! She could make a big pot of soup for Gayle's family. That would not only serve as a worthy project, it would help her friend. She and Ty could drop it off, and then head over to the playground for a bit afterward. It was perfect, really—she'd bought a ton of chicken when it went on sale this week. She could make enough to freeze some for their own future meals as well.

She pushed herself up from the table with renewed determination. Sliding the chair over to the fridge, she climbed up and pulled her old-school recipe box out of the top cabinet. She set it on the counter and flipped through the cards, her vision blurring slightly at the sight of her mother's neat writing. So many memories in this box. They didn't have a lot growing up, but her mom had done the best she could; home-cooked meals were not only the least expensive alternative to feed her family, they were also one of the many ways she demonstrated her love.

Of course, that ended the fall of Emily's freshman year of high school. Not abruptly; at first there were mountains of casseroles and baked goods from neighbors and friends, and the need to cook virtually disappeared. Then the deliveries dried up as people returned to their daily lives, and Mrs. Shea tried to sweep up the pieces of their shattered existence and fit them back into something resembling normal.

But each year became harder instead of easier, and her mother seemed to slowly fade as she ignored her own precarious health. By the time Emily graduated high school, she knew her mom was simply hanging on for her, going through the motions in a valiant attempt to get her to go to college and follow her dreams of becoming a vet. And so she did. Or at least, she tried.

She pushed away the melancholy thoughts with a tremendous mental shove. Like her own mother, she had to remain strong for Tyler. That involved ensuring that he had friends. *Real* friends. And at this stage of his childhood, nurturing friendships involved some effort on her part.

Grabbing the cutting board from the dish drainer, she paused at the sliding glass door to let Terence in. He regarded her coolly from his perch on the deck railing, his tail twitching suspiciously.

"In or out," she ordered.

His amber eyes glittered in the morning sun as he contemplated the decision. Finally, he leapt down and stalked inside, taking refuge under the kitchen table.

"Thanks a lot for the wakeup call, by the way." She slapped the chicken on the counter. "Let's see if you get any scraps."

She set her phone on the little dock, found an upbeat playlist comprised of songs her team used to dance to, and got busy slicing and chopping. Her feet automatically moved with the music, performing a stationary version of the old routines as she worked. Her body remembered every move; even after four years, dancing as though she were practicing for a halftime performance was still her favorite form of exercise. At least once a week, she would blast the music, and she and Ty would jump around together, with Tyler trying to mimic her intricate moves.

Unfortunately, dicing vegetables was not an engaging enough activity to keep her mind from wandering. By the time she was on the celery, the lyrics to a song had referenced a first date, and her memory grabbed the opportunity and ran with it. While she didn't welcome the painful tug on her heart, she didn't try to stop the flood—remembering their first date was infinitely better than picturing a search for bombs tucked away along Monday's race route.

It had been a mild day for late December, with the sun managing to keep the temperature above freezing during its brief journey across the winter sky. Brett had picked her up at noon, as promised, and when she'd assured him that she wasn't starving, he'd driven them clear up to the very tip of Cape Cod. Along the way, he chatted about the various towns they passed through in their journey along U.S. Route 6. When they reached Provincetown, he pointed out they had also reached the eastern end of the cross-country highway that originated in Bishop, California. Between Brett's knowledge of the area and his excitement over EOD school, the conversation flowed easily without dipping into the past. By two o'clock, they were tucked into a table by the window in a quiet restaurant, enjoying draft beers, fried seafood, and a picturesque view of the harbor.

After lunch, they strolled down Commercial Street in the fading light. Quaint shops filled with antiques, jewelry, and clothing lined both sides of the street, along with the restaurants and galleries. Despite the final Christmas shopping rush, a number of stores were closed for the season. But she pulled him into the places that were open, and rather than looking bored, Brett seemed more than willing to allow her time to browse through the merchandise.

At one point, they wandered into a shop with a surprisingly large assortment of sexual paraphernalia displayed in the back. Her eyes widened at the sight of one extreme device, but Brett had laughed it off with his easy manner.

"Don't worry," he whispered in her ear, sending a shiver down her spine. "We'll save that for our second date."

"I don't know," she replied, tilting her head as if deep in thought. Two could play this game. "It's pretty pricey."

He turned his gaze on her, raking his eyes over her body with agonizing deliberation. "Trust me, we won't need it."

Her attempt at nonchalance crumbled as her blood turned to fire. Heat surged in opposing directions, coloring her cheeks and flooding her belly. *Oh, this was bad*...she was falling fast.

As the sky darkened from indigo to an inky black,

Brett led her toward MacMillan Pier, where a Christmas tree made of a hundred lobster pots glittered with strings of white lights. His hand gripped hers tighter; she'd long ago removed her gloves in favor of feeling his touch on her skin. Pulling her closer, he kissed her hungrily until she was forced to come up for air.

"Someone's going to call the cops on us." Her breath formed little clouds as she panted.

"I think you're forgetting where we are."

"Oh. Good point." Things were definitely more relaxed in Provincetown. Still, there were probably laws against having sex in the middle of Lopes Square, and that's where she felt like they were headed.

"We could stay the night," he murmured, apparently reading her mind. He peered down at her meaningfully, threading their fingers together. "Find an open bed and breakfast."

A frosty breeze lifted her hair, cooling her flushed cheeks. "I can't. Kaitlyn's parents…" The words drifted off as she struggled to compose herself. "I need to be home at some point." She had too much respect for the Winslows to cause them to worry, and not enough courage to tell them she was spending the night out with her date. A guy she basically just met, at that.

The seemingly responsible decision to head back turned into a torturous test of restraint as they endured the hour-long drive home. Brett somehow managed to keep the car on the road while his right hand slid higher and higher up her leg.

When Brett finally jammed the gearshift into park in front of his house, they pounced on each other as if the world was ending. He pulled her onto his lap, wedging Emily between the steering wheel and his solid body. With deft fingers, Brett unhooked her bra and pulled up her sweater, and Emily moaned as his mouth surrounded her nipple. She squirmed against him, pressing her body against the hard swell of his erection. His hands slid down the back of her tight jeans, his thumbs hooking under the scant lace of her thong as his fingertips gripped her flesh.

"Come inside with me," he murmured, drawing his jaw across the tops of her breasts.

The rough burn of stubble against her tender skin chased away all coherent thought. All she heard was "come," and that sounded good. Very good. She hadn't realized how badly she needed this release.

He pulled back a little. "Come inside with me. I don't want our first time to be in a car."

Through a haze of lust, she noted that his voice held no arrogance at the mention of their first time. Just the solemn assurance of a foregone conclusion. It *was* going to happen—if not tonight, then very soon.

"Let's go." He reached for the door handle. "Quickly."

"Wait...what?" The meaning of his words finally pierced the fog clouding her mind. Was he seriously suggesting taking her into his parents' house in the state they were in? And then having sex there? She shook her head. "Your parents..." she managed, nibbling on his ear.

"There's a separate entrance to the basement. My bedroom's down there; we'll have complete privacy." He finished the sentence with a groan as her tongue continued its path.

"They might check on you."

"I'm a twenty-three-year-old man. They don't check on me. And I can lock the door if it makes you feel better."

"Let's just stay here."

"Em, I can barely move. I'm not trying to pressure you, really, but if we don't go inside, I should take you home. If I continue with this, it *will* happen in the car. And that's not the way it should be."

But should it be in the bedroom of his family's house? She couldn't really think of another alternative, and she was starting not to care where they went, as long as this aching need was slaked. "Yes, okay." She grabbed her sweater off the passenger seat. "Let's go in."

She barely felt the cold night air as they rushed down the hill leading to the backyard. All she felt was an overwhelming urgency, tinged with the slightest hint of doubt. This rash behavior was not like her.

It doesn't matter, she decided, silencing the inner voice. He was leaving soon, and she deserved to let herself go for once. Kissing him made her forget the pain of this past autumn. Hell, kissing him made her forget her own name. She couldn't even imagine what having sex with him would do to her.

Actually, she could. Wasn't that the reason her body was literally threatening to burst into flames? She followed him through an unlocked French door into the silent basement.

She allowed one last pragmatic thought to rise to the surface as he led her down a darkened hallway. "You'll take me home, then, after...?" *Wow, that sounded bad*. But she needed to make sure.

"Yes, I'll take you home." He pulled her into the

bedroom, turning to lock the door. The click of the button seemed to echo in the darkness with potent finality. The only other sound was the rasp of their tortured breathing.

"Unless...," he added, slowly walking her backward until her calves touched the bed, "I can convince you to stay."

The phone rang, interrupting both the music and her reverie. The knife flew from her fingers and clattered to the floor. *Brett!* She rejoiced silently, lunging for her cell. But the picture of the dark-eyed, raven-haired girl on the screen revealed the caller as Kaitlyn before she even yanked it off the dock.

"Hey," she said a bit breathlessly. She was suddenly acutely aware of the tingling heat between her thighs. Damn that man and her stupid hormones. Why did she have to remember everything with such aching detail? Sinking into a chair, she crossed her legs defiantly.

Kaitlyn's cheery voice greeted her as Tyler appeared in the doorway. "Is it Brandon?" he asked, his blue eyes shining with anticipation.

"No, baby, it's Auntie Kay," she said, shifting the phone away from her mouth. "You can say hello when I'm finished talking to her, okay?"

He frowned as he considered this consolation. With a nod, he turned and padded back into the living room, Larry the lamb dangling from his little fist.

"Sorry, Kay. He thinks he's going to the playground with his friend, but they already cancelled. I haven't broken it to him yet."

"Aww. I miss him so much. Poor guy. Do you have a Plan B?"

"Right now, Plan B is making soup." She sighed as her gaze fell on the knife she'd dropped. *And trying to cut off my toes in the process.*

"I can see how that might be less than fun for a three-year-old."

"Well, we're going to drop some off at his friend's house, since they're not feeling well. Then I'll drive around and case the local playgrounds until I find some kids for him to play with."

Kaitlyn laughed. "What about Brett? He always seems willing to play with you guys." Her voice held that suggestive tone she'd been using whenever they discussed Brett. Always the carefree optimist, Kay truly seemed to believe their two-week romance would somehow be rekindled.

"Kay. He *hates* me. I've told you that a hundred times this week. I've told you everything he's said to me. He's always willing to play with Ty. I'm just the repulsive chaperone he can't get rid of."

Now her laughter turned to a choking sound. "Jeez," she gurgled, clearing her throat. "You could never be repulsive. You look exactly the same as you did then, when he couldn't keep his freaking hands off you for two seconds. Unless you've changed drastically since Christmas."

Emily glanced down at herself with a shrug. Her toned legs shone with the tanning moisturizer she used religiously. Beneath the loose shorts of her pajama set, her belly was still firm and flat, thanks to daily sit-ups. Right now, her curls were secured in a messy ponytail, but otherwise her hair was essentially the same as it had been four years ago. No stylish cut worked for her; she had to keep it long in order to weigh the ringlets down into something she could manage.

"Physically, I look about the same," she acquiesced. "But you are well aware of what's different between us. And anyway, he's out of town on some kind of temporary duty." Her foot bounced nervously as she mentioned his trip to Boston, and she pulled in a calming breath. Even though she told Kaitlyn just about everything, she didn't want to mention her suspicions regarding Brett and the marathon. Any concern for his safety would just encourage Kay's fantasy.

And imaginary friends and frightening apparitions were off the table too, in terms of conversation topics. Kaitlyn and her parents should be enjoying their time together, not worrying about whether they needed to book her a stay in a psych ward.

"Temporary duty? Where?"

"I'm not exactly sure." *Mostly true, anyway.* Pushing herself off the chair, Emily carried her empty mug over to the coffee maker and poured a refill. *Time to switch the subject.* They'd spent more than enough time on her this week, anyway.

"So, how's the visit with your parents going?" After tossing the knife in the sink, she settled back down at the table. "And then I need an update on what's going on with that crazy woman at work." She pulled another chair toward her and put her feet up. Sipping her coffee, she leaned back and turned all her attention to her best friend.

Chapter 11

"Now, we're just going to drop the soup off at Brandon's house, because they feel sick. Hopefully the soup makes them feel a little better, but they need to rest. So Brandon has to stay home. You understand that, right?" She glanced into the rearview mirror as she turned the key in the ignition.

Tyler nodded and took a sip from his plastic cup. "Josiah has to stay home too," he said matter-of-factly.

Her eyebrows lifted. "Oh?" She peeked at him one more time before focusing her attention on backing out of the driveway successfully. "Why does he have to stay home?"

"He doesn't like the car."

"I see." Josiah didn't seem to like or understand a lot of things. Was this Tyler's way of telling her he didn't like or understand the recent changes in their life? Brett's sudden appearance was probably confusing, but Ty certainly seemed to enjoy his visits. In fact, the enthusiasm he showed toward Brett sometimes triggered a spark of jealousy within her.

How on earth could she help her preschooler express his concerns? "Do you have any questions, Tyler?" she tried. "Anything you want to ask me?"

She flicked her gaze to the rearview mirror again and caught him puckering his lips in confusion. Well, their counselor Drew probably didn't need to worry about losing his job. If only she could have him on-call 24/7 as opposed to an hour-long meeting scheduled once a week.

"Can I have pretzel sticks?" he said finally.

Releasing her iron grip on the steering wheel, she laughed with relief. "Maybe." She reached into the big bag on the passenger seat. "What's the magic word?"

His answer came automatically. "Please."

She passed back an opened box of thin pretzels as she slowed at a light. His request didn't mean there were no hidden issues, but at least an extra snack had been the first thing to come to mind.

"Now you ask a question." He crunched on a pretzel, swinging his legs in the car seat. Cleary, he thought this was a new game.

She bit her lip, considering. Maybe it was a mistake, but she wasn't about to pass up an opportunity like this. "Um…what does Josiah look like?" Her fingers tensed on the wheel again as she waited.

A beat of silence passed. "A boy," he announced proudly, as though he'd solved a puzzle.

Okay then. Well, what did she expect? An answer along the lines of "he looks like a filmy apparition that only certain people can see at certain times"?

"Your turn."

It wasn't, really, but they were almost there. "Let's see." She turned onto Gayle's street. "Do you remember which house is Brandon's?"

That was probably too hard. They'd only been here once, and that was just to drop Brandon and Gayle off after school one day, when Gayle had walked to the church for pick-up time and a sudden downpour had made walking home a soggy choice. "It has a blue door," she added, slowing down as they approached the Stevens' house.

"That one!"

"You got it." She pulled into the driveway and cut the engine. "Okay, I'm just going to go take this soup up to the door and give it to Brandon's mommy or daddy. I'll be right back, so you just sit tight and finish your pretzels. And think of a good question for me."

Gray clouds had moved in to turn the clear morning overcast. Emily retrieved the big bowl of chicken noodle soup from the backseat and shut the door with her sneakered foot. The house looked deserted, but two cars were lined up in the driveway in front of hers. She hurried past them toward the front walk. As she got closer, it was hard not to notice the rotting trim and flaking paint marring the front of the one-story rambler, but Gayle had clearly tried to spruce things up with colorful spring decorations. A pang of sympathy tightened her chest. She knew what it was like to live paycheck-to-paycheck in a place where so many people had so much.

She climbed the concrete steps, hesitating for a moment with her fist poised to knock on the faded blue door. What if they were all asleep? Maybe she should just leave the soup on the step and text a message to Gayle.

Suddenly the door swung open. Emily gasped, jumping back. The soup sloshed dangerously in the container she had clutched against her body with her free arm. She caught her balance and gripped the bowl with both hands, stifling a curse before it slipped out.

The man in the doorway stared at her, irritation flashing in his narrowed eyes. He was short but wide—

a bulky weightlifter who also enjoyed his beer, from the look of the bottle dangling from his fingers. The thick flesh of his arm strained against his T-shirt as he lifted the bottle to his lips. "Yeah?"

Even though he'd only uttered one clipped word, something about his tone and stance seemed menacing. A wave of unease rolled over her as she struggled to regain some composure.

"Hi. I'm…um, Gayle's friend."

"She can't come to the door right now. She's cleaning." He moved to shut the door.

"I—" *Wait, what?* Cleaning? Emily tilted her head, rewinding his comment. Had she heard that right? If Gayle was cleaning, she couldn't be that sick. Had she lied to get out of their play date? Maybe she really was upset about the scary tour.

"I brought some soup," she blurted out before he could actually shut the door on her. "I made way too much, so I thought maybe your family could use some." Instinct told her to avoid mentioning Gayle's apparent illness, but she studied the man's reaction for clues to the truth. Maybe this guy wasn't even the husband. What was his name? Joe? Perhaps this was a friend of Joe's. She hoped so, for Gayle's sake.

He didn't give any indication there might be sick members of the household who would benefit from some homemade soup. Instead, he reached for the container with a heavy sigh, as if being given some food were the biggest inconvenience in the world. "I'll let her know you stopped by…"

"Emily."

"Emily," he repeated. He nodded thoughtfully, as though he'd made a connection. "The friend from school?"

A sour taste filled her mouth at the recognition. This had to be Gayle's husband. *Creepy*. She swallowed hard and pasted a smile on her face. "Yes. The boys are in class together."

His return smile failed to reach his eyes. "She mentioned that."

"Actually, my son's waiting in the car," she said, hitching her thumb in the direction of the driveway. "So, I should be going."

"Bye, Emily."

She could feel his gaze on her as she retreated to the car. Was she imagining the hint of intimidation that came from his use of her name? Suppressing a shudder, she climbed into the front seat. *You're welcome, asshole*. She twisted the key in the ignition and jammed the gearshift into reverse.

Maybe she was taking his behavior too personally. Some people just didn't like surprise visits. She glanced back up at the closed door as she began to pull away.

A movement in the window caught her eye. The curtain twitched, obscuring a face peering from behind the glass. Gayle? Brandon?

Or maybe her overwrought mind playing tricks on her again. *What next?* She'd probably arrive home to find Josiah riding a unicorn around the front yard.

Thankfully, Tyler was absorbed in a picture book and appeared to have forgotten about the question game. *Good*. She wasn't in the mood. Still, she had to keep up her end of the deal.

"Okay, we're going to head to the playground for a while, and then we'll go home for lunch. And then a nap," she added, leaving the Stevens' house behind.

Chapter 12

Brett pulled into the driveway behind Emily's beige sedan and glanced at his dashboard clock. A quarter to five—so he'd have a little less than two hours to spend with Ty. The four days in Boston had felt like an eternity.

It was amazing how quickly Tyler had become an essential element in his life. How would he have handled being away from him for almost a year at a time? Even stateside between his two tours, he'd been stationed at Luke Air Force Base in Arizona—2,750 miles away from Cape Cod. Not being able to see his son on a daily basis would have been unbearably painful.

Still, he should have had the chance to experience that pain. Fresh anger flared in his chest as he climbed from the truck. He hesitated, looking into the backseat. During any downtime over the weekend, he'd worked on an Easter basket for Ty. But he realized as he assembled it that he didn't exactly know what was safe and appropriate for a three-and-a-half-year old. Or what was allowed, for that matter.

With a sigh, he shut the door, leaving the basket behind for now. He hated having to ask permission to give a gift to his son, but that was the situation Emily had created. A muscle twitched in his jaw as he slipped his uniform hat on and started up the walk.

He lingered in front of the door for a moment, debating whether to knock. Competing desires warred within him. She knew he was coming, and his son was inside. The aggressive side of his personality told him to walk right in—he had every right to be there, and his son should see that.

But unfortunately Tyler still didn't *know* Brett was his father...and entering the house as if he belonged there might suggest a level of familiarity to Emily that he didn't want to encourage. He shifted his weight, impatient with his indecision, and knocked firmly on the door.

Emily opened the door, and he noted her beaming smile seconds before she launched herself at him. His arms shot up reflexively, and he caught her in a tight embrace. A small sob escaped her lips as she pressed against him. His body answered with a deep, urgent throb of need.

Just as suddenly, she tore herself away. "Sorry," she whispered breathlessly, her brows pulled together as if she was just as surprised by her actions as he was.

He shrugged. "It's fine. Quite the...ah, welcome."

"I was just so glad to see you...in one piece." She bit down on her bottom lip as her hands plucked nervously at the fabric of her blue and white striped skirt.

Forcing his gaze away from her mouth, he cleared his throat. "So, you figured it out?"

"Well, don't be so surprised. It wasn't that difficult to put together."

"I'm not surprised at that. It's your reaction I'm having trouble with. I would've guessed you'd be wishing I didn't come back." The accusation hung between them, charging the cool spring air.

Her face fell. She swayed like she'd taken a physical blow.

A bolt of regret shot through him, but he drove his point home. "Well, you've got to admit—my demise would have solved a lot of your problems. Both then and now."

Tyler padded into the room, waving a large plastic Lego block. "Brett! Come see what I'm building!"

"He got some new Lego sets from the Easter Bunny," she explained softly, the hurt look still shining in her green eyes. She shifted her body to prevent Brett from entering the house as she called over her shoulder. "Go make sure it's all ready for us to see, Ty. We'll be right there, baby." Turning back toward the door, she stepped forward. "Can we talk out here for a sec?"

He moved back on the landing to allow some space between them. No need to risk more physical contact. His body was still betraying him, burning in all the spots where they'd touched.

She glared at him. Two bright spots of crimson colored her cheeks. "I never wanted you to die over there, Brett."

"No? I suppose you hoped I'd return so you could deal with this mess three years later?"

"I didn't exactly plan the way things happened. But there *was* the distinct possibility you wouldn't survive. That's what happens to the people in my life. They leave, and they don't come back." Her arms curled around her abdomen protectively.

He struggled to control his temper as blood thundered through his temples. "I came back. Twice." A dull pain traveled up his arms, bringing the realization that his nails were biting into the flesh of his palms. *Stay in control.* He exhaled, loosening his clenched fists.

"I know! And please believe me when I say I'm glad. I was worried sick this weekend when I figured out where you were."

"I really don't understand you, Em." He couldn't look at her for one more second. Her beautiful features were clouded with heartbreak. She was either sincere, or a very convincing actress. He lifted his gaze to the sky and was rewarded with the blinding glare of the afternoon sun.

She lowered herself onto the step, tucking her skirt beneath her. "Could we sit down? Please?"

At least he wouldn't have to look directly at her, then. With a nod, he sat down beside her. Her huge orange cat suddenly sprang up from the nearby bushes and landed with surprising agility next to Emily.

She drew in an audible breath as her hand traveled along the cat's back. "I...," she began, and then shook her head. A clump of orange fur had gathered in her fingers, and she released it with a shake. It floated away in a ginger cloud. She tried again. "It's hard for me to understand what I was thinking at the time. Even when I realized I couldn't go through with the...with terminating the pregnancy, I still didn't plan on keeping the baby."

Another surge of anger pulsed through his veins. "Excuse me?"

"What I mean is...I thought he or she deserved better than what I could give. There are so many couples, with careers and family support, who are desperate to adopt a baby. I decided to look into it after graduation."

"Without involving me in the decision? I guess that's a dumb question."

"It's terrible, I admit it. But I was still in panic mode, and I thought it would be easier. If you had contacted me, just once, to give me any indication you regarded me as more than a fling, I probably would have confessed."

"You're trying to put this on me again, Emily," he ground out, his voice low and dangerous. "Don't."

She stamped her sandaled foot against the concrete, sending the cat back into the bushes. "Well, I also knew you were taking the time to contact Miranda! What was I supposed to think?"

What? Miranda had been his high school girlfriend. For two years, he endured her wild mood swings and crazed jealously because she was also fun, hot, and always eager to have sex. Finally, he tired of her games at the age of eighteen, but she had never wanted to accept that it was over. Aside from polite conversation when he saw her out in a social setting, he would never have initiated contact with her. She was too hard to shake loose. This made no sense. "What are you talking about?"

"Before I went back to school…before I even knew I was pregnant, I was back at Black Sam's with Kaitlyn. You had left for Texas, but Miranda knew who I was. She cornered me and told me you two were back together, and you were going to try the long distance thing. She showed me a text from you—from EOD school!"

A headache was growing like an oncoming storm behind his eyes, and he knotted his brows together and rubbed his forehead. "She sent me a care package, the first week I was there. She must have asked my parents or my friends for my address and phone number, because I didn't give them to her. But she texted me to see if it arrived, and I texted her back a thank you."

Emily lifted her shoulders in a defiant "see?" gesture.

Incredible. "It was probably all of five words!" He pulled off his hat, scrubbing at his hair in frustration. "That was enough for you to believe her?"

"It was five more words than I ever got!"

"You never sent me a care package," he pointed out.

She threw her hands up. "I didn't have your address! Besides, we agreed no strings, remember? I do have some pride, you know."

Blowing out a breath, he forced his muscles to relax. "It's possible we both might have a little too much pride for our own good," he admitted. During those first few weeks, he *had* occasionally checked his phone, hoping Emily would break their agreement. He could have made the first move and let her know he was thinking of her—but he didn't. And then the pressure of the program truly did wipe away all thoughts beyond earning the EOD Badge.

He absentmindedly rubbed the inside of his left bicep, where an ink version of the badge was tattooed on his skin. They called it the Crab, due to the shape created by the four intertwined symbols: the wreath, the bomb, the lightning bolts, and the shield. It was a powerful insignia, and the only occupational badge awarded to members of all four services.

"Mommy?" Tyler's voice called from the other

side of the door.

She jumped up. "Oh! Sorry, baby, we were just talking. We're coming in now." Emily reached for the doorknob, lifting her eyebrows at him in an unspoken question.

He nodded as he pushed himself to standing. "I want to spend as much time with him as I can before you head to work. Let's go."

She opened the door carefully and motioned Brett inside with a tilt of her head. He caught himself noticing the sunlight playing against her blond curls as he followed her into the house. Good Lord, he needed help. Two minutes ago, they'd been at each other's throats.

"Careful," she said with a hint of embarrassment as they followed Ty into the kitchen. A pile of colorful magnetic letters were scattered across the floor. "More items from the Easter basket."

He leaned toward her, touching her lower back before he could stop himself. "I brought him one, too," he murmured in her ear. "It's in the truck. There's candy in it, so I thought I should ask if that's okay first."

"Oh, sure. I mean, I try to limit the sugar, but it's a holiday. I actually put colored chocolate chips in his pancakes Sunday morning." Her cheeks flushed with the admission. "It was a big hit. As long as nothing in there is a major choking hazard, it's fine."

She turned toward the fridge. "That was really sweet of you. I'm sure he'll—" Her voice dropped off in midsentence as she stood frozen, her hand reaching for the refrigerator handle.

He looked over as he seated himself at the table

across from Tyler. "What is it?"

Her trembling fingers pointed toward the letters lined up along the bottom of the fridge. "JOSIAH" was spelled out clearly among a jumble of other magnets. "The name. How did he spell that name?"

Brett glanced at Ty, who was busy trying to create an accurate portrayal of a picture on his Lego box. "You said he spoke early. He can't spell?"

She shook her head. "He has a few small words memorized. But he'd never be able to spell a name like that correctly. I'm not sure I'd have been able to spell it correctly if I'd tried." The pulse in her neck jumped as she drew in a breath. "Tyler. Can you listen to me for a sec?"

Tyler complied, setting the Lego down and swinging his legs restlessly.

"How did you know how to write this name?"

"Josiah told me."

Her lips pressed into a thin white line. She swung back toward the refrigerator door. "What about the word beneath it?"

Brett leaned closer to study the other set of letters. "GAOL," it read—a nonsensical word. Why was Emily getting so alarmed?

Ty scratched his blond head. "That's where he died," he explained as he turned back to his project.

Emily's knees began to buckle, and Brett shot up and caught her before she hit the floor. "Whoa. I've got you." He held on to her waist as he guided her into a chair. "What is he talking about?" he asked under his breath.

"Josiah's a ghost. Not an imaginary friend." Her face was ashen.

What? Was she having a breakdown? Maybe the constant exhaustion was catching up with her. "Em, calm down. He saw something on television, that's all. And that's not even a word," he added, gesturing toward the second line on the fridge.

She pulled the sleeves of her white sweater over her trembling hands. "It's a word. It took me a minute to put it together, but it's a word. It's an old way to spell 'jail'."

"I think it's probably just an accidental group of letters."

"No. You don't understand. That first day you were here...remember I said we had plans? I won tickets for a historical tour of Barnstable Village. We brought his friend from preschool. And the tour ended in the old colonial jail that's supposedly haunted."

He reached behind his head to rub the tight cords of muscle at the back of his neck. The headache was still gathering its forces, waiting for the chance to invade. "I don't really believe in that stuff, Emily." Turning, he pulled two glasses from a cabinet to the left of the sink and filled them from the tap.

"I know it sounds ridiculous. But in that jail, he started talking to someone who wasn't there. I think he brought some lost soul home with us."

He set one glass in front of her before moving back to lean against the counter. "I'm not trying to be a jerk, but do you hear yourself? Honestly, there has to be a logical explanation for this." He waved his hand toward the offending words. "He heard the words somewhere and made up the rest in his imagination. You've always said he's a sensitive and intuitive kid."

"He is." She drew in a shuddering breath. "That's

why Josiah picked him," she whispered miserably, her voice scratchy and raw. She reached for the water, her palm still wrapped in the fabric of her sweater.

He knocked back the rest of his own drink, willing the water to quench the flickering pain. "Maybe we shouldn't talk about this right now." He lifted his chin toward their son, who appeared to be engrossed in his Lego project. But who knew what his mind might be filing away for future use?

"Yes. You're right. I'm sorry…I guess I've had an emotional day. I need to start dinner. That's what I was meaning to do." She shoved her sleeves back up to her elbows as she rose from the chair.

"Right. You two need to eat before work. Why don't you sit back down, and I'll make something?"

"You don't need to do that." But a hopeful light filled her green eyes. "I was just going to make turkey burgers and fries. That's easy."

"If it's easy, I can probably handle it." He pulled open the fridge door and reached for the package of premade burgers. "See, the hard work's already done," he said, nodding at the plastic-wrapped circles of meat. The freezer above held a bag of crinkle-cut French fries. "Just point me to a frying pan and a cookie sheet."

"Only if you'll stay."

For one brief second, he took her remark as an invitation to stay the night. His mind conjured up an image of the two of them, tangled in her sheets. Then he remembered she'd be at work all night. On the heels of that realization, he remembered there was zero chance they'd ever end up in bed together again. She'd done something unforgivable. What was he thinking?

"I'd love to stay for dinner. Thanks." He turned

quickly, concentrating on the stove as he struggled to erase the lingering image from his brain. Damn his raging hormones. And her sexy legs.

"So," he asked, stabbing at the plastic seal of the package with a little too much force. "How does everyone like their burgers cooked?"

Chapter 13

Another counseling session that seemed to both fly by and drag painfully, culminating in little progress by the end of the hour. Her hands tightened on the steering wheel as she glanced in the rearview mirror. Brett's truck was right behind her, headed to her house. Their counselor, Drew, had decided they needed a few more sessions with just the adults before introducing Tyler into the mix. So she'd left him with a babysitter, since the Winslows were still in California.

Most of today's session involved Drew trying to convince Brett it was much too soon to tell Ty about their true relationship. Brett argued, insisting Ty was a mature and sensitive kid who could handle the news.

Emily tended to agree with Brett, but she was reluctant to dispute the opinion of a trained family counselor. After all, it was her brilliant parenting that had landed them all here in the first place. She did her best to focus on the discussion, but her mind kept wandering to the Josiah situation.

And when she wasn't worrying about the boy ghost currently sharing their home, she was trying to decipher the strange message she'd received from Gayle that morning. Since the Saturday morning soup fiasco, all her calls to Gayle had gone to voice mail, with no return calls. Texts had been short and sporadic.

She was terrified Gayle and Brandon might be

going through something similar to their imaginary friend problem. Could the same ghost haunt two places? Ty's account of Josiah suggested that the spirit preferred to stay at their home; however, he *had* traveled from the old jail to his new location. Maybe once he was attached to living people, he could just find them and materialize instantly. What did she know about how it worked?

But although Brandon had been in the parking lot, he'd never actually entered the jail. It was that creepy conversation in the cordoned-off cell that started this whole thing—she was sure of it. At least, that was the start for them. However, the entire group had walked through the old Cobb's Hill Cemetery before they'd arrived at the jail. Perhaps Brandon had encountered something there.

She really, really needed to talk to Gayle about this. If it was happening to both of them, they could help each other figure it out. At the very least, she wanted to apologize to Gayle for exposing the boys to this paranormal nightmare. It didn't seem like a discussion they could have via texts.

So this morning, Emily had sent a fairly insistent message, begging Gayle to find the time to talk to her in person. Since schools were closed this week for the April break, she couldn't try to ambush Gayle during drop-off or pick-up. She suggested a play date instead, at a location where the boys could play together out of earshot as they talked.

Gayle finally relented, agreeing to try to meet sometime next week when the boys were in school. Then she sent a final mysterious message: "Please stop texting and calling. It's making things worse."

Emily turned the words over in her mind again as she pulled into her driveway. Maybe Gayle's behavior had nothing to do with the ghosts of colonial boys. If so, they were caught in some major misunderstanding that wasn't being helped by the lack of communication.

Cutting the engine, she pushed Gayle's text out of her mind. Right now, she needed to focus on convincing Brett. He was taking additional time away from work to come back to her house, and she had to make him believe something she could barely accept. But the only way to gain his help was to present a compelling case. Tyler's imaginary friend was a ghost named Josiah, and they needed to find a way to get rid of him.

Despite their attempts to be quiet, their entrance woke Tyler from his nap. She silently hoped the real culprit wasn't their friendly ghost, whispering in his ear like some wake-up call from the supernatural world.

It was just as well, she decided as Brett took Ty into the kitchen to pour him some milk. They deserved some time together. Digging through her purse, she pulled out her wallet to pay the babysitter.

She calculated the hours in her head, added a tip, and handed a folded wad of bills to their sitter, Olivia. "Do you need a ride home?" Olivia's house was only a few blocks away, but she felt very protective of kids these days; at thirteen, Olivia still qualified in her book.

A horrible thought suddenly struck her—what if the ghost attached itself to Olivia? Ty had claimed Josiah was twelve, so a teenager would be a more logical choice.

But nothing in Olivia's demeanor suggested she'd witnessed anything spooky. While Emily didn't exactly understand the rules of the great beyond, common sense told her not everyone could communicate with spirits. She'd always believed Tyler possessed abilities beyond those of a regular child. But she'd been thinking more along the lines of the kind that would land him in the gifted and talented classrooms in elementary school, not an auditorium filled with desperate people seeking messages from late relatives.

"No, thanks," said Olivia, breaking into Emily's wildly racing thoughts. "My dad's home today. I texted him when I saw your car."

"Oh, okay. Perfect. So...did everything go...all right?" She searched Olivia's freckled face for signs of trauma.

She smiled, revealing bright cobalt braces. "Everything was great! We played a little after lunch, and then I put him down for a nap. We read a few books, first."

"Hello?" a male voice called.

Emily jumped, whirling toward the sound. Her heart slammed against her ribcage in a frenetic staccato beat. A head peered around the front door—Olivia's father.

His lifted brows indicated his shock at her reaction. "Sorry, it was open. I didn't mean to scare you."

Right. She'd left the door cracked in the hope that Terence, who'd greeted them at the steps, would venture inside. No such luck. "No, I'm just...wound tightly." She managed a weak laugh. "Come on in."

Stepping inside, Eric Tanner greeted his daughter. Then he turned to Emily, his forehead wrinkling with concern. "All okay?"

She nodded with a bit too much enthusiasm. Eric

was a nice guy, but she was in no mood for small talk. Her nerves really were shot, for a number of reasons, and she needed to have that discussion with Brett.

"Maybe you need to go out...do something fun?" he suggested, his tone edged with cautious hope. He scratched at his neatly trimmed beard.

Her stomach flipped. Oh, no, this was worse than small talk. Eric owned the little convenience store where she often stopped, and he was chatty with the regular customers. He'd told her recently his divorce had just been finalized.

"I just need some sleep," she hedged.

He didn't take her hint. "How about this Friday? I'm sure I could arrange for a sitter," he added with a wink.

Brett strolled in, Tyler by his side. Positioning himself right next to Emily, he extended his hand. "Brett Leeds."

Eric's gaze flicked between the two of them. He cleared his throat. "Eric Tanner." He shook Brett's hand as he tilted his head toward Olivia. "My daughter, Olivia."

"Yes, we met. Your fantastic babysitter, right, buddy?" he asked Tyler, who was leaning against his camouflage-clad leg.

The air around them felt charged, as though an electrical storm was brewing. Emily shifted her weight, willing a cohesive sentence to form on her lips.

"I'm sorry. I didn't realize you had company," Eric said, breaking the awkward silence.

Brett lifted a shoulder. "No problem. I parked on the street in case Em needed to drive Olivia home."

Her mind latched on to the use of the nickname.

Here and there, Brett was letting the shortened version of her name slip into the conversation. A tiny bud of hope bloomed in her chest every time he did it. She had to remind herself on a regular basis it was simply an old habit with little meaning. But this time, it sounded like a purposeful display of intimacy.

Tyler saved them. With a few noisy slurps, he finished his milk. He lifted the plastic straw cup toward Brett. "Can I have more milk?"

"Magic word," Emily responded automatically. This prompt seemed to restore her ability to speak. Where were her own manners? "So sorry, I should have done introductions. I've just been a bit overwhelmed with my work schedule lately. Unfortunately, they have me scheduled Friday night as well." She shook her head in a "what are you going to do?" motion as she ushered Eric and Olivia toward the door. "I need to go get Ty more milk, but thanks again, Olivia."

Once the Tanners were outside, she leaned against the closed door. What had happened to her normal, ordered life? Apparently Brett had already decided to take care of the milk situation. With a sigh, she pushed herself forward and headed for the kitchen.

"I hope this is okay." Brett screwed the plastic cap back on the cup. "I figured more calcium can only be a good thing."

She stared at him, too confused to speak. "It's fine," she finally managed.

"You got the okay, buddy." Brett handed him the drink, then turned his attention to her, pinning her with an icy blue gaze. "Is that someone you've been dating?"

Was he serious? Hysterical laughter bubbled in her throat. This was too much. She swallowed, fighting for composure. "He's just a friend."

"No wedding ring."

Her eyes darted to Ty, who was arranging letters on the fridge. "And? Are you jealous or something?"

"Just an observation." He folded his arms across his chest and regarded her coolly.

Desire surged through her, unexpected and unwelcomed. She dropped a hand onto Ty's silky head to steady herself. "Let's go put on a show for you, honey. Your d—" She caught herself at the last moment, before "dad" could slip out. What was the matter with her? The chaos and uncertainty in her life were seriously taking their toll. "Brett and I need to talk about grown-up stuff." Scooping Ty up, she settled him on her hip. She could feel Brett's gaze boring into her back as she carried him out.

He was washing out the coffee pot when she returned. "I thought you might want a cup of coffee for this."

She opened the fridge. "Maybe something stronger." Pulling out two light beers, she held up the bottles. "Care to join me?"

The corner of his mouth quirked up. "It's five o'clock somewhere." He accepted the bottle as he pulled out a chair for her. "We may as well sit."

Emily sank gratefully into the chair, sliding the Lego structures into the corner. "I realize what I'm going to suggest sounds absurd. But I need you to just listen, okay?"

Brett extended a hand in a "go ahead" gesture as he took a pull from his beer.

She blew out a breath, gathering her thoughts. "Okay. So I told you about the tour. That Old Jailhouse on Main Street—that's where we ended up. The guide said conditions were horrible and many people died there. It's supposedly haunted."

Pausing for a sip, she evaluated his reaction. His expression remained neutral, but she sensed an underlying impatience. Clearly he wanted to be spending his time here with Ty. She hurried on.

"Anyway, Ty slipped into one of the cells—they're roped off—and he was standing in the corner, talking to…no one. I'm sure now that's how this started. The next morning, he began the whole Josiah thing. Telling me how this boy had farm animals. And how he doesn't understand modern things, like trains, or cars, or the television. These things scare him because he's…from the past.

"Ty told his teacher that his friend was put to sleep underground, but he was lonely there. He missed his mom, I think. Don't you see? The spirit went back to the old jail, where he apparently died, and he's been there ever since. Until recently, when Ty offered to share his mommy. And then this lost soul attached itself to our son!" The final words tumbled out in a plaintive wail.

Tightening her grip on the bottle, she took another generous swig to steady herself. Beads of perspiration popped up along her hairline, and she swiped her arm across her forehead.

"I don't know, Em. It seems really farfetched."

"I hear sounds. I *see* things. And the cat…Terence is afraid of something in this house.

"Tyler talks to this Josiah. Sometimes out loud, sometimes in his head. And then he suddenly *knows* things. Things a kid his age wouldn't know."

He ran his fingers along the sides of his mouth. "You can't think of any possible rational explanations?"

She pulled her gaze away from his lips, flushing. How could she get distracted by his looks when they were discussing something so serious? It was his fault, for being so hot. She shrugged, picking at the raised letters of the glass bottle. "Well, I guess the other possibility is I'm having a mental breakdown. And while I realize that would be a fun option to explore, I just really don't think I'm crazy."

"I don't think you're crazy either. I just don't think Josiah is real."

The overhead lights flickered like a silent warning.

She froze, gaping at him. Her heart fluttered in her chest, mimicking the lights with its own electrical bursts.

He lifted his steady gaze toward the ceiling before turning it back on her. "Coincidence," he said firmly.

Tyler trotted into the kitchen, carrying the remote in one hand and the toy Air Force plane Brett had given him in the other. "Mommy, the TV is taticky."

"Static. Because the power went out, honey." She shot a glance in Brett's direction as she pushed her chair back. "I'll come fix it."

Brett drained the last of his beer and stood as well. "Let's ditch the TV for now and have some play time. What do you say, bud? We could use your Legos to build an aircraft carrier for your plane."

He squeezed her shoulder as he passed, sending a bolt of heat down her arm. "I'll think about everything you said, Em."

Chapter 14

His sneakers hit the pavement with jarring force as he ran through the base. He needed to pace himself, but he couldn't seem to slow the punishing rhythm he'd set. He'd told Emily he'd think about her ghost theory, which was the least he could do. But his thoughts kept veering into unacceptable places.

Instead of trying to suspend disbelief and consider Emily's argument, his mind just returned over and over to the events right before their discussion. That guy— Eric—had essentially asked Emily out, while he was in the next room. It made him crazy. Only jealousy, as absurd as that idea was, could be to blame. This realization infuriated him all the more.

He could not possibly want her. Not after what she'd done. But his body couldn't seem to get the message. Every hour he spent around her lessened his resolve. That fiery spark that had ignited the first moment he saw her was still there. It flared hotter and brighter each time he came near her. Seeing another man show interest in her only fanned the flames.

This was going to go south quickly if something didn't change. Sooner or later, his restraint was going to break, and he really didn't know what would happen then. A relationship between them, beyond one of co-parenting, was impossible. Not only because of their past, but also because of his present. Flashbacks and night terrors lurked in every shadowy corner of his mind. He had nothing to give any woman, now or in the future.

He was damaged beyond repair.

With a burst of speed, he sprinted the last half mile to the gym. Yanking open the door, he headed for the weight room to continue pushing his body to exhaustion.

*****

The steam bathed her face, opening the pores of her already freshly scrubbed skin. She swirled her fingers through the water, then adjusted the faucet to a cooler temperature. "Do you want bubbles?"

"Yes." Ty's reply came out muffled as he struggled with removing his shirt.

"Let me help you." She pulled off the shirt and helped him out of the rest of his clothes. "Did you have fun playing with Brett today?"

Tyler nodded enthusiastically. "We built a new train track." He lifted his little arms in the air, waiting for help into the bathtub.

She scooped him up, hugging him tightly before setting him into the sea of fluffy white bubbles. "I saw. Very nice," she said as she quickly soaped him up.

Brett had left before dinnertime, ostensibly to get his work out in. It was probably true—his physique certainly attested to regular exercise. But a nasty inner voice kept suggesting he probably also just wanted to get away from her particular brand of crazy for a while.

She'd followed his lead, though, on the idea that exercise might help clear her mind. Before dinner, she had pulled out the secondhand jogging stroller and headed out with Tyler. Now she was showered, in her pajamas, and ready to get them both to bed as soon as possible. Since Ty had awoken early from his nap, she figured he might not notice she was moving bedtime up a bit tonight.

"Do you like playing with Brett?" she asked, casting her gaze around the edges of the tub. Where was the big plastic cup she used to rinse him off? *Damn.* She'd taken it downstairs to run through the dishwasher. She needed it, especially with the soapy bubbles in the bathwater.

"Yes. But Josiah doesn't like him."

Huh? Goosebumps prickled along her arms. "Why not?" She turned and checked under the sink, to see if there was a container in there she could use for clean water.

"Brett says he's not real." His voice betrayed a hint of frustration.

The ghost had overheard their conversation? She did not want to get into this subject right now. But she owed it to Brett to try to mitigate the confusion. "Ah...it's just hard for Brett...and for Mommy, too...because we can't see or hear him." Exhaustion was creeping into her bones. And her search under the sink failed to produce anything of use. "I'm going to run down to the kitchen and get a cup. Just play with your toys for a sec. I'll be right back." She dashed out of the bathroom, running her fingers along the worn banister as her bare feet slapped each step.

She heard it as she crossed the living room, clutching the plastic cup. The solid thud of a door being shut. Running toward the staircase, she looked up to see the bathroom door closed.

"No!" She flew up the stairs, throwing aside the

plastic cup and lunging for the doorknob. Locked. "No, no, no!" Her shrill cries rang through the hall. "Tyler, are you okay?"

"I'm okay, Mommy," he called from inside the bathroom. His tiny voice sounded miles away.

A sob broke in her chest as she rattled the unyielding door. She banged the palm of her free hand against the wood. "Did you lock this door?"

"No. Josiah did."

Cold air snaked around her ankles, sending a shudder through her body. She slammed her foot down, as if she could banish the spirit by stomping at an invisible chill. Every cell in her body prickled with fear, but she needed to be careful. She had no idea what Josiah was capable of. Cleary the ghost was already angry with her for voicing doubt. Would he harm Tyler to prove a point?

"Okay. I want you to climb out of the tub and let Mommy in, Ty." *Oh, God, please, hurry.*

"I'm all wet."

"That's okay. I'll clean up the floor. Just be very careful getting out of the tub. Don't slip." She bounced on the balls of her feet, fighting against the rising hysteria. How could she have let this happen? She shook the door in its frame again, cursing her helplessness.

After an eternity of sloshing and squeaking, the knob turned under her damp palm. She rushed in, scooping Tyler into her arms. "Oh, thank God," she whimpered, squeezing his wet body into her chest. She rocked him, turning in small circles as relief flooded her veins, joining the adrenaline.

Foamy suds still clung to his skin, and she

reluctantly set him back in the tub after retrieving the cup with him still safely in her arms. She rushed to wash his hair and rinse him off, trying to appear outwardly calm. There was no need to alarm Tyler any more tonight, or to provoke their ghost into further displays of power.

But they were not staying here. Not tonight. She gathered Ty in a towel, stepping carefully over the puddles of water he'd trailed to the door. Once he was in his pajamas, she left him in his room—which had no lock on the door—and found her phone. Her fingers still shook as she scrolled to Brett's number.

"Hello?" His simple greeting carried an edge of concern. She didn't usually call him this late in the evening.

The words tumbled out as Emily crossed to the other side of the hallway. "Something happened. I was giving Tyler a bath, and I had to go grab something from downstairs. I know that's bad, but he's three and a half. I was only away for a second. But that…Josiah," she lowered her voice to a trembling whisper, "locked the bathroom door. I couldn't get in, and our son was in the tub!"

"Is he okay?"

"Yes, he's fine." Her breathless panting was making her lightheaded. She leaned against the wall. "But we're not staying in this house tonight. I just can't. The Winslows are still away, and I didn't know who else to call."

"Okay, calm down. Let me think."

His strong, clear voice gave her comfort, even through the phone. She gripped the cell in her hand and crept back toward Ty's room to check on him. He was sitting on his bed, showing a book to Larry the lamb. Her heart contracted painfully.

"There's not really room here. But my parents are still in Virginia. I'll meet you at their house, okay? Do you remember where it is?"

"Yes."

"I'll leave right now. Are you okay to drive, or should I come get you guys?"

A wave of gratitude rolled over her. Brett may not like her personally, but he was going to be there for them. "I'm fine to drive. I just have to change and pack a few things, and then I'll be right there." She straightened her back as the practical part of her took charge. "And Brett? Thanks."

Chapter 15

The car's headlights illuminated his dark figure, sitting on the front steps. He swirled the contents of the glass in his hand, knocked it back, and set it on the cement. He was up and striding toward her car as she braked to a stop behind his truck.

As soon as she cut the engine, he opened her driver's side door and leaned in. She could smell the sharp tang of whiskey mixing with the cool rush of night air.

"Everyone all right?" His gaze raked over her before he turned his attention to the backseat.

"He's asleep," she murmured. "But I explained where we were going, so hopefully he won't be scared if he wakes up. He was really excited, actually." She climbed from the seat, but Brett remained where he was, with one hand on her opened door and one hand on the roof. He loomed over her, trapping her against the car. Her breath caught as their eyes met in the darkness.

He stepped back. "I'll carry him in."

"Okay. Here, let me unbuckle him." She slipped by him and circled behind the car to get to Ty's car seat. Once Brett had hefted their sleeping child into his arms, she gathered the portable mattress and their bags.

"I'll take one." Transferring Ty's weight to one arm, he reached out for the heavier bag, looping it over his shoulder as he led her inside.

Their footsteps echoed in the empty foyer. She chewed on her lip, glancing into the adjoining rooms furtively, as though his parents might materialize at any time.

Brett motioned toward the door to the basement. "I thought we could put the two of you downstairs. That way you have some privacy," he added, his voice low. "There's that little office right next to my old bedroom. Ty could sleep in there. Or we can set him up in the same room as you, if you want."

She weighed the options. Sleeping in the same room with Tyler often led to a fitful night for her—every mumbled phrase and tiny snore he uttered woke her up. Besides, Josiah didn't like cars; she knew that well. He never followed them to the vet clinic. And she'd be right next door.

"No, the little office is fine. Thank you."

She descended the stairs behind Brett, her pulse thundering in her ears. Maybe this wasn't a good idea, but it was too late now. Memories flooded back as they passed the French doors she'd snuck through so many times during their two weeks together. A surge of longing pulled at her belly. *Oh, no.*

This wasn't just a bad idea—being here was downright dangerous. Should she ask to sleep upstairs instead? *No.* She didn't know what rooms were available up there, but she definitely did not feel comfortable sleeping in the Leeds' master bedroom. And to claim the upstairs felt wrong, anyway. She was stuck.

He led her into the little office, and she hurried to get the portable bed ready as he held Ty. Her hands were still trembling slightly, and she tried to hide her anxiety with quick, efficient movements. Thank God she had this routine down to a science.

"There's no lock on this door." He twisted the knob with his free hand to demonstrate.

"Good." She bit down on her lower lip before she could launch into another attempt to convince him the ghost was real. That could wait until tomorrow; they'd both had a long day. And he was being civil—he hadn't mentioned the absence of the lock to put her on the defensive, most likely. He was probably only offering her reassurance so she could rest easily.

"Done," she announced, pulling down the top sheet and blanket. She motioned for Brett to lay Tyler down as she searched the bag for Larry. Once the lamb was nestled beside him, she leaned over to kiss his warm cheek.

Bending down on one knee, Brett kissed his other cheek and ruffled his hair gently. He straightened up and looked at Emily. "Let's get you set up next door."

She swallowed hard. His old bedroom. He flipped the light switch as she followed him in, and she cast about for something to say to break the silence. "It looks the same."

He dropped her bag on the queen-sized bed. "I guess." Glancing around the room, he punctuated his short answer with a slight shrug.

"Sorry. I shouldn't have said that."

His eyebrows lifted. "Why not?"

She shifted nervously, rubbing her damp palms against the worn jeans she'd thrown on before leaving. "I just...didn't mean to bring up the past. But this room reminds me of what we had back then, and how it can never happen again." *Oh, God.* Had she really just said that? She dragged her gaze upward, forcing herself to look him in the eyes.

The air grew heavy with tension as they stared at each other. "'Never' is a pretty strong word," he finally said, taking a step forward.

She shook her head weakly, cursing the warmth filling her cheeks. "I'm just calling it like it is…you can't stand to even touch me."

"That's not true." His eyes flashed with a combination of frustration and desire as he closed the distance between them. "And that's the problem."

He gripped her upper arms, and she sucked in a breath. *What was happening?* Her mind spun as he steered her backward toward the wall.

"Every time I see you, I want to touch you." His voice was low and rough. "I want to throw you against a wall, like this, and do unspeakable things to you. That's the problem."

An inferno exploded inside her, a raging fire of raw need. The force of it left her almost breathless, and her words rushed out in a rasping plea. "It's not a problem. We're two adults. And…I've been on the pill for years now, so we're safe. We could just let it happen. What's the harm?"

"The harm?" His laughter rang with harsh incredulity. "I am still so angry with you—that's the harm. I'm not the same person I was. I could hurt you."

"No. I don't believe that. The only way you'll hurt me is if you leave me like this. I can't—"

His mouth slammed over hers, cutting off the words. The kiss was hard and bruising, as though he was extending a challenge. She responded with equal force, unleashing the frustration of years of abstinence.

He tore his lips away, cursing under his breath. His grip tightened on her arms. "I need to hear you say it."

A sharp twinge radiated up to her shoulders as his fingers pressed into her flesh, but her mind barely registered the pain. Her main thought simply involved getting rid of the sweater separating his hands from her skin. "Please." She groaned, arching toward him. "I want you."

He crushed her against the wall, seizing her lips in another agonizing kiss. He was trying to scare her off, but it wouldn't work. She was afraid of many things in her life right now, but she was not afraid of him. *Never*. She was only afraid he might stop.

His mouth trailed fire down her neck as she wrestled with the button of his jeans. The denim strained against his arousal, and she yanked down the zipper. But her arms were suddenly forced upward as he pulled the sweater over her head. Her elbow hit the light switch, and they were suddenly plunged into darkness.

He pinned her wrists against the wall with one strong hand, tearing at her lacy bra with the other. His mouth covered her exposed nipple, and a low moan tore from her throat.

An unbearable ache was building inside her, and she struggled to free her hands. When he finally released her wrists, he caught her by the waist instead, still trapping her against the wall. She clung to his neck and whimpered as he dragged his chin down her belly, his stubble scratching the delicate skin.

In seconds, her belt was undone and her loose jeans lay in a puddle on the floor. Her skimpy thong followed. Then he suddenly scooped her up, seizing her mouth again as she wrapped her legs around his waist.

He carried her toward the door and locked it quietly without breaking the kiss. Somewhere in the back of her mind, she remembered Tyler, sleeping in the other room. *Oh, God...what was she doing? What were they doing?*

Her mind clouded up, denying conscious thought. That was always the way it was with Brett. Somehow he took command of every one of her senses, until no practical considerations stood a chance. He was like a drug.

Her palms ran over the thick cords of muscle on the back of his neck, moving up to the bristles of his short hair. They fell together onto the bed in a tangle, and the weight of his upper body caused the air to rush from her lungs.

Why was he still wearing clothes? She was completely naked. She pulled at his T-shirt, and he reached back and tugged it over his head. The cold steel plates of his dog tags tumbled onto her skin. His T-shirt brushed her cheek as it landed beside her in the moonlit darkness.

His bare chest slid further down her body, the metal chain around his neck leaving an icy trail in the wake of his warm flesh. Suddenly he yanked her legs apart even wider. She braced herself for the rough, hard sex she both expected and craved. Instead, a gentle kiss landed high on her inner thigh. Then he was teasing her with his tongue, licking and sucking until she writhed in exquisite agony. *Don't make noise.* But the rasping screams broke loose as she came, and she pressed his discarded T-shirt against her mouth to muffle the sound.

He plunged inside her while her body rode the wave of contractions, and their hips fought each other until they settled into a rhythm.

She clung to him, digging her fingernails into his back as he drove her toward another release. Her muscles tensed. "Brett," she sobbed as she shattered again, and with one last deep thrust, he came with her.

Chapter 16

He collapsed onto her, groaning in her hair. His back was slick with sweat, and she slid her palms over the hard planes of muscle. Their labored breaths echoed through the room as they lay together, spent.

Then the moment of intimacy dissolved.

"Sorry, I'm probably crushing you."

He levered himself up and rolled onto his back. Their upper arms remained touching, but he managed to move farther away as he rubbed at his forehead.

Cold air settled over her exposed skin. She shivered, pressing her body into the comforter. As the hazy glow of ecstasy receded, reality settled over her chest like an iron weight. What now?

He answered her silent question by picking up on the physical part of her discomfort. "You must be freezing," he announced, climbing out of the bed. He pulled back the sheets and motioned her under. "I'll check on Ty." Pulling on his jeans, he crossed the room. "You get some rest."

Simple as that, he was gone. A tiny part of her heart held out hope for his return, but as the minutes ticked by, she knew she'd be sleeping alone. Curling into a protective ball, she squeezed her eyes shut. *I will not cry. I won't.*

Her throat began to swell, in clear defiance of her instructions. *Pathetic.* What did she expect? They agreed to have sex, they had sex. End of story. They took care of a physical need. Brett had no desire to stick around and hold her through the night. If he wasn't asleep somewhere else in the house by now, he was probably scrubbing off any traces of her in the shower.

She waited for the correct emotions to surface: regret, self-loathing, embarrassment. The ones he was surely battling right now. But the only thing she felt was pain—a deep, hollow loneliness pressing against the walls of her chest like a malignant growth. By the time she drifted off into an uneasy sleep, her pillow was damp with tears.

****

The sun was wrong. She struggled to wake up, pushing against the currents trying to drag her back into oblivion. Her brain felt muddled. Her body ached. *Where was she? Where was Tyler?* She shot up with a gasp. "Tyler?"

Memories of last night flooded back as she took in her surroundings. Brett's room. In Brett's *parents'* house. *And, oh, God...what they'd done.*

Her gaze fell on the clock on the nightstand. Ten o'clock! She brushed all that away and jumped out of bed. She needed to find Tyler, make sure he was okay. Where were her clothes?

There. In a pile by the wall. Blood rushed to her cheeks as she quickly crossed the room. Wincing from both the mental agony and the physical pain, she slipped back into the jeans and thin sweater she'd been wearing when she came over. Then she hurried into the adjoining office.

Aside from Larry the lamb, the inflated mattress was empty. *Oh, no.* She tore up the basement stairs and burst into the kitchen.

Brett's eyes widened as he took in her crazed entrance. His finger hung suspended over the screen of his phone. He was alone, sitting at the kitchen table with a cup of coffee.

"Tyler?" she demanded.

"He's right in there." He nodded toward the adjoining living room. "I found the box of grandkid toys." Setting his phone down, he reached for his coffee. His lips quirked as he looked her over.

She suddenly realized what her hair must look like after a night of wild sex followed by twelve hours of sleep. She plunged her hands into the mess, and her fingers snagged on the tangled curls. Her gaze shot to her wrist, in hopes of finding a tie, but no luck. Dropping her hands, she crossed the kitchen and peered in on Tyler.

"Hi, baby." Relief flowed through her as she finally received concrete evidence of his safety.

"Hi, Mommy."

A large plastic bin sat near the striped couch, and toys were strewn on the sage green carpet. At the moment, a vintage farm house stood open in front of him, and he was moving the plastic animals through the compartments.

Scrubbing her face, she rechecked the time on the microwave clock. Yes, she'd really slept in until ten. "Shouldn't you be at work?" she asked, leaning against the doorframe.

"I took the morning off. That might be pushing it after taking yesterday afternoon, but I knew you needed the sleep. And I wanted to spend time with my buddy."

"That was nice of you. You didn't have to do that."

He shrugged. "I have the leave. And it's not like I'm planning a lot of vacations." The chair scraped against the wood floor as he stood up. "So, are you going to tell me what happened last night?" he asked, crossing to the coffee maker.

Her jaw dropped as heat flooded her face. *What?* Was it possible he didn't remember? He *had* been drinking when she'd arrived. That didn't make a lot of sense, though…he hadn't swayed or slurred even one little bit. And the rest of his physical abilities…well, they certainly weren't compromised in any way. That thought unleashed another surge of flames. "I…I…we…," she stuttered, searching for the right words.

"No." He cut her off quickly, throwing his hand out, palm up. "No. I mean—at your house. The bathtub." Turning away, he filled a new mug with coffee. "Sorry. I'll have to heat it up." He slid the mug into the microwave and hit a few buttons.

She wasn't sure if he was apologizing for the misunderstanding or the cold coffee. Either way, she was grateful for the distraction. "That's fine, I'm not picky. And I could really use the caffeine. I think I may have actually gotten too much sleep. My body's not used to it." She forced a laugh as she accepted the steaming mug. If she drank it now, she'd probably spontaneously combust. But it was comforting to have something to do with her hands besides try to tame her hair.

He pulled out a chair for her and grabbed his own mug off the table. "So, tell me exactly what happened." The microwave beeped as he started it again.

She sank into the chair and took a tentative sip. The

warm brew washed away the terrible taste in her mouth, and she quickly gulped down half the cup. Her nerves finally began to settle, and as he took a seat across from her, she relayed the conversation she'd had with Tyler last night. Her stomach twisted when she got to the part about the door mysteriously locking. "I was back upstairs in less than a second. And I was terrified, but he was talking to me, so I knew he was okay for the time being. I told him to get out and unlock the door." She slumped back and finished the last of her coffee.

Brett scratched at the dark shadow of stubble along his jaw. "Is there any way Tyler could have done it? Locked the door, I mean."

"No. I mean, he said he didn't do it. He's never done that before. Why would he lock me out?" She spun her empty coffee mug, reading the inscription. "Proud Air Force Dad". Above the words, the star and wings symbol of the U.S. Air Force was etched in blue and silver.

"To stand up for his imaginary friend. A lot has changed in his life lately. Maybe he needs some kind of reassurance."

"Reassurance of what, exactly?" Crossing her arms, she lifted her eyebrows.

He blew out a breath. "I don't know. I'm new to this."

"Well, I'm not. Ty is not that manipulative." She needed more coffee. And possibly some food. Grabbing her mug, she headed over to the group of appliances sitting on the counter. Several tiles with small colorful handprints, labeled with names and dates, were propped up along the wall. Would the Leeds ever want Tyler's up there as well?

"All I'm asking is if it's possible. Was there water on the floor?"

She slammed the microwave door with a little too much force. "Yes. Because I made him get *out* of the tub to unlock the door." Stabbing at the buttons, she finally brought the machine to life. Apparently it planned to cook her beverage for seven minutes. That might be a bit much.

When he didn't respond, she spun back toward him. He was looking at her pointedly, his blue eyes revealing a hint of sympathy for her poor, confused state of mind.

"Fine," she snapped, yanking open the microwave door to stop the thing from incinerating her coffee. "I suppose, based on the evidence, it's *possible* Ty did it. I don't think he did, however. And I need you to promise, for his safety, that you won't say things about Josiah not being real in our house."

He spread his palms out on the table. "I can do that. It might not seem like it, but I really don't want to fight with you. In fact, I want to ask you something." He pushed himself to standing and ran his hands along the sides of his head. His bicep muscles bunched beneath the black and green tattoo. "I want to do something alone with Tyler this weekend. What do you think?"

Pain lanced through her. Hiding her expression, she reached for the mug. The ceramic seared her fingertips, but she only tightened her grip. "I think Drew would blow a gasket."

"I think you're right. But I'm not asking Drew. I'm asking you."

She sighed, leaning back against the counter. "I think Ty would love it."

"Really? You're okay with that?"

"Yes. Drew doesn't know Tyler like I do. He doesn't know you like I do." *Oh*. The blush that seemed to have taken up permanent residence under her skin returned as her brain registered what she'd said. Would this ever end?

Brett didn't seem to catch her unintended innuendo. Instead, his blue eyes shone with genuine gratitude. "Thank you, Em. I appreciate the vote of confidence."

A lump lodged itself in her throat. She nodded, lifting the mug to her lips. Outside, a police siren wailed in the distance, the perfect soundtrack to her inner turmoil.

This was it. Ty would start spending time alone with his father, and she'd miss huge chunks of his life. Weekends would become bargaining chips; holidays would be split between them.

And she'd only see Brett during the mandatory drop-off and pick-up exchanges.

Something in her expression must have given her away. Lines formed across his forehead as his brows pulled together. He cleared his throat. "I'm not doing this to hurt you, Emily. It's something that has to happen."

"No, it's fine. I mean, I understand. And it'll be great, because then I can get some research done. On the ghost thing." The words came out in staccato chirps, like some deranged bird. She probably sounded as crazy as she looked.

"Okay." He stared at her for another few seconds, perhaps waiting to see if she really was okay. With a small shrug, he gathered his things off the table, crossing the kitchen toward the sink. "Oh, and I made a few things I found in the freezer—sausage and hash browns. I realize those aren't the healthiest of choices, but there's not a lot of food here right now. Anyway, he seemed to like it. The leftovers are in the fridge; help yourself if you're hungry. I'm going to throw some laundry in, and then I've got to get back to the base."

"Okay. Thanks." Her gaze flicked toward the refrigerator. So, they were going to pretend last night didn't happen. Fine, she could play that game too.

No, an inner voice insisted as she studied the seashell magnets pinning family pictures to the fridge. *Tell him.* Tell him the rest, now. Maybe it wouldn't be enough for forgiveness, but it might make him hate her less.

She picked at a cuticle, debating as he stopped to wash his coffee mug in the sink. A million reasons not to have the conversation tumbled through her mind. He was in a hurry. Tyler was right in the other room. She probably looked like she'd been caught in a tornado.

"Brett," she began, hesitating. He turned, and she noticed how tight the shirt he was wearing was—most likely something borrowed from his father. Because his own shirt was down in the bed, left behind in his escape.

Anything she said now would seem like a desperate attempt to keep the door open for sex. She quickly changed tactics. "Um, I just wanted to say thanks. For letting us stay," she amended quickly.

He paused in front of her, his jaw line set in a hard line. "I will always be there for both of you. Always."

Chapter 17

He glanced back, checking on Ty once again as he pulled out of Emily's driveway. Thank God he'd somehow had the foresight to buy a pick-up truck with a backseat. Otherwise, he'd have to borrow a car to drive his son anywhere.

Tiny raindrops fogged up the windshield. It was a gray, drizzly day—not what he'd hoped for on his first Saturday alone with his son. But they would still have fun. Without the distracting temptation of his mother.

He shouldn't have done what he did on Wednesday night. And yet, all he could think about was having sex with her again. It was driving him out of his mind. He'd avoided both of them for the rest of the week, hoping some distance would help lessen this raging adolescent desire. It didn't work. From the second he saw her this morning, all he wanted to do was drag her upstairs and toss her on the bed. This, while his attention should be focused on his son.

What was it about her? Emily had always possessed some strange combination of strength and vulnerability he found irresistible. Physically, she was gorgeous. In bed, their chemistry threatened to ignite the sheets. Now, she was the mother of his child, which was no small thing.

And it could never work. She was also the woman who had kept his child a secret. He was a man who required special housing exemptions due to night terrors. Once, in the hazy days following the explosion, he'd attacked a male nurse who'd had the unfortunate luck to wake him from a horrifyingly vivid dream involving combat. A normal relationship would never be a possibility. At the very least, his screams would continuously deprive anyone near him of regular sleep. The worst case scenario involved an unconscious act of violence against someone most likely half his size. He'd learned later what he did to the nurse, even with his injuries and IV lines. There was no telling what he might do to an unsuspecting woman emerging from a deep sleep.

A dull ache flared in his knuckles, and he loosened his grip on the steering wheel. *Calm.* The last thing Tyler needed was to be exposed to Brett's anxiety. He flicked the wipers to a higher speed as he merged onto Route 6. "Ready for our big day, bud?" he called out, forcing all thoughts of Emily from his mind.

****

Emily locked the front door and collapsed onto the couch. She felt as worn out as the sagging cushions. The exhaustion, plus the depression over Tyler leaving with Brett, sapped every ounce of energy from her bones.

Maybe she could go back to sleep. Unfortunately, she'd tried to combat a sleepless night with hefty doses of coffee this morning, so it might not work. She was supposed to hit the library to do some research, but the effort it would take even to drive there seemed no less arduous than climbing Mt. Everest.

A heavy sigh escaped as she watched the rain spit against her living room windows. *Nope.* She was not going out there.

She pushed herself off the couch, a small smile touching her lips as she thought about the weather. Brett had decided to take Ty to the Cape Cod Children's Museum. On a rainy Saturday. She suppressed an evil giggle. He had no idea what he was getting into.

In the kitchen, she opened a can of tuna and cracked the sliding glass door. Terence usually ate outside now, on the back deck, but she'd been reluctant to put his cat food out in the rain this morning. She was hoping the combination of hunger and dampness might lure him inside today. "Here, kitty, kitty, kitty," she called, tapping a fork against the can.

Terence's orange head emerged from underneath the deck, right where the steps down to the yard didn't quite meet up with the flimsy wooden lattice trim. He stared at her suspiciously.

"Come on, T." She leaned down and waved the tuna enticingly.

After a short standoff, he slipped out of the hole and crept up the two stairs, his tail twitching.

"Gotcha!" she whispered, nabbing the scruff of his neck. She scooped him up and braced herself as she stepped into the kitchen.

No claws sank into her skin. He twisted in her arms, landing with a thump as she released him. Before he could dart back outside, she grabbed the tuna can and shut the door against the gray drizzle. She could almost feel her hair frizzing in her heavy ponytail.

She forked the tuna into Terence's dish while he slinked around the room, performing a feline security scan. Everything must have checked out, because he returned to his dishes and dug into his treat with alarming enthusiasm.

So Josiah wasn't in the kitchen. *Good.* He was probably somewhere in the spirit world, catching up on his sleep, since he'd been busy keeping her up all night with his antics.

She'd stayed up late to watch the Red Sox trounce the Yankees. That had been a mistake, especially since she'd worked the night before. When she finally went to bed, a repetitive knocking sound had her back up within minutes.

She rushed into the hall, pausing for a moment when the noise stopped. Her pulse thudded in her ears, and she tried to listen above the hammering of her heart.

Another series of eerie thumps echoed through the dark house. It was coming from Tyler's room. Two quick steps brought her to his open doorway.

Moonlight trickled in through the striped curtains, painting the bedroom in a silvery glow. Between the two windows, the empty rocking chair slowly rocked, the top rail of the seat hitting the wall each time it traveled backward. From the corner, Tyler's even breaths filled the silence between each creak and bang.

Wrapping her arms around her waist, she tiptoed toward the bed to check on his sleeping form. Somehow, the noise didn't disturb him. His thick eyelashes fluttered as he mumbled something unintelligible; then he rolled to his side, still deep in slumber.

She pulled the stuffed lamb from under his shoulder as she debated her options. Calling Brett after midnight wasn't one of them. Her first instinct was to get rid of the chair, but she saw several drawbacks: one, there was a child ghost sitting in it, and two, she didn't want to anger said ghost. Her stomach churned as the bathtub incident played in her mind like a horrible movie.

Still, the rocking chair couldn't continue its rhythmic banging against the wall. She took a few hesitant steps forward, shivering as the chill enveloped her. Her throat turned to dust as she prepared to address the boy ghost, and she swallowed hard. "Uh…Josiah? I have to move the chair. Just a little, to keep it from hitting the wall. You can stay." *Oh, God.* Would he understand? He certainly had heard her the night in the bathroom.

The chair's movement came to an abrupt halt. *Well, there's my answer.* Hysteria bubbled in her chest as she sank down onto her heels in front of the chair. Now for the hard part—she didn't want to risk touching any phantom body parts. With a deep breath, she reached out and grabbed the two wooden rockers.

It was like plunging her hands into a snow bank. Gasping, she yanked the chair forward a few inches. An image flashed through her mind—brown leather boots, worn and cracked—before disappearing so quickly it was impossible to tell whether her eyes actually saw the apparition or her mind simply manufactured it out of fear.

Her momentum continued to carry her backward as she released the chair. She sat down hard on the floor, the impact sending a jolt up her spine. Air rushed from her lungs with a whoosh.

A moment of silence followed, and then the chair began its slow rocking again. *Now what?* Carrying

Tyler out of the bedroom might appear hostile, like some type of abandonment. But she couldn't just go back to sleep in her room while this was going on. Sighing heavily, she trudged to her room and returned to the hallway with blankets and pillows to set up a makeshift bed outside her son's room. Throughout the night, the chair rocked, creaking like a pendulum marking off the hours.

Terence meowed plaintively, pulling her from her dazed reverie. "Hmm?" she murmured, blinking as the dreary scene outside the sliding glass door swam into focus. The cat made another demanding noise; his amber eyes glittered as he looked at her pointedly. The dish beside him was empty.

"Oh, okay." He was finally inside, surely he deserved a little more of his gourmet treat. She pulled the foil back off the can in her hand and dumped the rest of the tuna into his bowl. "Don't get used to it. This is a bit more high-end than regular cat food."

She ran her fingers along his warm ginger fur. "I don't suppose you want to come upstairs with me, huh, kitty?" Terence didn't answer. "Well, it was a rhetorical question anyway," she continued, well aware she was trying to engage a cat in conversation. Maybe she should call Kaitlyn before she lost her last shred of sanity.

No. She was too exhausted. And she wasn't ready to talk about what had happened with Brett. As it was, Kay was going to kill her for holding out this long. But that was a conversation that would end up taking a lot of time; it would have to wait until she felt ready to share. Right now, she was still reeling in humiliation.

"That's it," she told the cat. "I'm going to go take a

nap." She dragged herself up the stairs, holding on to the banister for support.

Chapter 18

The idea came to her as she stood at the sink, cleaning the breakfast dishes on Sunday morning. Yesterday's rain had finally moved on, and the sun was struggling to break through the remaining clouds. Emily chewed on her lip, chastising herself once again for failing to get any research done during her time alone on Saturday. The nap had done her a lot of good, but waiting for Brett to return with Tyler had caused her nerves to once again crackle with tension. In the end, the stress was completely unwarranted, since Brett barely uttered two words as he dropped Ty off. Truthfully, he had looked a bit frazzled—most likely the result of his first rainy weekend day at the Children's Museum.

There would be no chance for a library trip today. Even if it was open, Tyler wouldn't sit quietly while she pored over…what? What, exactly, was she going to try to find? The only clues she really had—the name Josiah and a place of death—were pretty vague. And those had come from a three-and-a-half-year-old.

She needed more to go on. Drying her hands, she glanced over at Tyler, who was wheeling a train under a Lego bridge on the kitchen table. She glanced around the room cautiously as she weighed the pros and cons of asking her son for help. While she didn't want to encourage him to communicate with a ghost, she had to find a way to get the ghost back to...wherever he belonged. A place where he could rest in peace. Away from her son.

"Hey, baby, I have a question. Can you talk to Josiah whenever you want?" Her hand drifted to her mouth, and she chewed on a cuticle as she waited.

The train track he'd constructed this morning followed the edge of the table in a complete circle. He walked around as he guided the train, releasing it when he moved around a chair and then continuing his path around the table. "If he's listening."

Okay. "Is he...ah...listening now?"

He stopped, raising his blue eyes to the ceiling as if he were concentrating on establishing the mental connection he seemed to share with the child ghost. "Yes," he said after a few tense seconds that stretched into hours.

Suppressing a shudder, she nodded. "Could you...ask him what his last name is? You know, like your last name is Shea? Maybe he could help you write it on the refrigerator." She pointed toward the magnetic letters on the fridge with a shaking finger.

Still clutching the wooden train, he padded over to the cluster of colorful letters massed along the bottom of the door like an alphabet army. He cocked his head in concentration, moving his hand over the magnets until he hit on the right one. "Josiah says he can't read good," Ty explained as his little fingers closed over an "M." "But he can spell his name." A hint of pride for his friend's abilities filled his voice.

Can't read well. She pressed her lips together, fighting the wild urge to correct a ghost's grammar. Her eyes tracked Ty's movements as he slowly lined the letters up.

The word "*Matthews*" took shape on the dingy white door.

"Josiah Matthews?" she confirmed. She twisted the towel in her hands. What next? "Can he tell you what year he was born? You can use the number magnets."

He stared off in the distance, and then frowned as he turned toward her. "He doesn't know." His forehead wrinkled as he listened to an inaudible voice. "He knows when he died," Tyler finally offered.

Oh, God. "Can you...use the numbers to write it down? The year?"

He picked at the number magnets. A one...a seven...a five. After another search, he looked up at Emily. "I need another seven."

It took a moment for his meaning to click. Then she understood: he needed another seven to complete the year 1757. A shiver traveled up her spine. Josiah Matthews had died before the Revolutionary War. This was surreal.

She pulled her attention back to Ty. "Oh...there's only one of each number, honey. I'm sorry. But I understand what you mean. The year would be 1757."

Although it had been weeks ago, she still clearly remembered the first time Tyler had mentioned Josiah—the morning after their trip to the Old Jail. He'd said his new friend was twelve years old. She quickly did the math: he would have been born around 1745. But why had a twelve-year-old died in a colonial jail?

"How did he die?"

It slipped out before she could consider the ramifications of such a question. Tyler's eyes drooped with dismay moments before his features went lax. In a hollow voice, he muttered, "Someone hurt him. He just wanted to share his food. His head…" The sentence drifted off as Tyler lifted his hand to the back of his blond head, pain clouding his expression.

No! She lunged for him, pulling him into a tight embrace. "Okay. It's okay. I'm so sorry. That wasn't a nice question. I didn't mean to make Josiah sad."

Tyler melted in her arms. "He's always sad. He wants his mommy."

She hoisted him up and settled him on her hip. "It's okay. I'm going to help with that."

Really? How, exactly, are you going to deliver a long-dead mommy to her long-dead son? She blew out a breath as she grabbed her phone's docking system off the counter. Now was not the time to worry about that. What they needed was an immediate subject change—and location change—before Josiah's memories caused Ty any more distress. She'd been foolish to even consider encouraging the communication.

She carried Ty into the living room and set her phone in the dock. "We're going to have a dance party, bud," she announced, forcing enthusiasm into her tone. "Ready?" She queued up a song, hit play, and went to grab her sneakers from under the bench near the front door.

Chapter 19

She was officially a stalker. She'd arrived at preschool early, dropped Tyler off in the classroom downstairs, and now she was hiding in the church's empty meeting hall. As moms climbed the stairs and headed for the exit, she peeked around to identify them by their backs. This was a new low point, she realized, but she *would* talk to Gayle today.

If Brandon was experiencing some of the same phenomena as Tyler, they could team up to solve this mystery. After yesterday's scare, she had no intention of asking Ty any more questions. He and Josiah were now apparently close enough to share emotions— maybe even memories. This had to stop, but she was at a loss on how to make that happen.

The idea of moving had briefly flashed through her mind, but she'd dismissed it for several reasons. First and foremost, she couldn't afford it. Secondly, she wouldn't repay the Winslows' kindness by moving out and leaving them with a haunted house. But the third reason was the most compelling: Josiah had followed them home from the jail. He might not like or understand cars, but he was willing to travel if the motivation was there. She didn't pretend to understand the mechanics of ghostly movement in the physical world, but she'd bet money she didn't have on Josiah finding a way to stay with Tyler, no matter where they were. Until Emily figured out how to reunite him with his mother, anyway.

Initial research on her computer had led absolutely nowhere. She had so little to go on, and communicating with the ghost through Tyler was not a safe option. Finally, she'd hit on the realization that there were people out there who did this kind of thing for a living. A quick search of "psychic mediums Cape Cod" had produced a name she recognized from the news a while back: Claire Linden Baron.

She probably couldn't afford it. And she really didn't want to ask Brett for money, especially for something like this. But maybe she and Gayle could pool their resources, if she could convince Gayle one or more ghosts may have followed them home from the tour.

There she was! Emily slipped from behind the doorframe and hurried to catch up to Gayle's retreating figure. As the other woman approached the exit, Emily called out, "Gayle!"

Gayle jumped and spun around, one hand clutching her chest. "Oh my Lord," she gasped. "You scared me!" She peered past Emily's shoulder, her forehead wrinkled in confusion.

"I'm so sorry." She held out her palms like she was trying to prove she had no weapons. What had she been thinking? Suddenly materializing behind a woman who may be dealing with a haunting was just mean. But she was desperate, and she was pretty sure Gayle would have avoided her if at all possible. She'd certainly managed to avoid the majority of Emily's calls and texts. "I didn't mean to scare you. I was just waiting for you and I got a phone call, so I ducked into the church hall to answer it. Um, you said we could talk today, remember?"

"Oh," Gayle mumbled, taking a step backward toward the door. Her head swiveled as she searched for an escape route. She resembled a cornered animal, trapped and frantic.

What on earth? "We could go somewhere for coffee," Emily suggested, aiming for a soothing tone.

Gayle's light brown eyes widened with alarm. "Oh, no, I'm not dressed." She gestured weakly at her rumpled white T-shirt and faded jeans. A thin navy cardigan served as her jacket, and she pulled it around herself protectively.

"Well, I'm not exactly ready for Fashion Week myself." She looked down pointedly at her black leggings and oversized plaid shirt. "But we can just go to my house, then. I have coffee. And I baked some banana bread last night."

"The thing is…I'm really busy this morning."

"One cup of coffee. It won't take long. You promised, Gayle." Emily added the last part firmly as she inwardly cringed. Gayle hadn't exactly *promised*, and she felt bad strong-arming this timid woman. But she had to do whatever she could to get to the bottom of this ghost business.

"Oh. Well, I guess that would be okay. At your house, right?" Gayle's brows lifted as she waited for confirmation.

"My house. I can drive us both—"

"Oh, no, I have my car. I'll follow you."

Sure you will. Emily nodded, fighting to keep her face free of skepticism. She led Gayle out the church's side door and into the weak sunshine. "I'm parked right there." She pointed to her car as she dug into her bag for the keys.

Throughout the short drive back to her house, she checked her rearview mirror compulsively, waiting for Gayle's car to suddenly peel away in a cloud of screeching tires and burning rubber. But the mud-splattered white SUV stayed right behind her equally dirty sedan until they were both parked in Emily's driveway.

Sunny yellow daffodils bloomed in clumps near the front steps, a stark contrast to the heavy tension hanging in the air between them. Emily forced an encouraging smile as she led Gayle into the house. She hoped Josiah wouldn't do anything to add to the stressful situation.

She kept a conversation about preschool and the weather going until they were both seated at the kitchen table, which she'd set with mugs of fresh coffee, cream and sugar, and plates of sliced banana bread. Reaching for the little white pitcher of cream, she struggled to find the right way to broach the uncomfortable subject of child ghosts. *By the way, Gayle, are you afraid you might be going crazy because a spirit from colonial times is now haunting your house? Well, I have good news—me too!*

She pressed her lips together, clamping down on the wild giggles threatening to erupt. *Just start at the beginning.* Her grip tightened around her mug as she finally broke the strained silence. "Gayle, I need to talk to you about the night we went on the tour."

Gayle's upper body curled forward, deflating like a popped toy ball. She kept her gaze on the tabletop as she shook her head slowly.

The knot in her chest tightened, but she pressed on.

"I know you're scared. But just tell me about what happened after, when you went home."

Gayle swallowed, and the dry clicking sound seemed to echo through the quiet kitchen. "I shouldn't be here. I think he suspects you know."

What? How strange. Did something happen to make Gayle feel threatened? The bathtub incident had certainly rattled Emily enough to call on Brett. Enough to make her flee to his house...

No. She needed to push that thought away immediately. *That* was never going to happen again.

She chewed on her bottom lip and pretended she understood, nodding her head sympathetically. "I do know some things. Tell me the rest."

Her eyes lifted, the brown depths swimming with tears. "There's nothing to tell. It was my fault. I said I'd be home by a certain time, and I was late." One of her shoulders lifted in a resigned half-shrug.

Huh? That made no sense. "But—"

Suddenly the truth slammed into place. Gayle's constant fear. Joe's aggressive behavior. The injuries and absences. The long clothes in unseasonably warm weather. Gayle wasn't being haunted by a ghost. She was the victim of domestic abuse.

Oh, God. She should have put it together sooner. She *would* have put it together sooner if her own life wasn't so chaotic.

Gayle twisted her trembling fingers as she continued trying to explain. "Listen, Joe's not a bad guy. He just likes things a certain way, and he has a short temper."

Emily fought to unlock her features from what was certainly an expression of horrified shock. Her mouth

154

snapped close, then opened again as the question fell out. "He…hurts you?" A vision flashed through her mind—Gayle's bruised jaw, the Wednesday after the tour. "Oh my God, he did that to your lip!"

"It wasn't a big deal." Silent tears rolled down her cheeks and dropped onto her folded arms, creating dark splotches on the navy cotton. "It looked worse than it was."

"It is a big deal! He's abusing you."

"No." It came out as a half-whisper, half-sob.

Emily ignored the denial. "Does anyone else know? Your family?"

"No family," she murmured, continuing to shake her head slowly, as if there would never be a question to which that gesture wasn't a suitable response. "My mom died from cancer when I was young. My dad…he tried…but alcoholism. He's on the streets now, I guess. Maybe he's dead, too." Her shoulders rose and fell in another weak shrug.

A fresh wave of sympathy washed over Emily. She knew what having no family was like. "What about friends?"

"I don't have any friends. Joe says I should focus on being a mother and a wife."

"I bet he does," she muttered. *No wonder he hates me*, she thought, her mind whirling in an effort to process the desperate situation. "There must be somewhere you can go…a shelter or something."

"He'd find me," she said, her voice dull and distant. Her gaze drifted back to Emily, and panic blazed in her eyes before she arranged her features in a grim smile. "I just need to try harder, and then everything will be all right." She stood abruptly, sending the chair skittering backward. "Goodness! I have so much to do, and here I am, chatting away the morning."

"But, Gayle—"

"I really do have to get going. Thanks, though, for the coffee." Backing away from the table, she dug into her pocket for her keys.

This was insane. Emily jumped up, glancing at the untouched coffee. What could she say to make Gayle stay? She extended her hands in a pleading gesture, but Gayle had already turned toward the entrance to the living room.

She skirted the table and caught up to Gayle as she hurried toward the front door. "Are you sure you can't stay?"

Gayle paused with her arm outstretched, reaching for the doorknob. She dragged her watery gaze up to meet Emily's. "Thank you, but no. I have so much to do; I really shouldn't have come."

"Yes, you should have." She put a gentle hand on Gayle's upper back as she looked into her eyes. "I'm your friend. You can trust me."

Gayle nodded, blinking back the tears. "Thank you," she whispered back as she pulled open the door. She managed a fragile smile before stepping outside.

Emily watched her walk to her car, fighting the urge to call out, "Everything's going to be okay." She really couldn't make that promise. She was sure as hell going to try to help make it okay, though. An image of Joe punching sweet, tiny Gayle in the mouth flashed through her mind, and anger flared. *Bastard*.

"Call or text me if you need me!" It was the best she could do at the moment—no promises, just an offer of help. Loosening her fingers from the tight fists they had formed, she gave the other woman a little wave as she climbed into her car.

Chapter 20

Tyler was asleep. Brett shifted on the little mattress, reaching awkwardly to stroke his son's hair. He'd come over later tonight, and when nine o'clock arrived, he'd offered to put Ty to bed. He'd even allowed Ty to pick out four books, instead of the usual two, but he'd only read the first few pages of the last one before Ty's breathing slowed to a heavy, even rhythm.

Brett glanced back at the colorful pages of the book—a simple story trying to impart the virtues of friendship. Apparently, the plot hadn't been quite exciting enough to keep Ty awake. He slid the book onto the pile on the floor and turned back to marvel at his son's beautiful features.

Sometimes it still didn't feel real. He wished he could tell people he had a son. *Friends share important news*, he thought wryly, mentally quoting the last book. Who exactly would he rush to tell, though? Brett didn't really have any close friends nearby at the moment. Technically, Brett was Air Force, and the Air Force's 102nd Intelligence Wing was one of the units located at the base. Occasionally, he met a few of the guys for beers. But it wasn't the same type of connection he shared with his EOD brothers.

EOD was comprised of members from all four branches of the military—Army, Navy, Air Force,

Marines. Once they came together in the program, they formed a new Brotherhood with extraordinary bonds. Brett had joined the military with the specific goal of following the EOD path; he'd chosen to enlist in the Air Force for the initial Basic Military Training because his brother Jeff was Air Force. In fact, Brett had first learned about the existence of the EOD program from one of Jeff's buddies who'd made that choice.

But right now, Brett was the only EOD stationed at Joint Base Cape Cod, which the locals still referred to as Otis Air Force Base. He had a feeling some strings had been pulled in the wake of the blast to ensure he'd be assigned somewhere close to home.

He didn't mind his current assignment—training and instruction on things such as explosive ordnance recognition and reporting, bomb threat search procedures and evacuation, and site vulnerability assessments—for the most part. But, God help him, he sometimes missed the constant adrenaline rush that came with the rigors of deployment. Unfortunately, that was a product of a very real danger, which often took lives. He'd lost many friends to what they sardonically referred to the "pretty pink mist." Then he'd watched his Team Leader explode in a hellish blast that was anything but pretty.

He jumped out of the bed, as if his memories could somehow contaminate his innocent son. His muscles sighed with relief at being freed from the strain of holding such a large frame on the little toddler bed. Somehow, he'd wedged his upper body next to Tyler, by request, and braced himself in that position with his legs.

Rolling his shoulders back, he bent down and

moved Tyler gently into the center of the mattress. He planted a kiss on one warm cheek as he tucked the yellow comforter around his chin. With one last glance back, he turned off the light and headed downstairs.

Emily wasn't in the TV room or the kitchen, but he heard typing coming from the little room off the back hallway. She used the enclosed space on this side of the front staircase as her office.

The door was slightly ajar, and he rapped a knuckle against the frame as he pushed it open. Emily jumped in her chair and twisted backward with a gasp.

Damn. He lifted a hand in a placating gesture. "Sorry." Was she always this tense? She'd never make it in his line of work.

"You shouldn't do that in a haunted house," she grumbled, swiveling around in the chair. She had changed into pajamas, and the short plaid shorts exposed most of her long, lean legs. Her skin shone bronze in the dim light of the desk lamp. For some reason, her toenails were painted a bright shade of turquoise.

He pulled his gaze back up to her face. "Tyler's asleep. I read him four books, but he didn't quite make it through the last one. Maybe I need to work on my narrating skills."

It wasn't the most hilarious joke, but he expected at least a smile. Instead, she nodded and glanced back to her laptop screen with a sigh.

He took a few steps closer. Pieces of paper with her neat handwriting lay scattered on the desktop. While he didn't want to open the door to more ghost talk, his curiosity got the best of him. "What's wrong?"

"Oh, nothing." Blowing out a breath, she pinched

the bridge of her nose. "Well, that's not exactly true. I found out today that one of the moms at Ty's school—my friend Gayle—is being abused by her husband. Both physically and mentally."

"What?" A bolt of rage shot through him at the thought of a man hitting a woman. No, "man" was not the right word for someone who would do that. His fingers curled into fists, and he took a calming breath to keep his temper under control. "And your friend—Gayle—just offered up this information?"

Her curls swayed as she tilted her head to the side. "Well…it was actually a bit of a misunderstanding. She thought I had figured it out already. But I really got the impression she wants help. I think she's just terrified to ask for it."

His mind caught on the word "help." *Oh, no.* He had a bad feeling about where this was going. "And is she going to get help?"

She glanced back at the laptop. "Well, that's what I'm trying to do."

Of course. "No. That's not a good idea. You should stay out of it. I'll go have a talk with him."

Her green eyes widened in alarm. "No! He's dangerous, Brett. He has no qualms about hitting a woman. If you go over there, one of you will get hurt."

He pinned her with his own steady gaze. "I can promise you it won't be me." Each measured word rang with deadly assurance.

An exasperated huff escaped as she folded her arms across her chest. "Brett, I've been looking stuff up all afternoon. That is not the way to handle this. She needs professional help."

He slid his hand to the base of his neck, kneading

the taut knot of stress. *Christ.* "You are not a professional in this area, unless I missed something. I don't want you getting involved."

"She has no one else!" She uncrossed her arms and lifted her palms, as if to demonstrate the veracity of her argument. "I'm just looking up options," she added, tugging her fingers through her hair. The movement raised her breasts, pushing her nipples against the fabric of her tight pajama top. "She needs to get away."

"Someone else can help her," he told her calmly, ignoring the tightening in his groin. This was ridiculous. She was discussing a serious topic that could put her in danger. And he was lusting after her while their son slept upstairs. *Unacceptable.*

She tipped her chin defiantly. "Listen to yourself. You didn't decide to let someone else go fight for our country. You spent two years in the desert, searching out bombs to keep our troops safe."

His blood went cold. "And I was highly trained to do that." Even so, years of experience still hadn't been enough to save Mac. He pushed the gruesome image of that fatal blast aside for the second time tonight. "You are not."

She leaned forward in the chair, putting her weight into the balls of her feet. The muscles of her legs shimmered beneath her skin as she bounced her heels against the floor. "Well, like I said, she has no one else. If Kaitlyn's parents hadn't helped me, I don't know where I'd be right now. I'm just trying to pay it forward."

"No, Emily. I don't want anything to happen to you." The words slipped out, but they were true. Not much scared him, but a thread of fear trickled through his veins at the thought of her anywhere near an abusive man. He suddenly realized he'd do anything to protect her, at all costs.

She cocked her head, lifting her eyebrows. "Really? I find that hard to believe."

"Stop." *Damn it*. She was like some kind of gravitational force, pulling him toward her. He closed the distance between them in three long strides. "You know I care about you."

She stood, looking up at him, her eyes flashing with challenge. "As Tyler's mom, you mean." The old clock on her desk ticked off the seconds as they faced off, the heat growing between them.

He pushed at the chair with a savage thrust, and it rolled away quietly on its wheels. Backing her toward the desk, he grabbed her shoulders. "As Emily," he growled, now angry with himself. But there was no resisting it. He crushed his lips over hers, allowing his desire to take control. His body needed her—it was as simple as that.

She wrapped her arms around his neck, returning his kiss with an answering hunger. Their lips and tongues clashed as they both fought to get their fill. His hands traveled to her waist, and he hoisted her onto the desk, pushing the laptop and papers across the slick surface.

"Hurry," she murmured, biting his lower lip.

He slid his hands up the smooth skin of her back. "Will he wake up?" His voice sounded thick and distant. Regardless of her answer, there was no stopping now. He pulled her thermal pajama top up, and she lifted her arms obediently.

She met his gaze as her curls fell around her bare

shoulders. "No. I just need you. Now."

Her words undid him. He yanked her shorts down and pushed his hips between her legs. The desk light shone on her smooth skin, and he kissed his way down the silky flesh of her abdomen.

"Oh!" She gasped as he buried his face between her legs. Her thighs locked around his head, and he slid his hands under her legs to pull her closer. God, the taste of her...he could never get enough.

Her hands flailed against his shoulders, beating him in the throes of desire. "Oh...please." She moaned, grabbing unsuccessfully at the shorn hair on his head. Finally, she dug her fingers into the skin of his back, attempting to haul him up. "Please."

He slid his tongue up the quivering flesh of her belly, pausing to suck on one perfect nipple. She shuddered, arching toward him. Her chest rose and fell with shallow breaths as she clawed at his back. God, he was hard.

Her chin tipped back, exposing the delicate column of her throat. The fluttering pulse beneath her jaw drew him. He gathered her curls in one fist, anchoring her head as he ravaged her neck. A low groan vibrated beneath her skin.

"Brett."

The sound of his name allowed reality to slip past the heavy haze of need. They were going to have sex. Again. It was a bad idea.

Too late for that thought. He mentally shoved it aside as he caught her mouth again. Releasing her hair, he reached behind and pulled at his shirt, breaking the kiss to yank it over his head.

She stared up at him, her eyes dark with desire.

Somehow she looked both wickedly sexy and heartbreakingly vulnerable. Her fingers touched the metal dog tags hanging from his neck before trailing their way down his chest. Lifting her lips back up to his, she worked the button on his jeans with slow deliberation.

It was too much to bear. He had to have her. Now. His hands tangled with hers, and together they tore off the rest of his clothes. The searing urgency returned, raw and potent.

He gripped the small of her back and pulled her forward, plunging himself into her, hoisting her up and riding the spasms as her body responded.

She came quickly, crying out, and he drove himself deeper as she clenched around him, finding his own release. They collapsed together against the desk, their ragged breaths filling the room, their limbs entwined as though their bodies were made to fit together. For one lingering moment in time, they were the only two people in existence.

She nuzzled the space between his shoulder and neck before lifting her head. Her gaze met his, her flushed features lit with hope. She didn't say it out loud, but the invitation was there, shining in her eyes. She wanted him to stay the night.

That could never happen.

He pulled his hands out from beneath her and held on to her waist, helping her down from the desk. Clearing his throat, he stepped back. "I should really get going. We start things early in the military. And my uniforms are at the base." He lifted his jeans, as though the civilian clothing served as proof of his story.

Her face fell, but she masked her disappointment

quickly. "Of course." She bent down and tugged her plaid purple shorts back on. The pajama bottoms covered next to nothing, and she crossed her arms over her breasts as she scanned the room for the top.

It lay on the far side of the desk, on the thick white rug beneath the windows. Mercifully, the shades were drawn. Had they been open, the desk lamp would have provided excellent lighting for anyone standing outside in the darkness.

The door to the room was open as well. What if Ty had woken up and come looking for them? They really needed to be more careful.

Listen to yourself, Brett's inner voice sneered, thoroughly disgusted. They didn't have to be more careful, because it couldn't keep happening. He pulled his T-shirt on as he retrieved her pajama top from its hiding spot.

He handed it to her, noting how she still kept one arm covering herself as she accepted the top. As if he hadn't just seen—and touched, licked, and kissed—her breasts. Should he turn away? He couldn't decide if that would come across as polite or rude.

Christ. How could this level of awkwardness follow something so intimate? *Because it's wrong*, the inner voice pointed out gleefully, *and you both know it*.

She fixed the problem by turning toward the desk to pull on her top. Then she slid the laptop back in place and closed it with a click. "I think I'll call it a night, too."

He nodded. "What are you going to do about all that?" Lifting his chin, he gestured toward her notes. "I don't want you putting yourself in harm's way."

"I heard you the first time." A hint of irritation

tinged her voice. She yanked on the chain hanging from the green lampshade, filling the room with shadows.

He didn't blame her for being confused. The mixed messages he was sending were confusing him as well. He wanted to insist she run any planned "help" for this woman by him first, but he knew that might be pushing it. Scrubbing his face, he followed her from the room. He could still smell her on every part of himself.

She led him through the kitchen toward the front door with purposeful strides. "I was thinking maybe I'll give her any information I find during pick-up and drop-off. Just handwritten, on paper. She can keep it and hide it if she wants, or rip it up and toss it at the church if she's scared. At least that way she'll know she's not alone, and that there are people out there who can help her. She's obviously thought about shelters, because she said he'd find her if she went to one. But there are ways to go into hiding, and I'm going to research all the options. I'm sure she can't do a search for that stuff—he probably checks her phone and her computer."

He understood her need to fill the silence; in fact, he welcomed it. And her plan set his mind at ease—minimal involvement on her part. They reached the door, and he struggled for the right parting words. "Bye" seemed too casual. "Thanks" would be downright insulting.

She stood off to the side, next to the bench by the door, arms crossed. Her lips were swollen, and red marks were forming on her neck like blooming roses.

He looked away, toward the top of the staircase. "Tell Tyler I said bye," he said, pulling open the door. The night air drifted in, cool and salty. Glancing back at

Emily, he added, "I'll call you tomorrow." That seemed safe enough, since it was true—she was, after all, still his only link to his son.

For now, anyway, he reminded himself as he stepped out into the darkness.

Chapter 21

"No!" Tyler kicked at her hands as she tried once again to put on his shoes.

That was about the twentieth "no" of the morning. Emily sighed and sat back on her heels. She hoped this wasn't the start of some new phase. Ty had never really been a child prone to tantrums—he seemed to understand, on some basic level, there was no room in their lives for time-consuming arguments. Plus, Emily usually stood firm, never giving in to any demands associated with a tantrum. Even at three-and-a-half, Tyler realized that type of behavior got him nowhere.

But this was different. Since they'd arrived home from work a little after seven this morning, Tyler had been moody and out of sorts. The moment she'd started trying to get him ready for school, he'd fought her. And then the reason came out, setting her nerves on edge as well. Not a great combination.

According to Ty, Josiah had cried all night while they were gone, missing his friend. Now, he wanted Ty to stay home, as some sort of consolation.

Tyler hated to see people cry—whether it was her, other children, or, apparently, a ghost. He'd always been an extraordinarily empathetic child. So now he was refusing to go to school, and the harder she pushed, the more he resisted her efforts.

"I don't wanna go!" His face turned red as he

peeled off a striped sock and threw it on the floor. He checked for her reaction as he tugged on the other one.

She pressed her lips together before a word she'd rather not teach him escaped. At this point, they'd be late anyway, and she hated that, even if it was only preschool. She'd definitely miss Gayle during drop-off. But if they didn't go at all, she'd also miss the chance to give her the notes during pick-up today as well.

It could probably wait until Friday. Gayle's problems were new to Emily, and she was anxious to help her friend. But Gayle had been living with it for who knew how long; it was unlikely she'd be ready to leave her home, or even her abusive husband, based on one list of resources. The desire to get away would have to build, and Emily would have to be persistent. She could do that. She hoped the situation wouldn't become more urgent in the next few days.

Clearly, Tyler sensed a win. He stood up, stomping up their stairs as fast as his little legs would carry him. "Staying home," he chanted with every step.

She watched him go, her heart tightening as she noted how he still held on to the banister for safety, despite his show of defiance. With another sigh, she turned to the little windows framing the door. Last night's high winds had blown the flowers off the cherry blossom tree in the front yard, frosting the lawn with bright pink petals.

Now what? She'd been planning on visiting the library while Ty was in school. That was out now. She couldn't try to rest until naptime. Maybe when the middle school let out, she'd see if Olivia could come over and watch Tyler so she could get a little more sleep.

Was that even safe for Olivia? A thread of helplessness coursed through her, sparking an answering anger. The emotions roiled through her belly, churning like sour milk. What options did she have? Even though the Winslows were finally back, she couldn't take Ty over there—Josiah wouldn't allow it. Her life was now dictated by an almost three-hundred-year-old ghost with a twelve-year-old mentality.

The fact that Josiah was exerting an increasing amount of control over her son was both disturbing and terrifying. What if he decided he wanted Tyler to join him in his lonely world of purgatory?

Bile burned through her chest, hot and bitter. Her mouth watered as her throat filled with acid, and she doubled over, clutching her stomach. This had to stop.

She lurched over to the bench beside the door, dropping onto the hard wood with a bone-rattling thump. *Deep breaths.* When the urge to vomit subsided, she pulled herself up with determination. She'd spent the last four years creating a structured, safe life for the two of them. She wasn't going to let a preteen ghost take it away.

Marching through the living room, she stopped in the kitchen to grab her phone off its dock before heading into the little office. She powered up her laptop as she settled into the chair.

It was time to call in a professional. Her fingers trembled slightly as she typed "Claire Baron—Gull Harbor" into the search box.

****

She stared out the window, waiting for Brett's truck to pull into the driveway. Not because she was afraid he'd wake Ty up; he knew all about nap time

171

now. She just didn't know what else to do with herself. She hadn't left the house in over twenty-four hours, since they'd returned home from work Wednesday morning to an angst-ridden ghost. This afternoon, they had their first counseling session for the three of them together. What if Tyler refused to go? Or rather, what if Josiah refused to let Tyler go? That would be tough to explain.

So she'd told Brett what was going on, and asked him to come over early as back-up. But she also wanted him here so she could tell him in person about the medium's visit she'd scheduled for the weekend. Brett was still convinced all the recent strange events could be attributed to a childhood phase or his sudden appearance in Ty's life. Perhaps if he were here to see the medium in action, he'd be more willing to believe…and to help them find a solution, before something tragic happened. Shuddering, she wrapped her arms around her middle and leaned her forehead against the middle pane of glass.

A gust of wind swirled more pink petals through the air as Brett's truck pulled in, making the world resemble a scene from a bizarre snow globe. She moved over to the mirror on the wall to check her appearance. Minimal makeup, as usual—she had neither time nor money for that. But she'd tried to cover the dark circles under her eyes, and then added a light dusting of bronzer to her cheeks to give her skin some color. Plus her regular lip balm with a hint of pink shimmer, and that was it. Her hair was doing its own thing, also as usual, but it looked calm enough not to need further attention.

She'd chosen the only seasonally-appropriate shirt

she could find that would hide the marks on her neck—
a tight, short-sleeved, cobalt blue mock turtleneck—and
paired it with tan Capri pants, wedge sandals, and silver
jewelry. Presentable enough for counseling.

She played with her long necklace as she pulled the
door open, sliding her mother's locket along the
dangling chain. Her thumb traced the beads of metal
embossed on the surface of the antique locket. It was a
beautiful heirloom, but every time she wore it, she was
reminded of all she'd lost. Although she hadn't looked
at the pictures inside for over four years, her mind
easily conjured up the images pressed into each half of
the circle: faded photos of her and her brother, their
childhood smiles gap-toothed and innocent.

"Hey," he said, pausing on the front step to wipe
the pink petals from his drab green boots.

He was wearing his uniform, which probably
meant he'd been pressed for time. "Thanks for coming
early." Stepping back to let him in, she glanced around
the living room. It looked as good as it possibly could
with its low budget décor. Since she'd been essentially
trapped in the house for the last day and a half, she'd
decided to at least devote some time to domestic
activities. Normally, she managed to keep things
organized, but this room had undergone a serious spring
cleaning. A fresh citrus smell hung in the air, and tulips
cut from her backyard brightened the coffee table.

"No problem."

He removed his hat and followed her to the couch.
A pitcher of lemonade sat on a platter beside the
flowers, along with two tall glasses. Turning toward
her, he raised his eyebrows.

She shrugged. "Want some?" she asked, reaching

for a glass. Maybe she'd gone a bit overboard, but it was only a frozen mix. Besides, going overboard beat going crazy.

He nodded, pacing across the wood floor. "Before I forget again, there's something I need to tell you, too. I kept forgetting to mention it because I don't think it's going to come as much of a surprise to you. But I got the results of the paternity test back, and I'm definitely Ty's father."

She handed him a drink and gestured toward the couch. "Yeah, I wasn't worried about that." Once he was seated, she tucked herself into the opposite corner, pulling one leg under her body as she turned to face him.

"I know. I just thought I should tell you before I mention it to Drew today. When Ty's not in the room, of course." He took a long sip. "My guess is he'll recommend finding a lawyer as the next step, so we can start hammering out child support."

Her muscles stiffened. "Tyler has never wanted for anything."

"I know," he said calmly. "You've done a great job."

She swayed backward, surprised at the validation. "Sorry. I guess I'm just a little defensive. Of course, I'll do whatever needs to be done to make his life better." Pulling in a breath, she steeled herself. "That's sort of what I need to talk to you about. I'm really worried about him, in terms of all the recent events. I know your position," she added hurriedly, before he could start denying Josiah's existence. Hopefully he'd remember his promise on that front. "But I truly believe there's a ghost in this house. And maybe that doesn't mean much to you, but I'm generally a pretty practical person, in case you haven't noticed, and I honestly have no doubt something supernatural is going on here."

"Okay." He shifted on the cushion, causing the springs to protest under his weight. "Is there…ah…something I can do to help?"

Here we go. She swallowed hard. "A few years ago, a psychic from Boston was all over the news here. You certainly wouldn't have heard about it overseas, but it was a big deal here; she helped solve an old crime in Gull Harbor by communicating with a ghost. She lives on Cape, now, and I called her. She's coming over this Sunday, and I was hoping you'd come too." A ribbon of sweat trickled down the back of her neck, and she tugged at her tight collar.

His ran his palm over his short hair. "Sunday?" A frown momentarily darkened his handsome features.

"Do you have something Sunday?"

"No. I mean, well, my parents come back on Sunday. That's all." He sighed, spreading his fingers out on his thighs. "I'm going to have to tell them, you know. Even if they can't acknowledge their relationship yet, they will want to see their grandson."

Her shoulders sagged, but she kept her face neutral. It had to happen sometime. "I understand. And it's fine. I don't think they'll be interested in speaking to me ever again, but it will be good for Ty to have some grandparents. Besides the Winslows, I mean."

He studied her for a moment. "What happened to your parents, Em?"

Crap. She should have seen that coming. She glanced at the clock. Only half past two, and their appointment wasn't until four. Tyler was still asleep.

Oh, hell. There was really no excuse she could think of, other than she didn't want to talk about it. But that wasn't fair.

She sighed, gathering her strength. "Well, when I was about two years old, my dad went out for the proverbial pack of cigarettes and never came back. My mom worked really hard to provide for us, but over the years, her health really suffered. She was a diabetic and it got harder and harder for her to manage her insulin correctly. She died of a stroke, apparently, when her levels fell too low." Pausing, she bit down on her lip as she drew in a breath. "No one was there with her. I was back at college. It happened about three months before I met you. Senior year."

His blue eyes widened. "Oh, God, Em. Why didn't you tell me?"

"I didn't want to talk about it. And you were leaving anyway." Her throat turned to dust, and she reached for her drink.

"For what it's worth, I'm really sorry. I didn't know you were going through that at the time." He scrubbed at his jaw. "I guess that sort of explains why you thought adoption might be the best option."

A searing pain burst in her chest. "Yes."

"What made you change your mind?"

"I really felt like the baby deserved more than a college senior with no family. And there were so many parents desperate to adopt him. So desperate, in fact, that as I started meeting them, I felt like they were trying to bribe me. I didn't want to sell my baby to the highest bidder. Then Kaitlyn told her parents, and they offered to help me." She blinked as hot tears pressed against the backs of her eyes. "In the end, it just came down to the fact that I loved my unborn baby, despite my efforts not to. I wanted to keep him. I wanted to hold him, and protect him, and watch him grow up."

"Why didn't you tell me then?"

The sob escaped. *Oh, God damn it*. "I tried. I was just too late."

"What?" He leaned forward, his voice jagged. "What are you talking about, Emily?"

"When I decided I couldn't go through with adoption, panic set in. I was living at Kaitlyn's, and the Winslows wanted me to have this house once the last of the summer rentals had left. At that point it was August, and I was due in the beginning of October, so I devoted every second I had to getting ready for the baby and saving money for our survival. Once I had him, I was going to find you. And I tried, I really did."

Her breath hitched as another sob bubbled in her throat. *Oh, please don't let me cry*. This was bad enough without her tears. Brett was a brave and dedicated soldier. She was the selfish, screwed-up emotional wreck who'd caused him all this pain. Bringing up the past was pointless—he'd never understand how things had been.

But she'd been left alone to deal with an unplanned pregnancy. Her entire life had changed, with all her carefully-laid plans for the future quietly dissolving as her belly grew.

"Tell me the rest, Emily." It was not a request.

She blew out a shaky breath and took a quick sip of lemonade before continuing. "I had Tyler on October sixth, a few days late. It took me a while to recover and get my act together, but my plan was to bring him to see you. To tell you in person, and show you your new son. Try to explain everything. I found the cheapest flight possible, and I got us to Lackland. I just assumed that's where you were…it's where you'd been right before we met, and you went right back there after Christmas for training. I screwed up, and all I can say in my defense is that I was a new twenty-two-year-old mother suffering from hormonal surges, exhaustion, and anxiety over telling you about the baby."

"You flew to Texas? With a newborn?"

"Well, I didn't have a lot of choice. I was breastfeeding. And I figured even if you didn't want to see me, you'd want to see him."

He shook his head. "I was only in Texas for the initial training. It *was* at Lackland back then, but the bulk of the training takes place at Eglin Air Force Base in Florida. That's where those of us who made it through the first phase went for the second phase."

"Yes, that's what I was able to learn." She dropped her chin, hiding behind a curtain of hair. The lack of common sense she'd shown still filled her with shame. Her feelings for Brett always seemed to cloud her judgment, both back then and now. "It was stupid and impulsive to go to Texas without confirmation, but I did remember how long the training was, so at the time it seemed best to show up and tell you something like that in person. And it turned out to be a mistake I couldn't afford, not just monetarily, but time-wise, as well."

He leaned forward, staring at the floor as though something down there could help him make sense of her story. "I don't know what to say. Christ. Did you come to Florida as well?"

A shuddering sigh escaped as she pressed her fingers to the corners of her eyes. The threat of tears still loomed, spurred on by humiliation and guilt. *Do not let them fall. You do not deserve sympathy.* "I was going to…but I didn't want to make the same mistake twice. I broke down and texted you. I mean, I tried to text you, but the number belonged to someone else at that point."

"I needed a better phone for deployment." Linking his hands between his legs, he continued to study the floorboards.

"I figured that's what happened, so I started making calls to Eglin. As you might imagine, they don't like to give out information about military personnel with top security clearance to random people on the phone. I didn't get very far."

He nodded, finally lifting his head. Wordlessly, he reached for his forgotten glass and filled it. Then he stood slightly and filled hers as well.

An intense wave of gratitude washed over her at the gesture. His hands were sure and steady as he set the pitcher down, while hers twisted in her lap like writhing snakes. She untangled them and took a shaky sip. "I was too embarrassed to ask your parents," she continued, warmth creeping into her cheeks. She managed another sip without dumping lemonade in her lap, and then returned the glass to the coffee table. "I just couldn't go over there and tell them I'd recently had your baby and thought I'd look you up and let you know. Especially since I thought you were with Miranda. I realize that makes me a coward, but that's the truth. So I put Kaitlyn on the job."

"'Coward' is a pretty harsh word. I can see how you'd want to talk to me before telling my parents about the baby." He pressed a fist into the palm of his hand, cracking his knuckles with a small series of pops. "I guess Kaitlyn was too late?"

"Right. You were gone. She got me an address to contact you in Iraq, but I truly believed getting a letter like that while you were overseas might do more harm than good."

"It wouldn't have been the ideal way to find out. But it would have been preferable to not knowing at all."

"I know. And I'm sorry." She lifted her gaze, forcing herself to look him in the eyes. "It's just…it sounds terrible, but I really didn't think you'd come back. It's such a dangerous job, and that's what happens to the people in my life. They leave or die…they don't come back."

"Why didn't you tell me this sooner?"

"I was going to that first day you came over. But you know how that went. And then I realized it was pointless, anyway. I tried to find you, but I failed. So instead I pretended you didn't exist, so I could live with myself. It's not like you're going to forgive me, so it doesn't matter." Her fist closed around the locket, and she pulled on it until the chain grew taut, the clasp biting into her neck through the high collar of her shirt. She focused on slowing her pulse as she awaited his judgment.

"It matters." His voice, low and firm, vibrated with its usual authority.

Her breath caught as a tiny bud of hope bloomed in her chest. It was something. Maybe it wasn't forgiveness, but it was something.

Upstairs, a door creaked open. She froze, but the soft footsteps that followed clearly belonged to her son.

Now, she just needed Josiah to leave Tyler alone long enough to get out of the house. Even Drew's drab office would be a welcome change of scenery at this point.

A smile touched Brett's lips as he pushed himself off the couch. Towering over her, he extended a hand to help her up. His strong fingers closed around hers, and he pulled her gently to standing. "I know that was hard for you," he murmured, rubbing his thumb across the back of her hand.

She swallowed and nodded, not trusting her voice.

"Look on the bright side. Now we get to go to an hour-long counseling session." The corner of his mouth twitched as he fought to keep a straight face.

"Brett!" Tyler picked up his pace, hurrying down the last few stairs with Larry the lamb dangling from his grip. He ran across the living room and launched himself at Brett.

He released her hand in time to catch Ty, swinging him up into his arms. "Hey! How's my best buddy?"

"Good."

"That's what I like to hear. Excellent. Because we're headed out for an adventure. First we have to go talk to someone for a bit, but then maybe we can go someplace fun for dinner." He glanced at her, lifting his eyebrows.

She nodded a silent "yes" as she reached out to rub Tyler's back. Suddenly she was struck by the image they created...the three of them huddled in a group, connected by touch. Any outsider would take one look at them and think—

Don't say it.

Family.

No. It would never happen. He was being kind,

because that was the type of person he was. He loved Tyler, not her.

Dropping her hand, she took a step back. "I'll go make sure we have enough distractions packed up, then. If you've never dined out with a preschooler, you're in for a real treat." She forced a wide smile as she turned away and headed up the stairs.

Chapter 22

She plunked down in her chair, carefully setting a full wineglass next to her laptop. Finally, she could see if her new idea would lead to fruition. As the computer came to life, her gaze traveled to the bottom right corner, where glowing numbers announced it was almost nine o'clock.

Another wild Saturday night. She really needed to get Tyler to bed. And get herself to bed, too, since she'd worked Friday night. But Tyler had become engrossed in a Disney movie, and she'd decided to allow him to finish watching. So she'd snuck in here to do some research, after pouring a glass of wine to help calm her nerves. The medium was coming tomorrow. Her foot bounced in time to the ticking of her mother's old clock as she waited for the page to load.

Her previous searches for "Josiah Matthews" pulled up a surprising number of modern-day people with that name, but no trace of a long-dead colonial boy from Barnstable Village. But this afternoon, as they'd driven home after visiting the Winslows, her gaze had traveled to a tiny family graveyard tucked into the woods.

These were common on the Cape—small family plots, surrounded by fences, with weathered headstones so old they were difficult to read. She drove by this one so often she barely noticed it anymore. But this time something clicked in her mind, and once she had Tyler fed, bathed, and settled in front of the television, she'd headed straight for her computer.

There were too many gravestones, and graveyards, for that matter, to search by simply walking around and looking at names. And she had no idea where this boy was buried—but he *was* buried—if Tyler's teacher had interpreted the story correctly.

Someone had to have listed all the names on headstones somewhere, though. At least the ones it was possible to read. A search for old cemetery records brought up a site entitled *Cape Cod Gravestones*, and the home page description read "Gravestones dated 1683—1880 or Later in Barnstable County, Massachusetts—Gravestone Records from the 15 Towns of Cape Cod." Bingo. She reached for her glass of wine and took a celebratory sip.

There was a caveat reminding users that while the site was an excellent source, it was not comprehensive, due to unmarked gravesites and missing headstones. But it was a start. While there was a suggestion to try finding a specific name by linking it to the site in a large search engine, there was no search box on the website itself. Her first attempt to find the name this way failed, but she wasn't about to give up that easily.

She clicked on the top list, which broke the cemeteries down into the geographical area known as the "Upper Cape," the towns of Bourne, Sandwich, Mashpee, Falmouth, and Barnstable. Sixty-nine cemeteries popped up, most with clickable links.

She scanned the Barnstable listing until her eyes caught on "Cobb's Hill Cemetery, aka Goodspeed's Hill Cemetery"—the graveyard they'd walked through during the tour. It was as good a starting place as any. There were thirteen links with date ranges, and she selected the earliest time period: 1715 to 1759.

And there he was. Down at the bottom of the list: Josiah Matthews, 1757, June 2, Age 12. A jolt of adrenaline sent her pulse racing. She'd found him! She scrolled though the names, looking for other people in the Matthews family.

Ten minutes later, her excitement had faded. No other Matthews were buried in Cobb's Hill during what would have been the appropriate time frames. She tapped a pencil against her lips as she stared at the screen. At least she knew where he was buried, now. And it made sense, really, that no other family members were there; that was why he was here, haunting her house, rather than resting peacefully with his relatives. His spirit didn't want to be alone, and he'd apparently wandered back to where he'd died—the jailhouse. Until he'd followed them home.

She picked up a research paper she'd printed out which discussed colonial crime and punishment in New England. Apparently, an eleven-year-old boy had been hanged in Boston in 1715 as punishment for three criminal offenses, one of which seemed to include playing in church. So she found it entirely plausible that twelve-year-old Josiah had been locked up in the old jail to pay for some childhood crime.

But where were his parents? Another idea surfaced, and she straightened her back with renewed determination. Setting the paper back on the desk, she typed "Barnstable Vital Records to 1849" into the top bar of her window. She'd found this site before, and spent hours reading pages copied from volumes of *The*

Mayflower Descendant. But when she'd looked for the surname Matthews in the death listings, she'd found nothing helpful. But there were pages and pages of family histories associated with births and marriages as well.

It showed up in the marriage records, under surnames "Maggs—Moses". A 1743 marriage between Ebenezer Matthews and Abigail Smith. It fit, based on Josiah's age.

Music blared from the kitchen, and she jumped in her chair. Her cell phone ringtone, amplified by the speakers of the dock. Who would be calling this late? Hurrying toward the kitchen, she congratulated herself on her success. Maybe it wasn't much, but it was something—and she'd found the information on her own.

And she could use it to verify what Claire told them tomorrow. She didn't think the woman was a scam artist, but her practical side was still tough to suppress. If someone had told her a month ago she'd be allocating funds from her tight budget to pay for a psychic's house call, she'd have laughed hard enough to justify skipping her daily ab crunches.

Kaitlyn's picture smiled at her from the screen of the vibrating phone. She grabbed it from the dock as she continued moving toward the living room.

"Hey." She leaned around the doorframe to check on Ty. He was asleep on the couch, despite the final enthusiastic production of the movie characters. Wooden trains were arranged in a line on the armrest, and both Larry and the toy airplane were wedged between his body and the couch. Her chest tightened as she gazed at his sleeping form.

"Sorry it took me so long to call you back," said Kaitlyn breathlessly. "I was in shopping hell. I had to find a dress for this fancy dinner tonight." She punctuated the last part with a heavy sigh.

Emily made her way back through the kitchen to the office. "You poor thing. A fancy dinner sounds terrible. We had macaroni and cheese and applesauce."

"Well, that sounds…color-coordinated, anyway."

"Yes, tonight's theme was 'yellow'." Picking up her wineglass, she swirled the straw-colored liquid. *Indeed it was*.

Kay's musical laughter rang out with the usual unrestrained glee. "Sorry, it's just that this thing is for Michael's work, and it's bound to be all small talk and schmoozing. In fact, I do have to start getting ready soon, so I can't talk too long." She dropped the phone, and muffled curses drifted through the connection. "Whoops. I'm trying to do too many things at once. Anyway, I heard you saw my parents today."

"We went over for a visit. I missed them so much." She sank into her chair and savored a sip of wine.

"Well, that makes one of us. That was a long visit. If my mom had dropped one more hint about grandchildren, I'd be calling from a mental institution."

She slid the rim of the glass across her lips as they curled into a wicked smile. "I'm with them. Have a baby. But move back here first, so Tyler can have an honorary cousin close by. And then I can have my best friend close by, too." *Oh, crap*. The words had slipped out before she could filter them—moving so far away from home had been difficult on Kay, and she didn't need to add another layer of guilt to Kay's plate.

But God, she missed having her here. An image of

187

Gayle flashed through her mind as she squeezed her eyes shut. Friday morning, she'd handed her a page of information she'd gathered, along with a quick reassurance that she was available to help at any time, if needed. When they returned for pick-up, Gayle had actually sought Emily out to chat. It was something, anyway—a sign of budding trust.

"Aww, I know, chickie. I miss you like crazy, too. Ugh, I really do have to get going. Michael will kill me if I'm not ready on time."

She knocked back another healthy swig of wine, debating. It was terrible, but she was going to do it anyway. "Oh, okay. I can catch you up on what happened with Brett another time. Have fun at your dinner, tell Michael I said 'hello'!" She sang the last sentence with manic enthusiasm, mimicking hanging up the phone even though no one was there to actually see her.

There was a beat of silence as Kay processed her words. "What? Oh my God. You are evil. Tell me. Did you sleep with him?"

"Twice." Her cheeks grew warm as she awaited Kay's reaction.

"Oh. My. God. I knew it! Didn't I tell you? When did this happen? How was it? Was it amazing? Are you two together now?" The questions flew from Kaitlyn's mouth in rapid succession, reminding Emily of those Whack-A-Mole games at the annual Barnstable Fair. She didn't know which one to hit first, and she truly didn't want to make Kay late.

"We're not back together. The first time was a few weeks ago, and yes I'm sorry I didn't tell you sooner. I'm not exactly thrilled with myself, since I'm pretty sure he still hates me. But yes, it was amazing. Beyond amazing."

"First of all, there's a fine line between love and hate," she insisted. "But he doesn't hate you. I know it. And second of all, I'm insanely jealous. I think *I* might hate you a little now, actually."

She giggled. The wine was going to her head. "Well, if you hate me, I guess I won't share the details."

"I am literally dying here, and Michael is yelling at me to get off the phone and get ready. Hang on." Kaitlyn's voice grew distant as she yelled back to her husband. "Jesus. Okay, I really have to go. I'll call you tomorrow, and you'd better answer."

Her good mood faded slightly. "Try to call early, okay? Like before ten." *After that I'll be very busy hosting a séance here.*

Kaitlyn sighed. "Before ten? That's seven here! I guess this will be worth setting my alarm on a weekend, though."

She shook her head as she closed the windows on her computer. "Just wait until you have those babies, Kay. You're in for a shock."

"Yeah, yeah. I'll tell you what. When you and Brett get back together, we'll both get pregnant. Then we can go through it together. All right, big hugs, talk to you tomorrow."

"Have fun tonight. Bye." She set the phone on the desk, running her fingertips over the smooth solid wood. Another yard sale find. And the scene of her last frantic sexual escapade with Brett.

She hoped it wouldn't be *the* last. What she'd told Kay was true—she wasn't particularly proud of her behavior. She'd practically thrown herself at Brett that night at his house. All the while knowing he resented her for what she'd done and that was putting it gently. But how could she fight it? She was still addicted to his touch, even after all these years.

It would end badly, though. How could it not? As soon as he didn't need her to facilitate visits with Tyler, she'd be cast aside—out of sight, out of mind. Out of his life, except for the mandatory contact that would come with raising their child.

Fresh pain joined the aching need stirring deep within her. She yanked her fingers from the desktop as though it had suddenly burst into flames. No time for this. She needed to carry her son upstairs to bed. Then herself.

She picked up her glass and switched off the light, moving through the shadows to the kitchen. Peering out the slider, she double-checked that Terence had plenty of water and food on the deck in case he grew hungry in the night. No doubt some nocturnal poacher would get to it first, but not much she could do about that.

"The medium's coming tomorrow," she whispered to no one, pulling on the door to make sure it was locked. *And so is Brett.*

She sighed, shaking her head. Somehow, she'd have to come to terms with the reality of the situation. Setting the glass in the sink, she headed for the living room to finish the night's tasks.

Chapter 23

Brett arrived first. She was still on the phone with Kaitlyn when his truck pulled in, and since they were talking about him, she figured she'd better end the conversation. At least she'd managed a segue at one point to discuss the Gayle dilemma. Kay had agreed Emily should do what she could to help the other woman, and she'd offered whatever support she could give from across the country.

Setting her phone on the coffee table, Emily crossed to the door and stole a quick glance in the little wall mirror. Hair secured by a striped headband that coordinated with her short-sleeved burgundy blouse. A simple, straight beige skirt that hit right above the knee, brown kitten heels, and her mom's locket. Hopefully it was an appropriate look for contacting restless spirits. Blowing out a breath, she opened the door for Brett so he wouldn't have to wait in the rain.

The steady drizzle pelted him as he jogged to the door, creating darker splotches on his navy shirt. He scrubbed the raindrops from his hair before stepping inside.

So much for the April showers leaving with April. At least it was warm. The humidity surrounded her like a steamy breath, and she shut the door against it. She checked her hair again in the mirror to see if it was expanding beyond the control of her headband. So far, so good.

"Hey." He glanced around the room. "Where's Ty?"

"He's on my computer, playing a matching game. It's sort of addicting, but at least it's educational. Although, if anyone could get his attention away from it, it would be you." She gave him a wry smile and led him toward the kitchen.

"Are you sure he should be here for this?"

They stopped in the kitchen, and Emily lowered her voice as she ran her hand along the back of a chair. "No, I'm not at all sure. But Claire—the medium—said it would be best if we decide after she can assess the situation. I mean, Josiah already talks to Tyler all the time, so I don't know if this could be any more damaging. But I have Ruth—Kaitlyn's mom—on standby. She's going to come by and get him if need be."

His brows lifted. "You told her about this?"

"Oh, no. I told her we were meeting with a family counselor at the house, and that we might need to have some time for just the adults to talk."

"So she knows about that, anyway."

"Yes. Thankfully, she hasn't passed any judgment on me. At least not to my face. But I guess it's safe to assume she always knew there was a father somewhere. I never hinted at immaculate conception or anything."

The coffee pot gurgled to life, and they both glanced over to the counter. Brett probably didn't think their resident ghost was fooling around with electricity again, but she offered an explanation anyway. "I programmed it to brew a little before ten so it would be nice and hot." She'd already set mugs, cream, sugar, glasses, and a pitcher of water out in the living room. She'd also put out a plate of biscotti and a bowl of grapes, even though she wasn't sure if this was exactly an occasion for finger foods.

Brett cocked his head, stuffing his hands into the pockets of his dark jeans. "Why don't I just take him somewhere if the medium decides he should leave?"

"I want you to be here. Because…" Shooting him a meaningful glance, she let the word hang in the air. She'd told him not to talk about his doubts at her house, where anything said out loud could further antagonize Josiah.

He shook his head, his grim expression speaking volumes. "It's not personal, Em. I just…can't go there."

Suppressing a sigh, she looked around the room as if she might catch Josiah eavesdropping in the corner. "I know I have no right to expect you to believe me based on some sort of loyalty. But you *know* what type of person I am…I was skeptical, too. Now, though, I've seen enough to be entirely convinced." She dropped her voice to a whisper. "He needs help. And I need you on board."

"I'm always willing to help you, Em. You don't need to convince me of anything for that. Just tell me what you want me to do."

I want you to believe me. She didn't think he would appreciate her circular argument, though. Pressing her fingers to her forehead, she tried a different tack. "Why is it so difficult for you to at least consider?"

His eyes darkened. "I've lost a lot of friends, Em. I need to believe they're resting in peace. Not stuck in some horrific purgatory, missing their families." He looked away, his jaw set in a tight line.

Pain sliced through her and caught like barbs in her chest. "I don't think that's the way it works. Claire said some spirits just miss their chance to cross over and…get lost. Either they have unfinished business, or they're confused, because of a sudden or violent death—"

Cords of muscle rose along his neck. "Emily. Getting blown up is sudden. And violent."

Oh, God. What was the matter with her? How could she be so insensitive? She struggled for breath like a fish thrown onto the sand.

A light knock rapped on the door, and she flinched. Her chest finally expanded as adrenaline raced through her system. "She's here."

He nodded. "It's okay. Go answer it. I'm going to say hi to Ty."

She sprang into action. It was raining, for God's sake. "Coming," she shouted, sprinting to the front door. Pulling it open, she greeted the handsome couple on her doorstep, trying to hide her surprise. For some reason, she'd just assumed Claire would come alone. "I'm so sorry for keeping you waiting. Please come in."

As she stepped back, her gaze traveled down, and she was hit with another jolt of shock. The medium was hugely pregnant.

"Thank you. I'm Claire. This is my husband, Max." She extended her hand.

"Thanks for coming. I really appreciate it. I didn't…um…realize…" She drifted off, unsure of how to finish the sentence. It was very apparent Claire was in the final weeks of pregnancy, but she hid it well beneath a dark gray A-line dress. Still, making comments about a new acquaintance's appearance during introductions might not be the best move, etiquette-wise.

"Max Baron," the dark-haired man said, shaking her hand as well. His blue eyes were piercing, a shade or two darker than Brett's.

"Don't worry, I have plenty of time," Claire said kindly as Max helped remove her raincoat. Drops of water glittered in her thick auburn hair like tiny crystals. She placed a hand under her belly, and a stack of bracelets jingled on her wrist.

"Don't let her fool you. She's due next week." Max touched the small of his wife's back, guiding her forward. While his tone was edged with real concern, his lips curled in an affectionate smile.

"He's a little protective these days, so we're a package deal lately." A deep smile lit her green eyes, radiating a joy that was almost palpable. "I hope you don't mind."

"Oh my goodness, of course not." Emily turned to drape the raincoat on the bench, freezing as the lights suddenly flickered. *Oh, God—it was starting already.* Would Claire be able to handle this in her condition? Guilt stabbed at her insides as she considered how to voice her concerns. She knew better than anyone that a pregnant woman wasn't an invalid, but this wasn't exactly tantamount to lifting something heavy or taking a brisk walk. This could be dangerous.

"Um, that happens a lot now." Wrapping her arms around her middle, Emily tipped her chin toward the overhead light fixture. "Sorry."

"Oh, don't apologize. I tend to elicit that type of response. The good news is that there's a very strong presence here. So maybe we'll have some luck."

Claire's eyes grew glassy as she gazed around the room.

"Are you sure this is a good idea? I don't want to cause the baby any distress."

"It's fine." Claire laid a hand across her husband's arm before he could add his opinion. "It is." She turned back to Emily. "As soon as I heard this case involved children—both your own child and the spirit of a young boy—I knew I had to do whatever I could to help. I'm feeling very maternal these days, as you can imagine."

Brett strode into the room. "Sorry. The computer lost power, and I had to get it started up again for Ty. You were right about that game."

"Hopefully it will keep him busy for a little while longer. Brett, this is Claire and Max, um, Baron."

Brett shook Max's outstretched hand, and there was a moment of tension as the two alpha males sized each other up. They were almost identical in height, and both solidly built, but while Brett's head was nearly shaved, Max wore his dark hair long enough to brush the back collar of his white shirt.

"Please, make yourselves comfortable." Emily untangled her twisting fingers and gestured toward the couch and chairs surrounding the coffee table. "Can I get anyone coffee?"

Claire lowered herself onto the couch, with Max's hand on her elbow for support. Her eyes closed as her fingers drifted toward her forehead. "No, thanks," she murmured. "I think maybe we should just start. This spirit is anxious to share his story."

Emily shot an alarmed glance at Max before joining Claire on the couch. "Are you okay? Maybe we shouldn't be doing this."

"I'm fine," Claire insisted again in the very same moment Max explained, "She gets headaches when she does this. But I can tell you now she won't leave until she's ready, so it's best to just let her do her thing." He frowned, but pride in her strength came through in his tone.

"A boy...like you said. He's been lost for a long time." Claire stared off into the distance, listening to a silent voice. "Josiah. Josiah...Matthews."

A shiver crept along Emily's spine. She glanced over to Brett as he lowered himself to the chair on her left. She'd filled him in on everything she'd learned from Tyler and her computer searches, along with which information she'd shared with Claire, and which she hadn't. And the last name Matthews was one of those pieces of information she'd held back.

Now his face paled beneath tanned skin. He leaned forward, fixing his steely gaze on Claire.

"He says he's not bad. His father...disappeared. Maybe drowned? I think he was caught in a storm while fishing. And he and his mother were struggling. They were hungry, and he...stole some food. He couldn't pay for it, so he had to serve his punishment in jail."

Emily sucked in a breath. *Oh, God.* Her heart hurt for the starving, fatherless boy, despite the havoc he'd wreaked on their lives.

"They didn't feed the prisoners much...it sounds like his mother brought food to him when she could. And then she suddenly stopped coming. He was worried. And very hungry."

The water in the pitcher trembled as Claire spoke, as if a mild earthquake were brewing under the coffee table. But her eyes were closed now, her beautiful face knotted in concentration.

"He knows stealing is wrong. But he was so hungry. He tried to take some of another prisoner's food. The man shoved him away, and his head slammed into something hard." Claire opened her eyes and glanced around the room. "That must be how he died. Some type of head trauma."

The goose bumps on Emily's exposed flesh tightened as cool air swirled around her. Shuddering, she pressed her arms into her ribcage and covered the skin above her knees with her palms. Did anyone else feel it, or was she imagining the temperature drop?

Brett noticed her small movements and turned toward her, his brow furrowed with concern. Something like indecision flashed across his face before his expression cleared. Shifting in his chair, he reached over and placed his warm palm on the back of her hand. His large fingers lined up in the spaces between her smaller ones, then curled inward until his fingernails slipped beneath her palm and pressed against the skin of her thigh.

Her own fingers folded at the knuckles, lacing with his, and she stared at their joined hands, stunned. He was touching her. Deliberate, prolonged contact, in front of people—not just the friendly squeeze of a fleeting, subconscious gesture or the frantic strokes of a goal-driven embrace, fueled by need. Somehow, it seemed even more intimate than sex.

Claire began speaking again, jarring Emily back to the present situation. Good Lord, how did Brett have the power to distract her during a séance in her own home?

"Okay, he understands on some level that he's

deceased. But what he doesn't understand is where his mother went. She wasn't at the graveyard when they brought him there. He was being pulled toward a bright light, but he fought it. He's proud of that." Claire glanced up, a weak smile lifting the corners of her lips.

Max slid his hand into the groove between her neck and shoulder, rubbing gently.

"So he went to his house. His mother never came. The animals were gone. So, he returned to the jail, in the hopes his mother would eventually find him there." Claire slumped back against the cushions, shaking her head slowly.

Max leaned down and filled a glass of water, handing it to her. "Anyone else?" he offered.

Outside, a sudden burst of rain drummed against the roof.

Claire sipped her water, pressing the fingers of her free hand against her temple. "I don't know what to say. He doesn't know where his mother is, so I can't communicate that to you. Something bad must have happened, otherwise she would have shown up to her son's burial. But this happened, when did you say? 1757?" She turned to Emily as she brought the glass to her lips again.

Emily nodded, wishing for water herself. The child's sad story had left a lump in her throat. But she wasn't about to let go of Brett's hand, so she'd silently declined.

"I'm not sure how easy it will be to find out where she is. But if we can, maybe we can reunite them somehow." Claire sighed with frustration. "I'm sorry."

"Don't be sorry." Emily's voice sounded brittle and scratchy. She swallowed. "At least we know what happened to him, now."

"Still." Claire frowned, clearly unhappy with the outcome. She settled her hands against the swell of her belly. "Is there anything you want me to ask? Anything you want to know?"

Guilt pricked at Emily's chest. It was something she thought she already knew, but she still needed confirmation in order to continue her search. While she hated to ask any more of the tired medium, she couldn't see any way around it. "Can you ask him his mother's name?"

Claire's pale cheeks flushed with color. "Oh, for goodness sake. Yes, I think that would be helpful to know, right? Pregnancy brain," she added, rolling her eyes and patting her stomach. She lowered her head as she continued her silent conversation, the dark red waves of her hair spilling forward to hide her face. "Abigail. Abigail Matthews." A grimace slid across her features before she could hide it, and she dropped her forehead into her hand.

"I think that's enough, babe." Max's tone held a new firmness as he crouched next to his wife.

Brett's grip tightened around her hand as their eyes locked. "Abigail" was the name Emily had found, and he knew it. More proof that Claire was a gifted psychic, not a fraud preying on desperate people.

"Can I get you something for your head, Claire?" Emily reluctantly pulled her hand free as she stood up, straightening her skirt. "Are you allowed to take some acetaminophen?"

"I am, thanks—but I brought some with me. In my purse, if you don't mind." She gestured toward the wooden bench by the door, where she'd left her large leather bag.

"I've got it." Emily crossed the room and delivered the bag, then retrieved the forgotten coffee from the kitchen. "Still hot," she announced as she filled mugs.

"Much better," murmured Claire, holding the steaming brew beneath her nose to inhale the scent. "It's a good thing my doctor didn't try to forbid coffee entirely. But still, I've already had some today, so maybe just a few sips." She gave her husband a playful smile.

"I feel awful that this was so hard on you when you're already probably fairly uncomfortable, if memory serves." Emily dumped cream into her own mug. Her hand still tingled from the warmth of Brett's touch.

"Don't feel bad. I wanted to help. I just wish I'd been able to offer a solution."

"Any new information is helpful. I'm going to keep researching, and I know I'll figure this out." Emily forced confidence into her voice, but honestly, she knew no such thing. What she did know, though, was that the medium had done something she had been unable to do—convince Brett. She debated saying something, but decided a comment like that might insult Claire. And it would certainly throw Brett under the proverbial bus.

"Good. I'll keep thinking, too."

Emily flashed a grateful smile. "If you have time, I'd love for you to meet my son. Our son," she amended, glancing at Brett.

"I'd love that. And then we're off to lunch. Another perk of today's visit is that it allowed me to pull my husband away from work for a while, and now he's going to take me out, right, hon? So we'll get to enjoy a little alone time before everything becomes about gearing up for tourist season."

Max helped her to her feet. "I hate to point out the obvious, babe, but I think there are some other impending limits to our alone time." He looked at her fondly, dropping his gaze to her belly.

Laughter filled the room, chasing away the last remaining threads of tension.

"Just wait," added Emily, leading them all toward the kitchen.

Chapter 24

She made them lunch after Claire and Max left, grilled ham and cheese sandwiches and the untouched grapes from her coffee table spread. Brett helped her clean up as Tyler devoted equal time to steering a red wooden engine around his plate and chewing his food. She didn't have the energy to tell him not to play at the table. At least she'd finally gotten him away from the computer screen when she'd introduced him to the other couple.

She closed the fridge, and suddenly Brett was standing right behind her. His hand closed around her wrist and he pulled her toward the office, the rough pads of his fingertips pressing into her skin. He closed the door partially and led her into the middle of the room.

Pain blazed in his eyes as he turned to her. "I need to apologize to you. I'm sorry I didn't believe you. On some level, I didn't want it to be true for selfish reasons. I don't know how to protect you two from a ghost. Protecting people is my job, and all my training is useless right now."

He was apologizing to *her*? After everything she'd done to him? The realization scraped her insides raw. "It's okay, Brett. I get it. And we'll figure this out, somehow. I just have to keep at it. There has to be more information out there—libraries, historical societies, maybe even some local history buffs. There are tons of cemeteries on Cape Cod. She could be in another town, or a little family plot. There has to be a record of her somewhere." She tipped her head toward the computer. "I just have to search harder."

His gaze followed her gesture, lingering on the desk. "This room brings back some memories." He touched her upper arm, trailing his fingers downward in a slow, agonizing caress. Stepping closer, he moved his other hand to her hip.

What was happening? She struggled to catch up to this sudden shift of reality. Not only was he touching her again, he was referencing their sexual exploits—a previously forbidden topic, according to the unspoken rules.

Her pulse skittered as she gazed up at him, speechless.

He pulled her closer, his rock-hard erection pressing into her belly. "I want you. Every...single...second...of the day."

Breathe. "It's the same for me." His mouth hovered above hers, taunting her with unbearable anticipation. She rose onto her toes, reaching for his neck, lifting herself up to him, until he captured her lips in a devastating kiss.

Tongues and teeth clashed as their bodies strained to meet, the layers of fabric an unacceptable barrier between their flesh. *Oh, God.* This kind of need was a force of its own.

It's like nothing's changed. But things had changed, of course. Starting with their son, eating lunch twenty feet away from them.

She slipped her hands to his shoulders, pushing at

the wall of muscle. "Brett," she managed between kisses. "We can't...Tyler."

He groaned as he dragged his jaw across her cheek. "No. You're right." But he didn't release her. "Maybe I could stick around for naptime?" His voice dropped even lower, rough with desire.

Oh. "Yes. An excellent idea."

"Mommy? I'm all done."

Laughing weakly, she collapsed against him. They shared a frustrated sigh, still locked in an intimate embrace. Warning flares ricocheted through her brain as she clung to him. This felt too good. Too much like they were an ordinary couple, united in parenthood, bound by love.

It was a dangerous thought.

She broke away. "I'd better go check what his version of 'all done' is." Straightening her skirt, she made her way back into the kitchen, Brett following her.

Only mangled bread crusts and two sliced grapes remained on Ty's plate. "Good job," she said, carrying the plate to the sink as Tyler returned from the living room carrying his sneakers.

"I wanna go outside." He plunked onto the floor and tore open the Velcro strap of one little shoe.

"What?" Rinsing the dish, she glanced out the window. Soft drizzle still splashed into puddles in the backyard, although a few rays of sunshine were struggling to break through the clouds. "It's raining, baby. You can't go outside."

"Outside," he repeated, a stubborn edge in his voice. He pushed his toes into the shoes, banging it against the kitchen floor in an unsuccessful attempt to get it all the way on. "Tag."

Great. He and Brett had played tag the other night, using a big plastic jungle gym in the backyard as base. Another military family had given the colorful structure—complete with holes to climb through and two small slides—to Brett, and he'd brought it over in his truck on Friday afternoon. Since then, Ty had been eagerly trying for repeats of the chasing game.

"We can't play outside when it's raining." She shut the faucet off and glanced at Brett, who was standing near the back door, looking from the soggy yard to his struggling son with a gleam in his eye.

"It's really warm out," Brett said, keeping the words low and neutral. But he spread his hands out in a "why not?" gesture.

Seriously? It was like having two preschoolers. "Because it's raining. It's almost nap time, anyway."

Tyler slapped the shoe against the floor a few more times. "Need help." His request was to Brett, and he waited, his features arranged in a determined expression.

Brett shrugged, the corner of his mouth twitching. "We won't melt. Let's all go play in the rain. It'll be fun. Come on, Em."

Oh, for God's sake. It did sound fun. And it wasn't like they'd catch their death from a romp in a warm spring shower. It might be messy, but childhood was supposed to be messy.

Brett had always been able to give her the gentle encouragement she needed to step out of the rigidly ordered world she'd created. Back then as well as now. He made her *want* to take risks and break the rules. It was their game, and she could still play.

"Oh, I have no doubt it will be fun." She sank to her knees and grasped Ty's shoe, pushing it onto his foot. "It's just that I liked your earlier suggestion better." Glancing up to him, she lifted her eyebrows.

Shock raced across his face before he recovered and flashed her a roguish grin. "Well, I'm full of good suggestions. For example, I'm thinking we're all going to need hot showers once we come back inside."

Blood surged to her cheeks. *Damn*. He always won. Visions of the two of them, naked in a steamy mist of sluicing water, filled her head as she wrestled with Ty's other shoe. *God*. Fastening the Velcro strip, she rose and yanked on her skirt. "Give me a sec to change into shorts, and I'll meet you at base."

****

It *had* been fun—running in the rain, splashing in the puddles. Every time Brett caught her, he'd managed a clandestine touch that had set butterflies loose in her stomach. And even Terence had shown up, taking cover beneath one of the slides so he could solicit some human attention when one of them was on base.

She'd bathed Ty fast enough to warrant a medal in an Olympic event. Brett had helped her get him down for a nap, both of them careful to avoid letting their own wet clothes touch Tyler's dry shirt and pants. Then Brett had gone to throw his things in the wash, since he had no change of clothing and dinner plans at his parents' house. Before he'd headed downstairs to the laundry machines, a towel in his hand, he'd given her a lingering kiss and a whispered promise to join her in the shower.

She shucked off her wet shorts and thong, telling herself the damp clothing was to blame for the tremors

207

quaking through her body. But that was a lie. The other few times they'd had sex, it had been sudden and spontaneous. Primal. Unavoidable. This time, they'd planned it in advance. Peeling off her shirt, she reached around the striped curtain to test the temperature. Hot. She stepped into the tub, gasping as the pulsing water seared her chilled skin.

Anxiety and anticipation warred within her as she tipped her head back beneath the spray. And then he was there, holding back the curtain, watching her with heavy-lidded eyes.

A rush of desire stirred the heat already throbbing between her legs. She lowered her head, sucking in a breath as her gaze fell on the enormous evidence of his own arousal. *Oh, God.* She moved back to make room for him to join her.

He stepped in, the water beading on the close-cropped bristles of his crew cut and running in rivulets down the hard planes of his chest. Somehow, even after everything he'd been through, his body had escaped the visible scars—the liver lacerations he'd suffered in the blast had healed without the need for surgery. He'd told her that one day, shortly after their first disastrous reunion. And it was true—his skin was miraculously unmarred. He was perfect.

She glanced away as her nerves hummed with uncertainty. Of all the things they'd done during those frantic two weeks, showering together wasn't one of them. Yet another first he was claiming from her.

She grabbed the tube of conditioner and squeezed the white cream into her palm. "My hair will be a tangled mess without this." Not very sexy, but true. Biting her lip, she smoothed it onto the top of her head.

"Let me." He slipped his hands around her waist and turned her away from him. His lips trailed across her shoulder as his fingers combed the conditioner through her long curls.

The intimacy made her shiver. With a soft moan, she pressed herself against him until his erection pressed solidly into the small of her back. "That feels so good."

"You feel so good." He nipped on her earlobe. "I've been thinking about doing this to you for an hour now. I'm not sure how much longer I can wait."

Reaching back, she wrapped her fingers around the length of him, stroking and squeezing. His hands moved under her arms to caress her breasts, and he made a low sound, a cross between a groan and a growl. "That's not going to help me last longer," he managed as he sucked on her neck.

A little thrill of power raced through her veins. "I don't think that's a problem. We have a good two hours, at least."

"Are you sure?" He licked at a trickle of water running down her collarbone. His hands slid down her abdomen, until one arm held her steady across her waist while his fingers slipped between her legs.

"I'm sure." She leaned forward to show him how sure, bracing her palms against the cool tiles of the wall and pressing the backs of her thighs against him. Lifting onto her toes, she arched her back and opened her legs wider.

"You're killing me, Em."

He pushed himself in slowly, filling her inch by inch.

Her calf muscles trembled and her belly quivered.

"It's a good way to go."

His hands settled on her hips, pulling her up and back, and she strained to lift herself even higher to accommodate for his height. He rocked inside her, anchoring her with a tight grip as he drove deeper and harder with each thrust. She gasped as the force of his rhythm sent shock waves rolling through her. Then he suddenly stilled, digging his fingers into her flesh as he came in hot, pulsing bursts.

"Holy God."

He hugged her fiercely, wrapping his arms around her abdomen. They stood that way for a moment, enveloped in a sultry mist of steam, his heart pounding against her back.

As he straightened, he pulled her backward, under the spray. "Close your eyes," he murmured, gathering her hair in his hands. "We've got to get you rinsed off. I'm not even close to done with you yet."

Chapter 25

A strange sound woke Emily. Her eyes flew open in the darkness, and she held her breath, listening. What had it been? All was quiet now, except the thudding of her heart.

She should be used to it by now. Claire's visit had really stirred Josiah up, apparently. All week long, drawers had been opening, door slamming, lights flashing—she'd finally removed all the batteries from Ty's toys to prevent the midnight theatrics. And while all this activity was disturbing on many levels, it didn't seem to be putting Tyler in any danger. For that, she was grateful.

She sighed inwardly as her ears strained to pick up a repeat of the sound. If only she had more time to spend trying to locate Abigail Matthews. It was hard finding a few uninterrupted hours in front of the computer when a three-and-a-half year old was in the house. When the opportunity did present itself, she had to make her office work a priority. Unfortunately, she couldn't tell the clinic she was unable to send out client bills due to a haunting.

Then there was the research she continued to do for Gayle. She'd printed safety plans up and even arranged for a free cell phone to give her on Friday. It would serve as a safe way to contact the counselors at the shelter without fear of having the number discovered on

Gayle's own cell phone. Emily hoped Gayle would find the courage to use it, so she could speak with people actually trained to help in these situations.

There. A floorboard creaked downstairs. The hair on the back of her neck rose as she swung her feet to the side of the bed. Shivering, she wrapped her arms around her middle and tiptoed across her room.

A soft rattle started up, and she paused, trying to identify the new noise. Her heart froze as she placed it—the front doorknob, twisting back and forth. Was someone trying to break in? *Oh, God.* She dashed back to the nightstand to grab her cell phone before peering around the corner to look down to the bottom of the stairs.

Ice filled her veins, turning her body numb. Tyler stood in front of the door, working the knob side-to-side with both hands in slow, repetitive movements. His silvery hair shone like a halo in the weak glow of the outdoor light.

She bit down on her lip before she could scream his name. If he was sleepwalking, she shouldn't suddenly wake him. At least that was the thought that came to her, some shred of random knowledge from a parenting magazine she must have buried away in her subconscious. And the door was secured with a deadbolt he probably didn't have the strength to turn. Everything was okay.

Except it wasn't. She crept down the stairs, shuddering as Tyler continued to twist the knob as if in a trance. Her son had always been a heavy sleeper. Nighttime wanderings were never, ever a concern before.

She reached out, gently taking his hands and

turning him from the door. "We have to go back to bed, baby."

He stared past her with wide, unseeing eyes. "I have to milk the cow." His fingers curled, mimicking the motions of his chore.

No. Her stomach heaved with a sickening roll. Even though the words only confirmed what she'd known—that this was related to the child ghost—hearing Josiah's thoughts come out of her son's mouth was too much to bear. Did Tyler think he was the colonial ghost? Or had Josiah's spirit somehow invaded his little body? If that was the case, would she get her son back? Bile flooded her throat, and she clapped a hand over her mouth. Shallow breaths puffed out her nose as she choked back the bitter fluid.

Okay. She needed to calm down. Swallowing hard, she lifted him into her arms and carried him back up the stairs. "I'll take care of the cow today," she murmured, just in case he could hear her.

She paused in the hallway. Now what? Either she brought him into bed with her, or she set up camp outside his room again. Neither choice was ideal, but she preferred to stay in a routine as much as possible. He already spent several nights a week on a blow-up mattress in the office of a vet clinic. Plus, taking him out of his room might just provoke their resident ghost.

With a shaky sigh, she laid him back in his toddler bed, tucking the covers around him tightly, as though that might be enough to keep him in place. Not that it mattered much, since she'd be on the floor in the hallway, blocking any escape routes. Sleep was unlikely, but she had to try.

She dragged herself back into her bedroom to get a

pillow and blankets. She hoped Tyler wouldn't remember any of this in the morning.

And hopefully, he'd be himself in the morning. She said a silent prayer as she curled up on the wooden floor.

****

By nine-thirty in the morning, she was almost in tears. The only thing preventing a complete breakdown was the overwhelming relief that Tyler seemed completely unaffected by the previous night's events. He was his regular self, full of energy. She, on the other hand, could barely hold her head up. The exhaustion weighed her down like an iron anchor. And she had to work tonight. Just the thought of it made her want to crawl into a dark hole somewhere. Maybe Terence had room under the deck.

Sighing, she pulled her forehead off the cool glass of the slider. Tyler had already begged her once today for a game of chase out back. Instead, she'd told him "maybe later" and parked him in front of the television. She certainly wouldn't win any Mom of the Year awards. But she just couldn't do this on her own anymore. Not with a ghost in the house.

Dropping into a kitchen chair, she hit the keys to dial Brett. He was probably at work, but she had no other options.

He answered quickly. "Hey Em. Everything okay?" Calling him during work hours wasn't something she usually did.

"No. I mean, Tyler's fine," she quickly amended. "I'm...not." Her voice wavered as she filled him in on the night's events, and she drew in a deep breath. *Pull yourself together*. "After I put him back to bed, I didn't sleep at all. The whole thing was really unsettling. And I have to work all night tonight, and I just don't know how I'm going to manage…" Pressing her lips together, she swallowed against the tears gathering in her throat.

"Okay. We'll figure something out. Let's see…how about Kaitlyn's mom?"

"I called her already. I mean, I knew you were at work. She can watch him, but only until around three. Then she has somewhere she needs to be. Stan—Mr. Winslow—isn't all that comfortable watching him alone. I could go get him when Ruth leaves, but I was really hoping to get a full eight hours of sleep. I just don't know how I'm going to function if I don't get some rest."

The tap of fingers on a keyboard drifted through the phone connection. "Hang on, let me check something. Okay. Do you think Kaitlyn's dad could just hold the fort down until about four? I could be over to their house by then."

Her shoulders sagged with relief. "I think he could do that. It's right after nap time, so if I bring a DVD, that should keep Ty busy. You'll be there by four?"

"Yes. I'll do something fun with Tyler for an hour or so, and then we'll pick up a pizza and bring it over in time for you to eat before work. Does that sound good?"

The tears found their way out, trickling down her face and dropping to the table. *Damn it.* She nodded, although he couldn't see her. And thank God for that. Swiping at her nose, she regained some composure. "That sounds better than good. Wonderful. Amazing. Thank you, Brett."

"I'm happy to do it. He's my son, too. Emily, I'm

here to help." His tone was kind, with no hint of resentment. "Just tell Mr. Winslow I'll be there as soon as I can make it out of here, okay?"

"Yes. Okay. I'll see if Ruth can come get him now. I don't think I have the energy to even drive over there. His bag and car seat will be at their house."

"No worries, Emily—I've got this. We'll be fine. Get some rest."

Chapter 26

She jammed the car into park in front of the church. *Crap*. She was running a bit behind this morning—not exactly late, but not early enough to ensure she wouldn't miss Gayle. And she had the cell phone from the shelter in her purse. She really wanted to get it to Gayle before the weekend, just in case.

Pulling Tyler from his car seat, she hurried up the walkway. *Thanks a lot, Josiah*. Once again, it had been a battle of wills this morning. They'd been gone all night, and their resident ghost didn't want Tyler to leave again.

Too bad. She had renewed energy, thanks to eight hours of solid sleep yesterday. Preschool would be over at the end of May, and she was paying a lot of money for it. While she did feel bad for the lost and lonely spirit, she wasn't about to let him completely dictate their lives. So she'd dug in her heels, and here they were.

There. Gayle's stroller came into view. Since their house was only a few blocks away, Gayle often walked in nice weather. And today was a glorious spring day, full of sunshine and a crisp breeze.

She ran into Gayle on the stairs, and conscious of the other mothers, she made her comments vague. "Hey! I have something for you. Will you wait for me in the meeting hall? I just need a sec to get him situated."

Entering the classroom, she helped Ty with the zipper of his jacket and watched as he hung it on his peg and joined the circle. Something was bothering her about Gayle's appearance, but she couldn't put her finger on it. There'd been no visible bruises, but Gayle was wearing a long-sleeved shirt. And a scarf.

The scarf. That was it. There was a light wind, but it was warm out. And the scarf Gayle was wearing was not a stylish accessory. It was thick, heavy winter-wear, wound tightly around her neck. Trepidation roiled through her as she dashed back upstairs to the church meeting hall. *Please, please be there.*

Gayle was waiting, gazing at notices posted on a bulletin board. The cavernous room was deserted, as it always was on weekday mornings. Still, they tended to huddle in the back corner when they met, partially hidden by towers of plastic chairs and folding tables. Anyone watching probably thought they were making drug deals or trading prescription meds.

Emily's footsteps echoed in the quiet as she approached Gayle. "Are you okay?" she whispered, following her into the corner.

Gayle nodded, not quite meeting Emily's eyes. "Yes. I just have a cold." The words came out like sandpaper, coarse and raspy. Her hands fluttered to the scarf. "Sore throat."

It would have worked on anyone who hadn't been researching domestic abuse. But Emily knew exactly what she was trying to hide. Strangulation. Visible signs were not always there, but Gayle was hiding something under that thick scarf. Her voice was the only other proof Emily needed. Things were escalating.

Gayle's expression was guarded, but the look in her brown eyes acknowledged the truth. She understood Emily knew what had happened. Her head dropped as she curled her arms around herself protectively.

"I am so, so worried about you." Emily lowered her voice to the barest breath of a whisper. "You know this kind of behavior is a precursor to homicide." All the notes Emily had printed listed the same frightening statistics—abuse victims who'd been strangled were seven to nine times more likely to be murdered. It was a horrific red flag in an already terrible situation.

Gayle continued to stare at the floor, saying nothing.

Don't judge. Don't pressure. It has to be her decision. Emily took a deep breath. "I have the phone I told you about. You can use it any time to call the people who can help." Her fingers trembled as she slipped it into Gayle's hand. "And you know what to do if you decide to leave, right? I have another copy of the notes on safety planning if you need them."

She shook her head slowly. "I just don't know how I can leave my husband...my house. My entire life."

"I know it's hard. But your life is in danger. And Brandon needs his mom. He needs a safe and healthy environment." She chewed on her lip, hoping she wasn't going too far. But she sensed this moment was a turning point. "You have the strength to do this when you're ready. The people at the shelter know what they're doing. No one will know where you are. They'll protect you and help you make a new life. Just remember you're not alone, okay?"

A hoarse sob escaped as Gayle's shoulders shook. She lifted her head, blinking back tears. "Why are you bothering with me?"

"Not too long ago, I was in a really tough situation. The only reason I made it through is because my friend and her family stepped in to help me. My life would be very different if they hadn't. I had to make scary choices, but they told me I was strong enough to do it. You are too, Gayle. I'm just here to remind you of that, and support you in any way I can."

Gayle's harsh breathing filled the silence as she stared at the phone in her hand. "Thank you." She slipped the phone into the pocket of her jeans.

"You're welcome. Now, you have somewhere safe to hide that?"

She nodded. "I should...get going." Taking a step back, she tilted her chin to the back exit of the meeting hall.

"I'll go through the front," Emily assured her. That was their usual practice, ever since the day Joe had caught them coming out of the building together after pick-up. He'd said he was there to "surprise" Brandon, but Emily was certain he'd been checking up on Gayle. While he'd played out a nice-guy routine in front of her, even shaking her hand, Emily had felt the dark, menacing waves of suspicion and disapproval rolling off of him.

Gayle paused, her hand on the steel bar of the door. "Thanks again, Emily...for everything."

"Of course. I'll probably see you at pick-up, but if not...just remember, I'm here for you if you need me." She gave her friend one last encouraging nod. "A phone call away."

****

Another counseling session over. Since he and

Emily were now getting along, and Tyler seemed perfectly happy with his presence in his life, they'd mostly discussed the monetary arrangements that would eventually need to be drawn up by a lawyer while the receptionist kept Ty entertained outside of Drew's office.

A serious waste of time on a gorgeous spring afternoon. Everything he had belonged to his son now. He couldn't imagine a scenario where he'd deny any financial help requested, even over and above the eventual legal requirement. Especially since Emily was so practical.

He was just grateful he had money to give. He'd always lived fairly simply: he'd lived at home while attending Cape Cod Community College, and then paid off his tuition working for two years at a local marina before deciding he'd had enough of boats. After that, he'd followed his brother into the Air Force. He'd saved a lot during his years overseas, since he didn't have a family to support. Plus, his dangerous job offered an additional hazardous duty pay. While he wasn't rich, money wasn't one of his worries.

After fighting their way through the traffic caused by weekend visitors trying to navigate a narrow bridge leading to a chaotic rotary—one of only two ways to get onto Cape Cod—they'd officially declared it Happy Hour. Emily decided on a Mexican theme of nachos and margaritas, so they'd stopped at the liquor store and then the little market near her house.

Emily had looked flustered when she'd come out of the store and climbed back into his truck, and a combination of persistent questioning and words spelled out to keep Tyler from understanding had finally revealed the reason: that guy Eric—the owner of the market, apparently—had been inside, pestering her for a date this weekend.

It bothered him more than it should. Even now, as he wrestled with their son on her couch while she mixed up margaritas, he was struggling to tamp down on the irritation. Ridiculous. She'd turned the guy down—again—and she didn't seem interested in pursuing a relationship with him. Besides, it didn't matter; he had no claim on her.

Did he even want one? Would she? In bed, their chemistry was undeniable, but that would only get them so far. Beyond sex, however, they were spending a great deal of time together, even though they both knew Ty was fine on his own with Brett. Even Drew had okayed that much.

And they were having fun together. At least from his perspective, they got along not because they had to for Tyler's sake, but because they enjoyed each other's company. Still, there were things between them, a wide gulf of pain and mistrust that might never be bridged.

"Margaritas are up." Emily carried two full glasses toward the couch, taking careful steps as the liquid sloshed dangerously close to the wide rims. "Nachos will be out of the oven soon."

"Okay, buddy, that's enough roughhousing right now. I don't want to spill on the couch." He accepted the drink, moving over to make room for Emily.

She gave him a wry smile. "It's not exactly my most prized piece of furniture." Lowering herself down, she sipped at the light green liquid. "Oh, strong."

"Sounds perfect." He gave her a nod once he'd tried it himself. "It is perfect. Hey, little man, let's show

Mommy the pictures we took yesterday."

By now, most of his close buddies at the base knew he had a son. He didn't provide the details, and they didn't ask…one of the best qualities of his male friends. But when he'd requested ideas for fun places to take a preschooler yesterday, they'd offered up plenty of advice. When he'd picked up Tyler from the Winslows, they'd headed to a local co-op farm where visitors could look at the animals.

He set his drink down on the coffee table and picked up his phone. Opening his photos, he scrolled back to start at the beginning. "Some pictures from Coonamesset Farm yesterday." He held the screen so she could see, and Tyler scrambled onto his lap to look as well. He was a big fan of cell phones.

"Oh, they're so cute!" She leaned forward as Brett slid a few pictures of the bunnies across the screen. "I wish I'd been there with you guys."

"You needed sleep," he reminded her. "Lots of new babies there, though." A picture of piglets sleeping with a large sow popped up next. Then Ty on a little tractor.

"I wanna ride the tractor." Ty pointed to himself on the little red vehicle.

"We'll go again soon, bud. And we'll take Mommy this time." He flipped to the next picture, a brown mallard duck, floating on the farm's pond, surrounded by tiny ducklings with fuzzy yellow heads.

"That's the mommy," explained Tyler. "And the babies." He reached out and slid his finger across the screen to bring up the next picture—a close up of a male mallard, his emerald green head iridescent in the afternoon sunlight. "And that's the daddy."

"Very good, buddy. We talked about how you can tell from the color of their feathers, right? The daddy ducks have the bright green feathers on their head and neck."

"Are you *my* daddy?"

Emily gasped as her margarita spilled down the front of her blouse. "Oh, sh—" Catching herself mid-curse, she snapped her mouth closed and stared at Brett, wide-eyed.

His heart stopped. Tyler tilted his head up to him, his inquisitive blue gaze so much like his own. What was he supposed to say? Resorting to humor, he tickled Tyler's sides. "Are you saying I have a green head and neck?"

Ty giggled, squirming on his lap. Outside the open windows, the breeze knocked the long metal bars of Emily's wind chime.

He continued to distract Ty as he looked to her for help. Was this the opening they needed? Or was it best to get past the question, and deal with this another day?

She bit her bottom lip. Closed her eyes and nodded.

His normally steady hands shook slightly as he turned Tyler to face him. "That's a good question, buddy. I *am* your daddy. I had to go away to fight the bad guys, but now I'm back."

"That's what I thought." Tyler nodded, confirming this to himself.

Brett braced himself for the barrage of questions likely to follow, forcing himself to recall Drew's advice for dealing with kids this age: give simple, truthful answers, straight to the point. Three-year-olds didn't need lots of adult justifications. Blowing out a breath, he grabbed his margarita and gulped it down.

But the questions didn't come. At least, none related to Brett's role as a parent.

"Can I play with it now?" Tyler asked, reaching for the cell phone.

What? It took Brett a moment to respond. He glanced over to Emily, who shrugged. A dazed expression slackened her features, and she wiped at the damp spot on her shirt with an ineffectual, repetitive motion.

The oven timer buzzed, snapping her out of her bewildered state.

"Nachos are ready." She sprung off the couch and rushed to the kitchen, as though an extra second or two under the heat might turn the chips to ash.

"I'm going to…help Mommy." He studied his son, who only nodded as he opened one of the apps Brett had downloaded for him. Tyler knew exactly which icons led to which games, and his little fingers manipulated the phone with practiced ease. Amazing.

Brett picked up his glass and wandered into the kitchen, his head buzzing with the combination of shock and tequila. "I think I need a refill."

Emily set the baking pan on the stovetop with a rattle. "Could it really be that easy?" She opened her hands, still covered with bright red and yellow oven mitts.

"You always said he was a sensitive kid." He located the margarita pitcher and dumped some into his glass. "But, no—it can't be that easy. Maybe it will be for now, but there will probably be things to deal with in the future."

"Wait till Drew gets a load of this." Her shoulders shook with suppressed laughter as she pulled off the mitts. The giggles finally escaped, and she tossed the oven mitts in the air and strode over to Brett. Taking the pitcher from him, she tipped it back and drained what was left.

His own laughter broke free as he raised his glass, drinking deeply. "I think we're going to need to make more of these. Good thing I don't have to drive until much later."

She slapped the empty pitcher down on the kitchen table. "Hey, after today's events, you don't have to drive at all, really." Her eyebrows lifted as a suggestive smirk played across her mouth.

Oh, no. There it was. His strangely exuberant mood imploded, sucking the laughter from his chest. He cut his gaze from hers, glancing around the room as an awkward silence spun out. Electronic beeps drifted in from the living room.

Doubt crept across her beautiful features as she quickly backtracked. "I only meant, ah, if you wanted to stay over...it probably wouldn't impact Ty in a negative way." Turning, she opened one of the cabinets and pulled out two small plates.

Damn it. Of course he *wanted* to stay over. He wanted to drag her upstairs right now and toss her into bed. He wanted to rip off her wet blouse and taste the sweet saltiness of her skin. He wanted to ravage her for hours, finally falling into a dreamless sleep once they were spent. To awaken in the hazy morning light with her in his arms, kissing her slowly until she was ready for him again.

But that could never happen. And he didn't know how to tell her that without unleashing everything he fought to keep contained. The guilt he carried would break him if he let it out. After all the punishment he'd laid on her, she'd see that his failings were worse. Deadlier.

It wasn't your fault. There was no evidence of the hidden IED—the signs are only in your dreams. The mantra from his obligatory PTSD sessions floated through his brain, but he could never quite accept it. Mac had been a husband and a father. It should have been Brett.

You're a father, too. He wanted to stay, not just to be with Em, but to protect them both. That was his job; it was the life he'd trained for. Instead, his wild screams would terrify them in the midst of nights already filled with fear. And if the dreams were exceptionally intense, he might hurt Emily as she tried to calm him.

No. It was too risky for her and Ty. Too painful for him. Aside from the potential danger, he just wasn't prepared to expose his weakness. He'd resigned himself to a lifetime of solitary nights during the long hospital stay.

A pink flush rose on her cheeks as he hesitated. But he hadn't anticipated this. Now that Tyler knew, she'd expect him to want to stay over after sex. Eventually, she'd grow tired of his excuses and put an end to this aspect of their relationship. And that was probably for the best.

"I…wish I could." True enough, but now he searched for the lies to back up his statement. Because if he stayed with her until Tyler went to sleep, they'd end up in bed together, if he had any say in the matter. He wasn't about to just turn around and leave her after that, especially on a Friday night when she knew he didn't have work in the morning.

"The thing is…some of the guys on the base set up a poker game for tonight, and I said I'd come." It was tomorrow night, actually, and although he was considering it, he hadn't made any type of commitment. But it was the first believable thing that came to his mind. "So I'll probably have to get going soon."

"Oh. Of course." She hid her expression behind her curls as she shoveled at the nachos with a rubber spatula. Sliding a heap of chips smothered in cheese onto a plate, she offered it to him along with a strained smile. "Well, I'm sure there will probably be a ton of food there, but if you want to hang out for a bit longer and snack on these, you can. I'm just going to see what I can find for Ty's dinner." She crossed to the far side of the kitchen, opening the pantry door to rummage inside.

He strode back into the living room, anxious to escape the tension. What was happening here? His son had just acknowledged him as his dad, with minimal confusion, it would seem. He should be settling in for a night of quiet celebration with the two people he most wanted to spend time with. Instead, he was headed out to an imaginary poker game.

Tyler continued to play with Brett's phone, engrossed in the game.

He set his plate of nachos down and paced the room. What he needed was a long, hard run. Let the ache in his muscles replace the ache in his heart. "Let's finish up with that, buddy. We can go set up a new train track in your room before I have to go."

Chapter 27

He'd had a horrible night. The workout had exhausted him physically, but the guilt over leaving Emily and Ty invaded his subconscious anyway. One nightmare after another woke him from a restless sleep. In one particularly awful dream scenario, Mac had been carrying Tyler as his foot hung over the buried IED.

He shuddered, slamming his hand against the truck's steering wheel. The horrifying image was now burned into his brain. He'd met his parents for an impromptu lunch, and they'd expressed concern over his dark mood. He'd explained he was tired—certainly true, if not the full story. Even if he'd wanted to explain, they didn't know about Tyler yet. He knew they'd be supportive, as always, but he didn't want them to condemn Emily, and that was bound to happen. At least as part of their initial reaction.

The thought of that discussion weighed on him, adding another layer to his exhaustion. He reached for the heavy-duty coffee he'd stopped for, hoping the potent brew would also wash away the gloom clouding his mind. He was almost at Emily's, and he wanted to enjoy his time with his son.

And Emily. She'd cheerfully responded to his texted request to come over after lunch, even asking how his poker game was. Another jagged splinter of guilt lodged itself in his chest. At least he was safe from the lies today—she had to work tonight. In the meantime, he had a few hours to hang out with them. He hoped holding Tyler in his arms would lift his spirits. Holding Emily in his arms was too much to hope for, however. At least he could help her. Last night before he'd left, he'd jury rigged the two doors leading outside to be childproof in case Ty had gone wandering in his sleep again. Thankfully, he hadn't, although Emily reported waking during the night to the loud banging of kitchen cabinets opening and closing.

He wasn't sure if she'd want him to remove the cabinet doors from their hinges to put an end to the source of that nuisance. At the very least, though, today he would install more secure mechanisms on the front and back doors. He glanced at the bag from the hardware store sitting on the passenger seat. After lunch, he had stopped and bought a safety bar for the slider and a hinged metal lever for the front door. Both devices had childproof features, and he would also mount them high enough to remain out of Tyler's reach for many years.

If only he could solve the ghost problem so easily. Clenching his jaw, he pulled into Emily's driveway and cut the engine. The little house appeared so quaint and peaceful. He stared at it as he finished his coffee, searching his mind once again for a way to stop the haunting. He'd move them in a second if Emily would allow it, but she insisted it would do no good.

He grabbed the bag and strode up the walkway. It would pain him to suggest it, but maybe they should hire another medium. The one from last weekend had claimed she couldn't speak to this Josiah ghost's mother—maybe a stronger one could. At least Claire had refused any money for her visit, insisting she hadn't done anything useful. That in and of itself gave him a little more faith in the whole process.

Knowing Emily, though, she'd probably sent the other woman a gift card of some kind. He would have to make sure he got some more money into her hands without hurting her pride. God, she'd probably try to pay *him* for the hardware supplies. He shook his head as he reached out to test the doorknob. Locked.

Good. He'd been on her since the Wednesday night incident to make sure the doors were always locked, even during the day. Even if Ty somehow managed to figure out the deadbolt, it would slow him down. He already knew how to flip the flimsy lock on the sliding glass door, but that at least led to a fenced-in backyard. Could he open the gate? Another thing Brett would have to check on today.

He tapped his knuckles against the door quietly, in case Tyler had gone down for a nap after all. But Emily had said he slept in and was refusing to go back to sleep after lunch. While he waited for her to answer, he glanced down to the shadowy spot where the steps met a large bush—one of Terence's favorite hide-outs. Sure enough, a pair of amber eyes glittered up at him from between the new green leaves.

The poor cat couldn't even come in the house. While that wasn't the most pressing issue, he knew it was upsetting Emily. One more reason to come up with the solution.

She opened the door wearing a wide smile, a white lacy top, and tiny cutoff denim shorts. His gaze dropped down beyond the frayed hems, traveling the length of her firm, tanned legs. Desire clenched like a fist in his belly as he brushed against her, stepping inside.

"Sorry, I was in the office. Trying to catch up on billing for the clinic." Reaching up, she tightened the high ponytail on her head, exposing a line of skin above the low waistline of her shorts.

Not helping.

Thankfully, Ty's excited voice rang out from the top of the stairs. "Br—Daddy!"

His heart contracted at the new name. Joy flooded his veins as he glanced back at Emily.

"We've been working on it," she murmured, her emerald eyes shining. She tucked a stray curl behind her ear.

He mouthed "thank you" to her before calling out, "Hey, buddy! I love hearing you call me 'Daddy'. Coming down to see me?"

"I have new books in my room. Mommy said you'd read them to me."

A hint of pink rose on her cheeks. "I hope you don't mind. We went to the library, and he picked out literally two dozen books while I was trying to talk to the librarian. Since I couldn't get him down for a nap, and I really needed to get some work done, I told him to line them up in order of how he wanted them read. It kept him busy for a while."

"No problem. I'm happy to do it." He set the bag down on the bench by the door. "I'll be right up, buddy, okay?"

"Don't worry; I don't think you'll have to read all twenty-four." The corners of her mouth tilted up. "He'll probably get antsy after a few. Or he'll go the other way and fall asleep."

He really wanted to kiss those lips. He looked

away, scrubbing at the weekend scruff on his jaw. "Did you find anything out? At the library?"

She sighed. "Well, I don't know if I told you, but I'd already discovered that the Barnstable Historical Society doesn't open until mid-June. I think there's a treasure trove of information there, but I can't get to it. The librarian did give me some names of local historians and genealogists, though, so I can try that. She pulled a few books they had on local history during that time period, and she requested a few more through the library sharing network. So, I guess we'll see what I find. Hopefully, tonight will be slow and I can read at work. But right now, I *have* to get this billing done."

"Go," he ordered her, resisting the urge to pull her in for a kiss before sending her to the office. "I've got this." He paused on the third step to watch her walk away.

It didn't surprise him that knowing he could never have her—not fully—made him want her all the more. That was human nature, wasn't it? What did surprise him was the one-eighty his feelings had taken in two short months. Although really, it was more like a full three-hundred-and-sixty degree circle since they'd first met. He knew then he could fall in love with her, if the circumstances had been different. Now, he was falling hard, and he had to stop it. That was the only way to spare himself the pain, because soon enough, she'd move on to someone who wouldn't potentially kill her in her sleep. He set his jaw as he reached the landing, turning left toward Ty's bedroom.

"Wow." Starting at the threshold of the doorway, a line of colorful picture books marched across the room until they met the disabled electric train set. From there, the line continued perpendicular until it reached the bed, where Tyler bounced happily.

"Okay, little man, which end are we starting from?"

He pointed straight down, to the first book at the edge of the bed.

"Bucky the Bulldozer, huh?" Brett leaned over to pick it up, surveying his options. The little bed didn't fit his large frame very well, especially for an extended reading session. The rocking chair was gone—banished to the corner of the office, where it had been laid on its side. But Emily had piled a fluffy blanket and a few pillows under the windows, presumably as a temporary replacement. He spread the blanket out, propped a pillow behind his back, and leaned against the wall. Patting the spot behind him, he called Tyler over.

Emily had been right. After four stories, Tyler grew restless, and soon they were instead playing a game that involved throwing pillows at each other. As they wrestled, Tyler's little hands found the metal chain around his neck, and Ty pulled the dog tags out from beneath his black T-shirt. He studied one of the two identical steel plates, his brow furrowed.

"What's it say?"

"My name. And some other stuff. It's like a...ah...nametag, for work."

"Fighting bad guys?" He picked at the black rubber silencer lining the tag with his thumb.

"Well, yes, sometimes. These ID tags are part of my uniform, but sometimes I forget to take them off when I'm not at work."

Tyler released the chain, sitting back on his heels. "Mommy has some too."

"Yes, she probably wears a nametag on her shirt for work, right?" He slipped his dog tags back beneath the neck of his T-shirt.

"No…like those. But she doesn't wear them."

He frowned. "I think you mean a necklace, bud," he said, picturing the long silver pendant Emily often wore. "And you're right; she probably doesn't wear her necklace to work."

"I wanna wear it. Like you." He ran from the room, swerving around the trail of books, one bare foot slapping against the wooden floor planks. The sound echoed through the quiet house, joined by the creak of Emily's bedroom door opening.

Brett stood, searching for the missing sock as he straightened the pillows. Emily was probably not going to be too happy if Ty was going through her jewelry, but he didn't quite feel comfortable enough to follow Tyler into her bedroom. Besides, she was organized enough to have made anything she didn't want played with childproof.

He wandered out into the hallway, peering through the doorway to Em's bedroom. Tyler was standing by the open drawer of her nightstand, trying to pull a chain over his head. A long beaded chain with two matching tags, one hanging off the main chain by a smaller loop. Dog tags.

Giving up on propriety, Brett entered the room and knelt by his son. "You do have some. Can I see?" He took the chain from Tyler and turned the tag to read the five lines of information embossed on the steel plates:

SHEA
TYLER M.
034-24-1579

A NEG
PROTESTANT

What the hell? A gray haze blurred his vision as he tried to process what he was seeing. Why would Emily buy military dog tags for their son? His stomach burned as the remains of the bitter coffee turned to acid. Folding the tags into his palm, he brought his hand to his forehead. There had to be an explanation. Some kind of birthday party favor? No, something like that would never include such personal data. A gift from someone who knew about Tyler's parentage, then? Maybe an attempt by Kaitlyn to connect Tyler to his father in some small way?

But they weren't Air Force tags. No branch of service was indicated—that meant Army tags. Of course, Kaitlyn might not have known any better, if this was her doing. Maybe she meant well, but he didn't like thinking of his young, innocent son owning military spec dog tags. None of this felt right. The headache that had been hovering behind his eyes all morning sent up a warning flare.

"Hey, buddy, I'm going to give you mine for a sec, okay? We'll trade." A vise tightened in his chest as he placed his own tags over Tyler's blond head. Then he pulled out his phone, unlocking the screen. "Can you play one of your games for a minute?" He handed off the phone and lifted Tyler to set him on Emily's bed. "I'll be right back, little man."

He found her in the office, sitting at her desk, fingers tapping on the computer key board. A half-eaten energy bar lay on top of a pile of paperwork, and her blond curls swayed from the ponytail as she paused for a sip from her coffee mug.

He waited until she'd set the hot drink down before tapping on the door frame. Still, she jumped slightly in her chair as the unexpected noise pulled her from her work.

"Oh!" She swiveled around to face him. "Everything okay? Did he fall asleep?"

"He's fine. I gave him my phone to play with for a minute." Lifting his hand, he opened his fist to let the dog tags fall until they dangled from his fingers. "Why does Tyler have dog tags with his name on them?"

Her face paled. "Where did you get those?"

"Ty was looking at mine. Then he went into your room and pulled these from a drawer by your bed."

"They're not his." She shook her head slowly.

"That doesn't make any sense, Emily. His full name is on them."

Her lips trembled as she cut her gaze away from the suspended chain. "I named Tyler after my brother. They're his."

A brother. Suddenly, the statement that had niggled at his brain for weeks, never quite reaching the surface, came back to him. *My mom worked really hard to provide for us*, she'd said, the day she finally told him what had happened to her parents. The "us" had lodged itself into his subconscious, but then she'd gone on to explain how she'd searched for him at Lackland, and that one tiny clue to her past had been completely buried under all the other emotional revelations.

"You have a brother in the military?"

Muscles moved along her neck as she swallowed. "I *had* a brother. And yes, he was in the Army."

Oh, no. "Tell me what happened, Emily."

She shook her head more vehemently, sending her

ponytail swinging. "It hurts to talk about it. I named my son for him, and I can't even set his pictures out. I have to keep them in a *box*. Isn't that awful? But I keep the tags next to my bed so I can take them out and remember him." Her voice continued to rise until a sob broke free, and she pressed a hand to her chest. The tick of the old clock marked the seconds as she struggled for control. She exhaled, her shoulders falling. "I guess Tyler's pulled all the stuff from the drawers he can reach enough times to know about them."

He waited, forcing himself to ignore the tears glittering in her eyes. His sympathy for her was outweighed by the need to know. By now, he understood she was the type of person who bottled up her pain, sealing it away in a dark corner of her mind so it couldn't hurt her. Hell, didn't he do the same thing? A defense mechanism, yes, but sometimes a necessary one.

So he couldn't exactly fault her. And yet, his situation was much different. Surely she didn't carry the belief that maybe she could have prevented her brother's death. And it was just as unlikely that she'd actually witnessed the incident that ended his life, only to relive it in nightmares over and over again.

"What happened to him?" He pushed her again, because she probably needed to tell the story as much as he needed to hear it. He deserved to know what happened to their son's namesake.

"Oh, shit," she whispered, dropping her head into her hands. "Do we have to do this right now?"

His armor cracked a bit. Crossing the room, he reached for her wrists and drew her up. "Yes, we do." His tone was firm but gentle, and he wrapped a steady arm around her waist. "Let's go sit down in the kitchen. I'll get you a refill." He grabbed her mug from the desk and led her out of the room.

Once she was seated at the table, he poured two mugs of coffee for them, running upstairs to check on Tyler as they heated in the microwave. Then he joined her, setting the dog tags on the table between them.

She stared at the chain. Wrapping her hands around the warm mug, she blew out a breath. "Remember when I told you how my dad left when I was young?"

He nodded, but she wasn't looking at him. "Yes, I remember." He shifted his chair closer to her, reaching out to rub her shoulder.

She flinched at his touch before leaning into it with just the slightest motion. "I was two years old. I don't remember him. My older brother Tyler was six, so of course it was harder for him. We had these neighbors, the Conleys...they had a son, Kevin, who was the same age as Tyler. They played together a lot. Over the years, Mr. Conley became sort of a surrogate father for Tyler. He would include Tyler in all the guy activities he did with his own son: sports, fishing, Red Sox games. Tyler loved Mr. C." She paused, lifting the mug to her lips. "Then Mr. C. had to fly to Los Angeles for a business trip. On September 11, 2001."

"Oh, Jesus."

"He was on Flight 175 from Logan. Kevin and Tyler were seniors in high school that fall. After the attack, they vowed to join the Army as soon as they graduated so they could go fight Al Qaeda."

He cleared his throat. "When did he die?"

"March of 2003. In Afghanistan."

"Hostile action?"

She nodded, swiping at the tears rolling down her cheeks. "An ambush."

"Oh, God, Em...I am so sorry." He moved his hand to the back of her neck and kneaded the knots of tension with his fingers. "How old were you?"

"I was fourteen—a freshman in high school. That was when my mom began fading away. She went through the motions for me, I know, but a part of her also died that year. Somehow she managed to keep herself going until she got me off to college, though. I don't think it's a coincidence that she died shortly after I turned twenty-one."

He scrubbed his jaw with his free hand. "Are you saying...suicide?"

"Honestly, I don't know. I really don't think she'd have done that to me on purpose. She always put her kids first. I think it was just a matter of knowing I had safely reached adulthood, and that it was finally okay to let go. Her illness had been taking its toll for a while, and I guess she was tired of being so vigilant when her heart had been broken for so long."

His own heart hurt for her. But he couldn't ignore the other less altruistic emotions churning inside him. Why was he just learning about this now?

"You've been through a lot of tragedy, Em. I get that. But I wish you'd shared this with me when we first met."

She laughed, the sound completely devoid of mirth. "Seriously? How could I have told you my brother had been killed overseas? You knew you were going to be deployed to Afghanistan or Iraq almost immediately after school. You were so excited about getting into EOD. I just couldn't imagine telling you my brother had been killed seven years ago in essentially the very same war you were going off to fight!"

"I wasn't exactly naïve to what happens in war, Emily. Even back then. But this certainly sheds some light on why you were so certain I wouldn't come home."

Shaking his hand off, she pushed the chair back and stood. "I told you…the men in my life leave, and they don't come back! They die, or they disappear."

"Still, you should have told me. In these past few months, anyway."

She thrust her arms out. "Why? So you can have better insight into my emotional scars? It's not like it matters. All these things played a part in my screwed-up decision-making process, but the end result is still the same. What I did is still unforgiveable."

There it was—that guilt and self-loathing he knew so well. It was even more destructive than the grief. He pushed himself to standing as the last shred of anger he had toward her, buried deeply now but still alive, burned away into harmless ash. "No. It's not."

She froze. "What?"

"I forgive you, Emily. I played a part in this mess too. But I don't want to hold on to any more anger or regret. And I don't want you to, either. I forgive you, so forgive yourself."

Her face crumpled as he closed the distance between them. She stiffened in his embrace, and he pulled her in closer, pressing her face into his chest. Her back heaved silently beneath his hands.

"I can't…" she sobbed, trying to break free.

He held her tightly as she repeated the words. He understood the double meaning: it wasn't just that she couldn't forgive herself—she couldn't let him comfort her, either. To get that close to him emotionally meant leaving herself vulnerable. She'd spent her entire life building a protective wall, and each crack in the foundation was terrifying.

"It's too late to stop it, Em." He softened his tone to a soothing murmur, breathing the words in her ear. "I'm already here. I'm Tyler's father. You know I can't promise nothing bad will ever happen to me. No one can promise that. But I will never abandon either of you. Never."

The hitching sobs grew louder before finally subsiding. When she quieted, he took her shoulders and pushed her back gently. Cupping her face, he wiped the remaining tears from her cheeks as he kept his gaze on hers, looking for answers to a multitude of questions in her red-rimmed eyes. Was she okay now? Could she forgive herself and start to heal? And did she trust that he would be there for them?

She nodded, suppressing a final shudder.

He didn't know if that was an answer to any or all of his unspoken questions. But it was a reassuring gesture, at least—good enough for now. "Okay. Let's get you some rest before work. You can't go in like this—you're a disaster." He shook his head in mock dismay, hoping to lighten the mood.

She produced a watery smile. "I bet." Sniffling, she allowed him to lead her toward the staircase. "I'll be fine by seven, I'm sure. I can't call in sick—that's reserved for when Tyler or I have an actual illness."

"Don't forget you have me now, too. I can always stay with Ty when he's sick." He released her waist and caught her hand as they climbed the stairs. "And right now, I can keep him busy while you get some sleep. You can fit in a solid two-hour nap and still have plenty of time to get ready. I'll find something for dinner."

No electronic beeps chimed in her bedroom, and sure enough, Tyler lay curled on his side, asleep, his hand still loosely clutching Brett's phone. His long lashes fluttered as he mumbled something incoherent.

Emily sighed. "Finally. My guess is either the game got boring, or your phone ran out of juice." She nudged the drawer of her nightstand closed with her knee.

"Probably the latter. I forgot to charge it last night." He gently tugged the phone from Tyler's lax grip and tried the power button. "Yep, it died. Those games suck up a lot of battery power."

"Don't I know it." She sank down on the bed just beyond Tyler's feet.

He shrugged, setting the phone on her nightstand. "Makes no difference to me. I'm not exactly expecting a lot of calls."

She shot him a wry smile. "Because the only person that constantly bothers you is sitting right here."

He grinned back at her. "Well, anyway, this is convenient. You want me to carry him to his bed?"

"No. I'm just going to curl up next to him." Lifting his lower body, she managed to slip the covers from beneath him and then settle them over him without disturbing his slumber. She crawled over his sleeping form, glancing up at Brett as she slid her bare legs between the covers. "Will you…stay with us?"

His chest tightened. "Of course I'll stay." He circled around the bed to the other side and climbed in beside her.

"I should set my alarm," she murmured, pushing herself up to her elbow.

"No, it's fine, I won't fall asleep." It would be hard, after the night he'd had, but he would have to make absolutely certain he didn't drift off. Both Emily and his son were going to be right near him—they did not need the additional trauma of waking up to his screams. Having a ghost in the house was enough to worry about.

He wrapped his arm around her as she dropped her head back down to the pillow, hauling her against him until her back pressed against his chest. "You get some rest—I'll keep watch. If Tyler wakes up, I'll take him downstairs. And I'll make sure you're up in time for work."

"Thank you." Her voice was fading. "I'm kind of emotionally drained."

"I bet. Just close your eyes. I'm here."

Chapter 28

Emily opened the front door, taking a cardboard drink holder out of Brett's hands. "Wow. I feel like I'm at a spa or something."

He lifted his eyebrows as he stepped inside. "It's an orange-mango smoothie and a breakfast panini," he pointed out, holding up the brown bag. "Hardly spa fare."

Shrugging, she led him toward the kitchen. "You made us dinner last night. You're bringing me breakfast this morning, and now I get to sleep all day while you watch Ty. Feels like a spa weekend to me. I just need a fluffy white robe."

She glanced down at her attire as if she really might find herself wrapped in a pristine robe. No such luck. At least she'd managed to change out of her dirty scrubs, though, into something only slightly more glamorous: black spandex running shorts and a faded Red Sox T-shirt. But hey, she was just going to sleep.

"Do most spa weekends include working a twelve-hour night shift?"

She laughed as she set the drinks on the table. "Good point. At least it went by fast—we were super busy."

"Well, maybe if you play your cards right, you'll get a massage later." A roguish smile flashed across his face before it disappeared just as fast, and he suddenly made himself busy pulling the sandwiches out of the bag.

What was going on with him?

"That'd be nice," she said, injecting her voice with a noncommittal tone. "I'll go pry Tyler away from the computer." She strode toward the office, her sleep-deprived mind spinning drunkenly.

He was hiding something. While she wasn't exactly going to win any prizes for volunteering personal information, whatever it was loomed like a shadowy obstacle between them. He'd seemed to balk at the idea of staying over Friday night, but his explanation had made sense. After all, he'd been spending a huge amount of his free time with them for the last few months. He had probably been chaffing at the bit for a guys' night out.

Then Saturday, he'd miraculously forgiven her. She'd had to work, so sex hadn't exactly been an option…yet, he'd held her for hours as she slept, curling his body around hers protectively, which somehow felt even more intimate than everything else they'd done.

Today, he'd made a suggestive remark within the first five minutes of conversation, only to seem like he suddenly wanted to take it right back.

Did he regret what had happened between them? Now that Tyler knew the truth, maybe Brett thought they should just be friendly co-parents.

Or maybe, now that he had forgiven her, he wanted to start over. Her heart fluttered with hope. Their last courtship had been rushed. He'd wooed her for less than twenty-four hours before she eagerly jumped into bed with him. But they'd both known their time together had been limited.

Could he really want to try for a long-term relationship with her? After everything that had happened? If so, perhaps he wanted it to begin as a grand romance, with no lusty trysts to confuse things. When Kay got engaged, she spent one crazy month trying to convince Michael that they should remain celibate until the wedding to make their big day more meaningful. He'd played along good-naturedly, knowing she'd eventually crack, which she did.

She smiled at the memory as she peered in at Tyler. Maybe it was possible that Brett still wanted her...but the other option seemed more likely. He'd probably gotten her out of his system already, and now she was just Tyler's mom. The flirtatious comment had been a slip—just Brett being Brett. Her good mood leaked away on a stream of exhaustion.

"Time to shut it down, baby. Br—I mean, your daddy is here. He brought you a strawberry smoothie and a bagel with cream cheese."

"Daddy!" He jumped up and ran past her, headed for the kitchen.

Wow. A tiny sliver of jealousy pricked at her, even as she rejoiced at how well Tyler was adjusting to all this. She trudged across the room to turn off the computer. At least it had been the somewhat-educational matching game. He'd be with Brett all day, so she'd indulged him in some screen time this morning.

She forced a smile back onto her face as she went to join them. No matter what happened between her and Brett personally, she felt confident they could work together to raise Tyler successfully. That was what she should be focusing on, anyway. That and getting rid of this ghost. She'd arrived home from work this morning to a blaring television set and a blown fuse in the kitchen. Who knew what had gone on during the night?

Tyler sat at the table already, swinging his feet as Brett unpacked the food. She pulled the drinks out of the cardboard holder, pausing to inhale the rich scent of Brett's coffee. "I'm jealous," she said, gazing longingly at the insulated cup as she passed it to him.

"No caffeine for you right now. Drink your healthy smoothie." He made a production of enjoying his first sip, his lips curling in a wicked grin over the plastic top.

She pretended to pout as she accepted the panini. "I hope you burn your tongue."

He laughed. "You need your sleep. But I'll bring you one when I come back."

"You don't need to do that. I can just brew some here." *If Josiah doesn't blow out my entire electrical system when you take Tyler away again.*

"I'll bring you some." His voice was low, threaded with some emotion she couldn't quite identify. "Just call me when you wake up. But no rush. I can take the mattress for naptime, right?"

The memory of yesterday's nap drifted through her mind—lying in the middle of her bed, with her hand on her sleeping son's side while her own body was cradled in Brett's arms. She'd never felt so safe and content. *Bliss.*

"Em? Is the mattress packed up?"

She snapped back into the present. "Oh. Yes. I packed everything you need into the bag I take to work. The mattress inflates easily—just turn the dial."

"I think I can handle it." His lips formed a

withering smirk, but the playful light in his cerulean eyes ruined the effect.

"Okay." She drew the word out, playing with the straw of her drink. "But I seem to recall a lot of trouble with the car seat harness, Mr. EOD tech."

"I don't remember that." He feigned confusion, taking a bite of his sandwich. "So, buddy," he continued as he turned toward Tyler. "When we finish breakfast, you and I are going to a Nature Museum."

"The one in Brewster? That sounds like fun. I miss all the good stuff."

He cocked his head, the corner of his mouth twitching. "I'm not quite sure how to take that."

There it was again. Warmth flooded her cheeks, and she grabbed her frozen drink. How to respond? She'd ignored his earlier suggestive remark, but in the past, she'd never shied away from giving it right back to him. Their banter had always flowed smoothly, keeping them both laughing. "Well, I'm willing to reassess the situation based on how the rest of spa day goes." She lifted her eyebrows as she sipped her smoothie.

His gaze lingered on her lips, curled around the straw. "I think I can promise a happy ending."

She struggled for a clever comeback as more heat traveled through her body. Damn it—he always won. A muffled meow saved her, and she turned in her chair to look at the sliding glass door. Terence sat on the opposite side of the glass, his orange tail swishing.

Jumping up, she hurried to the door. It had been fairly quiet this morning, spirit-wise, and she was hoping to get him inside for a while. She removed the new safety bar and slid the door open. "Hi, T. Come on in and get some food." His bowls were stationed near the door, and she shook a little plastic tub of cat treats. "Here, kitty, kitty, kitty," she repeated in a high, sing-song voice.

Terence craned his neck, scrutinizing the kitchen. Apparently he didn't like what he saw. He turned from the door in a feline huff and leapt gracefully onto the deck railing.

"Fine." She sighed, leaving the glass door open as she slid the screen door into place. The cool morning air smelled of new grass and fresh flowers, and fat bumble bees were already buzzing around her blooming azaleas. "I'll try to get him in again once you go," she decided, walking back to the table.

Brett crumpled his sandwich wrapper into a ball. "Are you suggesting he doesn't like me?"

"He doesn't like Josiah," Tyler explained, his mouth full of bagel. He looked at the empty seat directly across from him, tilting his head as though listening to a silent voice.

Brett glanced at her as an icy shiver tiptoed down her spine. She tugged at her shirt hem, casting about for the right thing to say to avoid upsetting both her own child and the child ghost. "Well, he's not always comfortable around new people, right? He's a cautious kitty. He lived on his own for a long time, so he's not always ready to trust."

"Cats scare the rats away." Ty licked the last of the cream cheese off his fingers.

"Yes, that's true." *And what scares the ghosts away, Josiah?* Emily turned to the sink, hoping Josiah couldn't somehow access her unkind thoughts as she wet a clean dishcloth. After wiping Ty's hands and mouth, she instructed him to throw his trash away. "So, on that note," she said to Brett under her breath, "I think I'll just go make sure his stuff is all ready to go."

Once Brett had moved the car seat into his truck and secured Tyler, she waved one last time and shut the door. Flipping the lock, she leaned against the column of little windows and watched them drive away.

A few pink petals still clung to the cherry blossom tree in the front yard. The remainder created a decaying brown carpet around the base of the trunk; the few that had traveled farther were smeared along her walkway. She really needed to do some yard work. Now that the new growth had appeared on her hydrangea bushes, she could finally prune last year's papery blossoms without risking future flowers. She chewed on her lip. Maybe she could just spend an hour…

No. She needed to do the one thing she absolutely couldn't do when she was alone with Tyler—sleep to her heart's content. That was the whole point of today. Nodding to herself, she climbed the stairs. She'd start one load of wash. Then she'd try again to get Terence inside. At this point, she was worried he would just abandon their house all together for more hospitable lodgings.

Grabbing the laundry basket from her closet, she stopped in the bathroom to add a few towels before heading back downstairs. If she had success coaxing Terence in, she'd try to carry him up to her bedroom so he could snooze with her for a few hours. She could even start one of those books on local history, once she'd climbed into bed. While it was unlikely there'd be a chapter devoted to the ill-fated Matthews family of 1700s Barnstable, at least she'd learn more about the customs and events of that time. Even a little clue might help. And some background knowledge might help her sound like less of a nutcase when she called the historians—

"Where's my wife?" A burly man stepped from behind the kitchen wall into the doorway.

She froze, her heart leaping in her chest. *Joe*. A million thoughts raced through her mind, stretching out the moment. Gayle's husband was in her house. Alone. Gayle had done it. She'd left.

And Joe knew she was involved.

Admit nothing. She grasped on to the one thought that gave her a way out. "Joe? What's wrong? Is Gayle missing?"

He took a step closer, pinning her with a menacing gaze. "Where is she?"

Think. How did he get in here? The back door. She hadn't bothered with the flimsy lock on the screen—she was coming back to try to get Terence. "I...don't know."

"I think you do." He narrowed his eyes, wiping his hands on dark blue uniform pants. His bulky arms strained the fabric of a tight white undershirt. "See, I got home from work to find my wife and kid gone. She left her cell phone on the table, with everything deleted. But I've seen your name on there enough times to know you're involved in this. Is she here?" He flicked a glance to the staircase.

Warning sirens screamed in her head. She bit her lip, clutching the laundry basket in front of her body like a protective shield. "No, she's not here. But my...boyfriend's upstairs."

An ugly sneer twisted his lips. "Funny, because

I'm pretty sure I just watched him leave with your son. Now, one way or another, you're going to tell me where she is." He edged forward, closing the distance between them.

Run! She flung the basket at him, spinning around as he emitted a gratifying grunt. She raced for the stairs, but he tackled her from behind, and suddenly she was falling. The air rushed from her lungs in a painful gasp as she hit the floor, his body weight crushing her bones. *No!* She struggled futilely, fingers clawing at the floorboards, as his hand grabbed a fistful of her hair.

He yanked her head back, hissing in her ear. "Where…are…they?"

Chapter 29

Tyler cried out, the sudden, sharp sound almost causing Brett to veer into the neighboring lane. *Jesus Christ.* "What's wrong?" he called over his shoulder, panic coursing through his veins. He steadied the steering wheel, frantically flipping his gaze between the road and the back seat.

"Ow," Tyler wailed, shaking his head. His heels banged into the seat cushion.

"Hang on, buddy." He swerved over to the side of the road, drawing a few honking horns in his wake. Jumping out of the truck, he ran around to the opposite side and yanked open the back door. "What is it? What's wrong?"

Tears streamed down Tyler's flushed cheeks as he sobbed. "Mommy!"

"Ty! Are you hurt?" Brett's fingers deftly unfastened the three-point harness as his mind whirled. What had happened? His gaze swept the car seat, searching for something pinching or poking Tyler's skin.

"Mommy hurt!"

What? Was Tyler suddenly experiencing some sort of separation anxiety? They'd been alone together, away from Emily, many times at this point. This made no sense.

Ty threw his head back, banging it against the

cushioning of his seat. His eyes rolled up until the blue of his irises disappeared. He moaned as his mouth went slack.

No! Years of training for emergency situations counted for nothing when his son was having some sort of seizure by the side of the road. Brett dove for the cell phone stashed in the cup holder by the driver's seat, praying he could get an ambulance in route before the sight of his lifeless son triggered a paralyzing flashback.

Ty moaned again, blinking as he returned to consciousness. "The man is hurting Mommy. Come back." The words sounded distant and monotone—a recitation of someone else's instructions.

Brett froze, his finger hovering over the cell phone screen. *What man?*

It suddenly slammed into place. The abuser. Emily's friend's husband. That had to be it. "What man, Tyler? How do you know?"

His smooth forehead wrinkled. "Josiah says. It's hurting my head," he added, returning to his own speech patterns.

Oh, God. Josiah was trying to communicate with Ty, from a relatively far distance, as the ghost witnessed whatever was happening at the house. "Tell him we're coming," Brett pleaded, furiously jamming the harness buckles back together. He had to stop Tyler's pain. He had to get back to Emily. He had to call 9-1-1.

His muscles trembled with the need to move. The adrenaline dumping into his system begged him to take off running toward the house. But his brain fought for control, reminding him that driving would certainly get him there faster. And not only did he have to drive, he had to drive *safely*—his son was in the truck.

"We're going to help Mom," he repeated as he shot around to the driver's side and leapt into the seat.

He gunned the engine, cursing under his breath as he waited for the traffic to clear. Then he peeled out, tires screeching, and swung the truck around in an illegal U-turn.

Gripping the steering wheel with one hand, he tried to split his focus between the road and his phone. Emily first. He hit her speed dial number, his heart pounding in his ears along with the unanswered rings. Maybe she was asleep, and this whole thing was a mistake.

He flicked his gaze to the rearview mirror. Tyler's wide eyes stood out against his pale face like a pair of blue moons. A river of mucus ran from his nose. His son might not completely understand the situation, but he was terrified. This was real.

Brett navigated a turn before returning to his phone, dialing 9-1-1 with his thumb as he inched the speedometer a few ticks higher. He told the operator he suspected a break-in, rattling off Emily's address. Then he explained he was driving and hung up before the operator could ask any more questions. He couldn't afford to split his attention anymore. He was almost there.

Chapter 30

His breath was hot in her ear. And, God help her, she could feel the stirrings of his arousal against her bottom as he lay sprawled over her. Subduing her was turning him on. She had to get away, quickly.

"I don't know," she cried, driving her elbows backward to get her hands under her shoulders. She bucked her hips as she tried to lever her chest up, but she was no match for the dead weight of his prone body. A sharp, fiery current of panic surged through her.

He tightened his grip on her hair and slammed her forehead to the floor. Pain exploded behind her eyes, sending her to the brink of consciousness. She fought to stay awake as he flipped her over, pinning her by the wrists as he used the length of his legs to restrain her lower body. She couldn't kick, couldn't hit. She was helpless.

He leaned over her, bringing his face close enough for her to see the sheen of sweat on his skin. "You want to play rough? Is that it?"

She shook her head, her skull rocking against the floor. "No. I don't know where Gayle went. Maybe she just had errands—"

He released one of her wrists, striking her across the jaw with his closed fist. Her teeth rattled as a gray haze settled over her vision.

"Don't lie to me again."

One of her hands was free. She gathered her strength, aiming her palm at his nose as she snapped her arm up. He bellowed, rearing back to dodge the blow. His features darkened with rage, and he clamped his hands around her throat, keeping his face out of her reach.

Air. She needed air. He would strangle her to death, right here, on the floor of the Winslows' house. The house she shared with Tyler. She clawed at his hands, prying with her fingers, fighting the pressure of his deadly grip.

No use. He was too strong. She flailed wildly, slapping at his arms. The room grew black as she struggled for breath.

Suddenly the television came to life, the upbeat theme song of a cartoon piercing the scratchy hum filling her ears. His hold loosened as his head swiveled toward the sound.

She sucked oxygen into her burning lungs, struggling to stay conscious. Panic was her enemy, yet there was no other possible reaction to having her air supply cut off. *Think*. Curling her fingers into claws, she tried to scratch at the skin of his arms.

"Who did that?" he demanded, even as he pressed down again, making it impossible for her to answer. He barely seemed to feel her short nails, digging weakly into his flesh.

"Emily!"

Brett's voice drifted through her mind, a comforting reminder that Tyler was safe, with his father. Brett would take care of Tyler after she was gone.

"Emily!"

Louder this time. The furious rattle of the front door dimly registered against the pounding of blood in her ears. *Brett was here?*

Glass shattered, and the pressure on her neck disappeared. She gulped in the air, each breath searing her tortured throat. Then the rest of the crushing weight holding her down vanished as well, as Joe scrambled to his feet and ran for the kitchen.

****

Brett yanked his elbow back, thrusting it forward again to knock out the remaining shards of glass in the rectangular window closest to the deadbolt. Emily was on the floor, struggling beneath a man—just as Tyler had described. The coward had his hands around her neck.

Fresh rage boiled up, the crimson haze turning everything bloody. His fingers found the deadbolt, and he flipped the lock, swinging the door open with a crash as the man fled toward the back of the house.

Brett barreled toward Emily, dropping to his knees to cradle her head. "Are you okay?"

She nodded, rubbing the crimson ring staining the base of her neck. "Tyler?" she whispered, her voice gravelly and raw.

"He's locked in the truck. He's safe." His gaze tracked the path the other man had taken. Every primal instinct he had demanded he go after the bastard who had dared to put his hands on Emily…and once he caught him, all bets would be off. But he couldn't leave Emily. Thankfully, the cops were on their way…and since they probably wouldn't use sirens to alert an intruder of their presence, it was possible they were already here.

"Go," Emily moaned, waving her arm toward the front door. "I'm okay. Please watch Ty."

He glanced back toward the open door, torn. "If you lie still and rest, I'll get up and stand by the door, okay? Then I can keep an eye on both of you."

"I'll stay put. Just go!" Her voice gathered strength, vibrating with anxiety.

He released her gently, jumping up to rush to the door, his shoes crunching on the broken glass scattered across the floor. The truck stood in the driveway, undisturbed.

"Ty's safe," he assured her, scanning the street in both directions. No sign of the attacker, but a police car slowed to a stop a few houses away.

As two officers emerged from the vehicle, he suddenly realized what he would look like to them. He'd called in a break-in, and here he was, standing in the doorway, bleeding and half-dressed. He'd ripped his T-shirt off and used it to cover his elbow as he broke the window, but a few shards had still pierced his skin.

They were already drawing their weapons as he bent to retrieve his shirt. He quickly tugged it over his head, assessing his options. Tyler was in the car, and he would witness this. But the cops were not going to like it if he darted back inside. And the sooner they cleared him, the sooner they could focus on both finding the real assailant and getting medical help for Emily. Frustration burned through him, but he knew better than anyone how important it was to secure the scene.

"Show me your hands!" the older officer demanded.

He raised his hands in the air, praying Tyler had

pulled a book from the pouch attached to his car seat.

"Come down the steps and get on the ground!"

"Brett, what's going on?"

Damn it. Holding his arms aloft, he called to Emily without moving his head. "Just stay put. The police are here. I called them to report the possible break-in. They don't know who I am, so just hang tight until they ID me."

He reached the walkway and sank to his knees, slowly hinging forward until he was prone on the ground. Grinding his teeth together, he forced himself to stay silent as they cuffed his hands behind his back. If he cooperated, this would be over soon…but every second allowed the true assailant to get farther away.

"Who are you?"

"Staff Sergeant Brett Leeds, U.S. Air Force. I called in the break-in. My son is in the parked truck. His mother is injured inside and needs medical attention. I surprised the man who attacked her, and he may have left the house through the back door. My wallet is in my back pocket."

Drawing deep, calming breaths, he tried to focus on what was important as the younger officer frisked him. Emily was safe. He'd made it in time. And apparently, he had a ghost to thank for that.

Chapter 31

It was after eight o'clock at night when they finally pulled back up in front of her house. It felt like three days had passed, though, since she'd been preparing to put in a load of laundry and then sleep the day away. Since the attack, she'd been poked, prodded, scanned, swabbed, observed, questioned, and photographed. Strangulation was now a felony in Massachusetts, the Crime Unit reminded her as they gathered Joe's DNA from her skin and nails. They'd need all the evidence they could gather to charge him, once they caught him. *If* they caught him. She shuddered as Brett cut the engine.

"Are you okay?" His voice was sharp with concern as he studied her face through the shadows.

"Yes. That was just a really unusual spa day."

He made a choked sound, somewhere between a laugh and a sigh. "God, Emily. I can't believe you're joking about it."

She pretended to pout. It had now been well over twenty-four hours since she'd slept, unless she counted dozing off a few times at the hospital. The weekend's roller coaster of emotions, the bone-deep exhaustion, and the various pain meds were combining to make her punchy. "You don't think I'm funny?"

He shook his head, the corner of his mouth quirking up. "No, I do. Your sense of humor is one of the things I love about you."

Her stomach flipped as the "L" word hung between them in the darkness of the truck's interior. From the backseat, Tyler's even breathing punctuated the silence. He'd fallen asleep almost immediately after they'd picked him up from the Winslows'.

Did he even realize what he'd said? She studied the hard planes of his profile as he stared out the windshield, seemingly lost in thought. It wasn't as if he'd actually said "I love you," but still, his comment made her chest ache with a potent mix of hope and fear.

She was still unsure of his feelings toward her, even after his actions today. He hadn't left her side, except for the ambulance ride, and that was at her insistence. She didn't want Tyler to see her carried away on a stretcher, so she'd begged Brett to contact the Winslows and get Tyler over there before he witnessed anything else traumatic.

But once he'd dropped their son off, he'd arrived at the hospital and remained with her throughout the long hours of exams, procedures, and interviews. She wanted to believe it was more than kindness...but then again, maybe it was just that he knew she had no one else.

Say something. "Well, I guess we'd better get him inside. We've all had a long day." She turned to look at Tyler as she gingerly touched the tender mound of flesh on the left side of her face. She was truly a mess. A large knot protruded from her forehead, purplish bruises stained the swelling along her jaw, and red contusions on her neck marked the placement of Joe's fingertips.

At least the only illumination at the moment was coming from the dim glow of the light outside the front door. Mr. Winslow had probably left it on for them when he came by to board up the broken window. Or, who knew? Maybe it was Josiah, welcoming them back. She wouldn't be surprised, after the story she'd heard from Brett.

Brett scrubbed his chin, flicking his gaze between her and Ty. "I'd carry Tyler in, and then come back to help you, but I don't want to leave you alone out here. Not with that maniac on the loose."

"I can walk. Although I'll admit I can't wait to crawl into bed. I just hope I can sleep."

He paused, his hand on the door handle. "We can still go to a hotel if you'd feel safer."

"No, no. I want to sleep in my bed, and I don't want to disrupt Tyler's routine any more than necessary. And you'll be here."

With a gun. Apprehension trickled through her veins. The idea of a gun in the same house as her child filled her with dread. But Brett was a trained soldier, and she trusted him, so she hadn't argued when he'd stopped by the base to pick up his weapon. He swore he could leave it unloaded and still have it ready in seconds if he needed it. And he loved Tyler just as much as she did. He wouldn't do anything to endanger their son.

"I'll be here," he assured her, his voice low and firm. He climbed out of the driver's seat and came around to open her door.

She took his arm as he helped her out of the passenger seat. The cool night air washed over her bare skin, and she huddled inside the stiff white hospital blanket they'd sent with her. "Thank you for staying. I don't want him to have the power to drive me out of my house. And honestly, I really don't think he'd be stupid enough to come back here."

"If he comes near this house, it will be the last bad decision he ever makes."

A shiver slid down her spine. She nodded, wrapping the blanket across her chest like a cloak.

Brett slung both his bag and Tyler's over his shoulder before lifting Ty into his arms. When they reached the front door, he pulled her house key out of the pocket of his cargo shorts.

"Stan made sure everything was locked when he was here," he said, turning the doorknob. "But I'm going to do another check of the house, once we get you two upstairs."

Her gaze dropped to the bag he'd retrieved from his quarters. The gun was in there, along with whatever else he'd packed. She swallowed, wincing as pain flared along her jaw and down her throat. "Are my pills somewhere?"

"I tucked them into Tyler's bag." He lifted his shoulder slightly and tilted his chin toward the staircase, gesturing her forward.

The laundry basket sat in the hallway at the top of the stairs, filled with the dirty clothes she'd been meaning to wash. Could that only have been this morning? She followed Brett as he carried Ty into his room, stepping over clusters of trains and books to get to the toddler bed.

"Hang tight in here for just a few minutes."

He laid Tyler on the bed, shrugging off the bag she'd packed this morning for their outing. He took the other one with him, stopping first to check Ty's closet. Then he shut the door behind him as he left the room.

He was back by the time she'd changed their half-awake son into pajamas. "All clear," he announced as he followed her into the bathroom to help her finish Ty's bedtime routine.

Once they'd tucked him in, Brett steered her into the hallway, his hand resting lightly on the small of her back. "Now *you* need to get to bed."

"Will you…come with me?" She stared at the floor, hating the doubt in her voice.

"I'm going to stay downstairs and keep watch. Just in case."

Warmth flooded her cheeks. "Oh. Okay."

His fingers settled beneath her chin, tipping her face up with a gentle touch. "Hey," he murmured, forcing her to meet his gaze. "It's not that I don't want to. But I'm not taking any chances tonight." His eyes darkened as he studied the bruise on her jaw.

She closed her eyes, trying to twist her head to hide the swelling. "Don't. I look awful."

He slid his hands into her hair and held her steady. "You look beautiful. And alive. God, I could have lost you." His voice thickened as he stepped closer. He lowered his head, brushing his lips against hers.

Her breath caught as his mouth moved against hers in a tender exploration. Not their first kiss, no…far from it. But the first one since he'd returned that wasn't sparked by the heat of their desperate passion. Instead, this one burned with the slow scorch of deep emotion. Her bones turned to liquid as the flames consumed her, and she leaned into his solid chest.

After one last lingering kiss, he pulled her into a tight embrace, nearly crushing her ribcage with the force of it. He buried his face in her hair. "Okay, you really need to get to bed before I can't stop myself from carrying you in there myself and doing things to you that don't involve rest."

She groaned as he released her. "Rain check?" she asked, running her hands from the small of his back to his waist.

"Count on it." He shot her a roguish grin before his expression turned serious. "But tonight my job is to keep you both safe."

"I know. Just remember…a lot of weird things go on here at night. I'm guessing after the exertion of connecting with Tyler today, our ghost is as worn out as I am. But if not…please don't shoot up my kitchen cabinets or anything."

His eyebrow lifted. "Your faith in my abilities is concerning."

Oops. She flushed. "I'm sorry. I'm mostly kidding." Rising up on her toes, she kissed away his frown.

"I hope so," he said, filling his tone with mock indignation. "Luckily I did mention how I enjoy your sense of humor earlier." His mouth curved into a smile as he dropped a quick kiss on her lips.

She twisted her fingers into the hem of her shirt. God, she was still wearing the same skimpy clothes she'd been in this morning. Exhaustion dragged at her body like quicksand. "I'm just…scared." Her gaze sank to the floor.

"I know," he said, settling his hands on her shoulders. "You have every right to be shaken up. You were attacked by someone who's still running around. There's a ghost in your house. And now I've brought a gun into your home. But on the off chance he comes back here with his own weapon, I need to be prepared.

Okay?"

She nodded.

"I'm an excellent shot. I'm well-trained. And I'm staying awake, so there's no chance of him taking me by surprise. But my guess is he's well on his way out of this state by now."

He turned her toward her bedroom, kneading the muscles between her shoulders and neck. "Go sleep. I'm on duty."

Chapter 32

Brett sat on the sagging couch, staring at the gun in his hand. He'd brought his personal weapon, a Glock 19, and true to his word, it was not currently loaded. But the magazine rested on the cushion next to his other hand—as he'd told Emily, it would take him only a second to slide it into place. And once she'd fallen into a medicated slumber, he'd fastened a paddle holster onto his belt, so he could move about the house with his hands free if needed and still have his gun. He'd be ready if that bastard returned.

He rolled his head forward, wincing as the bones in his neck cracked. In all likelihood, it would be a quiet night. Joe would have to be truly crazy to come back here, especially with Brett's truck parked in the driveway. And if that wasn't enough of a deterrent, the possibility of the occasional police cruiser driving by the house should keep him away.

Still, he couldn't disregard the nagging feeling he was mistakenly ascribing rational thought to someone who didn't deserve it. Someone with a tendency toward violence on an average day, who was now seething with rage and humiliation.

The shades were drawn in the living room, but moonlight trickled in from the unbroken glass framing the front door. Fresh anger coiled in Brett's chest as his gaze raked over the piece of plywood nailed across the broken pane on the right side.

The coward who put his hands on Emily needed to be locked up. Or dead. The very fact that he was still out there, posing a threat to the people he loved—not to mention Gayle and her son—made Brett's blood boil. His mind replayed today's events for the hundredth time, searching for a way he could have kept watch over Emily and Ty while also chasing down Joe. As usual, no magic solution materialized. He had done the right thing—the only thing he could do in the situation. But the frustration gnawed at him.

The green numbers on the VCR glowed in the darkness—it was already a little past one a.m. Probably time to brew some more coffee. He was hesitant to turn the lights in the kitchen on, however. That would advertise the fact that he was awake, and some primal part of him actually hoped Joe would show up here tonight and try to break in. Then he could end this. Although he didn't relish the idea of firing a weapon inside this house.

He worked his jaw, trying to relieve the tension. Adrenaline was keeping him up, but more caffeine wouldn't hurt either. Five minutes is all it would take.

The faint creak of wood interrupted his thoughts. He froze, his ears straining to identify the sound. The back deck? It was probably just the cat. Or another animal. Or an old plank, settling.

Another creak. He rose from the couch slowly, popping the magazine into the well of his Glock in one fluid motion. The distinctive double click pierced the silence as he chambered a round. Hugging the doorway, he angled his body just enough to bring the kitchen slider into view.

Beyond the glass, a shadow shifted. An indistinct figure, darker than the surrounding night. He was here. He'd actually returned, unable to admit defeat.

Brett's muscles stilled as his finger curled around the trigger. The back slider was locked, but more importantly, the safety bar was lodged in place above Tyler's reach. If Joe had noticed, he'd be looking for another way in. Scenarios flipped through Brett's mind as he anticipated Joe's next move.

An arc of weak light suddenly fell across the deck, accompanied by a muffled shout. Joe's face was a pale blur as he spun away from the door.

Shit! The neighbors! Of course they were rattled after today's events…someone was up and noticed a suspicious figure creeping around the backyard.

He wasn't getting away this time. Brett raced across the room, anger and frustration burning through his veins. Surely the alarmed neighbor would have called the cops, but it would take them precious minutes to get here. All Brett had to do was catch him and keep him subdued until they arrived. Then it would be over; Emily and Ty would be safe.

He eased out the front door, scanning the yard. Branches cracked to the right, by the fence separating the other neighbor's property. The wooden boards shook as a dark figure clambered over it. Joe had crossed the backyard to avoid the glow of the floodlight, and now he was only fifty feet away. Brett had no doubt he was faster and stronger than the man he'd seen choking Emily this morning.

With a sharp twist, Brett ensured the bottom lock was engaged as he pulled the door shut behind him. He leapt off the steps, shoving the gun into his holster as he ran across the lawn. Adrenaline surged through him like a current. A few long strides and he was past the far corner of the house. Skirting a clump of tangled brush, he crossed onto the neighbor's property and vaulted over a low scalloped fence into their backyard.

He landed unevenly, his right sneaker hitting a rock protruding from the ground. A bolt of pain shot up his leg as his ankle twisted, his foot rolling inward. *Damn it!* He regained his balance, a low grunt escaping through his clenched teeth.

Joe slowed, stumbling slightly as he turned to look back at his pursuer. A dog barked in the distance, and Joe sped up, cutting diagonally across the lawn toward the far end of the house.

Brett shot across the yard, ignoring the throb in his ankle. Joe was headed for the street, and if he had a vehicle there, Brett had to catch him before he got to it.

The black sweatshirt and dark pants Joe wore merged with the night, but Brett's vision compensated, focusing and sharpening until the only thing he could see was his quarry. His pulse jackhammered in his temples. But then Joe vanished, disappearing around the corner of the house.

Brett's well-trained muscles responded with a burst of speed. The neighbor's fence opened to the front yard with a wide arbor instead of a gate, and he shot through it without slowing. Joe's bulky form appeared again, dodging the cars in the driveway and heading for the street.

Almost there. He could hear Joe's labored breathing now. With a final push, he closed the distance between them and launched himself at the man who had injured Emily.

He tackled Joe, the impact sending them both crashing to the ground with bone-jarring force. They rolled onto the road in a tangle of limbs, and Brett used the momentum to gain control. As he pinned Joe beneath him, part of his mind registered the frantic barking of a dog. Lights flicked on.

"Let's see how you like it," Brett growled. His fist slammed into Joe's jaw with a gratifying crunch. The vibration traveled up his arm, carrying with it a pleasant jolt of pain. *Good*. He landed two more blows, fueled by images of Emily's bruised neck.

Joe flailed beneath him, his own punches glancing off Brett's chest and arms. Blood poured from his nose and mouth, and the whites of his eyes shone with panic.

Red and blue flashes suddenly lit up the night, accompanied by the blinding white glare of a spotlight. Brett froze, his arm cocked, as the cop car pulled to a stop in the middle of the street.

"Police!" came a shout, followed by, "Break it up!"

"Show me your hands!" an officer ordered, shining a flashlight over them. His right hand hovered over the gun holstered in his uniform belt. "Now!"

A mixture of frustration and relief flooded Brett's system. His part was over. Joe would be brought in. But until the situation was sorted out, Brett would be considered just as dangerous as the actual criminal here. Even more so, since he was carrying a weapon currently concealed by his shirt.

"I'm armed." Brett lifted his hands into the air. "I have a Class A License. US Air Force."

Both officers quickly drew their own service weapons, each barrel aiming at one of the men.

The male officer kept his gun trained on Brett as he

barked out instructions. "Keep your hands where I can see them, both of you, and lie down on the ground. Where is your weapon?"

"Hip holster. Right side."

"Okay. Officer Snow will cuff you, and then she will disarm you. Any other weapons on either of you?"

"No, sir."

"No," echoed Joe.

Brett could hear more front doors opening as he slowly stretched out on his belly. He was about to be handcuffed for the second time in twenty-four hours. How was this happening?

All because of the pathetic excuse for a human lying perpendicular to him on the ground. Out of the corner of his eye, Brett could see blood seeping from Joe's face onto the pavement. A knee settled on his back, and cold metal snapped around his wrist once again.

Suddenly Joe rolled to his side, reaching into his pants pocket. He withdrew a small pistol and levered himself up in one quick motion.

"Gun!" shouted the covering officer as Joe swung the barrel toward Brett.

A shot rang out, and Joe fell backward, his arms spread eagle. The gun clattered against the asphalt.

Shit! Brett's heart lurched. What had just happened? Christ, he'd nearly been shot. The echo of the blast filled his ears, joining with the rush of his pulse to drown out the tense conversation around him. His other arm was yanked back, and his wrists were linked in cuffs. Officer Snow removed his gun and hauled him to his knees.

"Shots fired," the male cop was saying into his

radio. "We need rescue here."

Neighbors peered out through windows and doors as Officer Snow led Brett to the cruiser. "Against the car," she instructed, patting him down once he turned around. She opened the back door. "Okay. You'll need to stay in here until we can get you to the station."

Two more cruisers raced toward them, and ambulance sirens wailed in the distance.

"Wait." Brett shook his pounding head. "I..." He tried again. "Can it wait until tomorrow? That maniac tried to strangle my...girlfriend earlier today. She was in the hospital all day, she's heavily medicated now, and our son is asleep in the house. I need to be there for them."

"You're saying this man assaulted your girlfriend earlier?"

"Yes. The police were called. An emergency restraining order was issued, but no one was able to find him to serve him. And then he came back, tonight. All the information should be in the reports, so maybe I could just give you my ID and my information now, and come in tomorrow? So I can get back to the house tonight."

Her brow furrowed with sympathy, but she shook her head. "Sorry, but no. There's been a police shooting. You'll need to come down to the station immediately and give your statement." She gestured toward the backseat as the ambulance pulled up.

No, no, no. He sucked in a deep breath. He had to stay in control. "Can we go by her house, then, first? It's only right up the street." Tipping his head, he gestured toward the dark house.

"We'll make sure she's all right. She may have to

give a statement as well."

Deep breaths.

Beyond the cluster of uniformed officers, paramedics transferred Joe onto a gurney. He'd be on his way to the hospital, accompanied by police.

"Okay. Okay. Just tell her he's not a threat to her anymore."

****

The sirens intruded on her chaotic dreams, drilling into her drug-enhanced slumber. The pain did the rest, spiking and ebbing, gathering strength with each assault. Was it time for more pills? She groaned, struggling to open eyes as heavy as lead weights.

Too hard. Each attempt made the world tilt drunkenly. She needed to just go back to sleep, but colorful lights flashed around the blinds of the bedroom windows. What was going on?

Joe. Brett. Did something happen? She forced her eyes open as panic swelled in her ravaged throat.

Sudden pounding rattled the front door, and she bolted upright, her heart seizing. Despite the stiffness of her muscles, she was out of bed and across the room in seconds. Barreling into the hallway, she ignored the knocking and raced toward Tyler's room first.

He was asleep, impervious to the noise. Thank God. She pulled the door shut and ventured to the top of the stairs. Below, the living room was immersed in darkness, but a bright light shone through the window panes around the front door.

"Barnstable Police!" a voice called, punctuated by more pounding.

Why wasn't Brett answering the door? *Oh, God.* She hit the light switch and flew down the stairs.

The deadbolt wasn't locked. Terror ripped through her stomach like poison. Every instinct demanded she fling the door open and learn what horrific events had transpired. What tragedy had occurred while she slept, oblivious? Useless.

But she forced herself to hesitate. "Hang on!" she yelled, peering cautiously through the window. Should she ask for ID? Two patrol officers in uniform stood on her steps, and a cruiser with illuminated headlights sat parked in her driveway. She couldn't stand it. With a shaking hand, she yanked open the door. "Is Brett okay?"

"Are you Emily Shea?" a middle-aged officer with heavy features and a salt-and-pepper crew cut asked.

"Yes. What's happened?" She craned her neck, searching the activity down the street for signs of Brett.

"Is this your house?"

"Yes! Yes. Where is Brett?" She clutched at her chest. This was torture.

"So you know Staff Sergeant Brett Leeds?"

"Yes, of course! He's my son's father. He was here, guarding us from the man who broke in here earlier today. And now he's gone! Please tell me he's okay!" The two men swam in front of her as her vision turned gray. *Please, Lord, no.* She couldn't lose Brett too. She needed him. Tyler needed him.

"He's okay," the second officer assured her, gesturing with his chin toward the living room. "But we need to speak with you. May we come in?"

She slumped with relief. "Oh. Ah…yes. Come in." Brett was okay; they wouldn't lie to her, would they? Stepping back, she glanced down at her attire. A short-sleeved, cropped T-shirt and plaid boxer shorts. She wrapped her arms around her middle as the officers entered the living room.

"I'm Officer Mendoza," said the younger man. He was Hispanic, with dark eyes, thick black hair, and olive skin. "This is Officer O'Brian. Is there anyone else in the house?"

"My son is upstairs, sleeping. I just checked on him." She shuddered, hugging herself tighter. "Could you just please tell me what happened?"

"There was an altercation between Sergeant Leeds and the man who apparently attacked you yesterday—a Mr. Joseph Stevens. Mr. Stevens drew a weapon and was shot by one of the initial responders. Because this is a police shooting, we're going to need you to come down to the station with us and give a statement." Officer O'Brian's thick lips pressed together as his gaze traveled over her injured face and neck.

Joe—shot? She wobbled, reaching out to grab the back of the armchair. "Uh…that's not going to be possible. My son is asleep upstairs, like I said before." If Brett was okay, why wouldn't they tell her where he was? For God's sake, she was his…what? She frowned, sending a flicker of pain along her swollen jaw. Maybe she wasn't legally bound to Brett, exactly, but he was her son's father. She deserved to know his whereabouts.

"Is there anyone who could watch him for a bit? Half the neighborhood is up," Officer O'Brian pointed out, tipping his head toward the windows. "Otherwise, he'll have to come with us."

She weighed her options. Joe was in the hospital, with a gunshot wound, apparently. He wouldn't pose a threat. Their resident ghost had been quiet tonight—as least as far as she knew. Protecting her son from additional trauma seemed more important than inconveniencing someone, even though she hated to put a neighbor in this position. And no way was she waking up the Winslows after all the help they'd already given her today. Or yesterday? Surely it was the early hours of Monday morning now.

"I could call Mrs. Darling. She's helped me out a few times and she lives a few houses down, where all the…activity seems to be." She planted her hands on her hips, hoping she appeared defiant despite her skimpy pajamas. "But first, I'm going to need to know where my son's father is." Pain flared again as she set her jaw.

Officer O'Brian nodded. "Staff Sergeant Leeds is also at the station giving his official statement. You can see him once you've given yours. We'll drive you over, once you've arranged for childcare."

She released the breath she'd been holding. *Thank you, thank you.* Her knees nearly buckled, and she fought to remain upright. "Can I change first?" And maybe grab a few ibuprofen—something to take the edge off without knocking her out.

"Certainly." Officer Mendoza waved an arm toward the staircase. "We'll wait here."

Chapter 33

The pain woke her, along with the desperate need to use the bathroom. Blinking groggily, she lifted her head to find the clock. Ten-fifteen in the morning. At least she had managed six solid hours of sleep. She had finally been reunited with Brett at the station after giving her statement, and Officer Zeh had dropped them home around four a.m. She vaguely remembered Brett helping her up the stairs, placing a pair of pills in her hand, and tucking her in to bed.

Grabbing the amber bottles off her nightstand, she plodded through the hallway and into the bathroom. Upstairs, all was quiet, with the exception of her stomach. The rumbling growls of hunger sounded like some kind of primitive language.

As she downed the pills, she caught her reflection in the mirror. *Good God.* What a train wreck. She studied her face, blinking repeatedly in the hopes that her image might adjust to something a little less terrifying.

No such luck. She quickly patted concealer and powder on the bruising, and then tamed her wild hair into a topknot, with curls hanging around her face to help hide the lumps and swelling. That was as good as it was going to get for now. At least the light in her house had to be more forgiving than the fluorescent glare of the police station last night. Sighing, she took another swig of water.

She made her way slowly down the staircase, wincing as her muscles groaned with every step. *Damn.* Everything hurt, especially without fresh terror masking the pain.

Joe had been gravely wounded—shot in the chest—but she still felt vulnerable. The fact that he'd taken such a chance last night—returning to her house, with a gun—was deeply unsettling. Surely he was unable to move, and yet she couldn't stop picturing him stripping off tubes and needles, rising from his hospital bed, and coming for her. Or Tyler. She wouldn't be completely comfortable until he was locked behind bars.

Downstairs, the television was off, the living room deserted. The kitchen held signs of life—a pot of coffee, a box of cereal, and a few glasses and utensils on the table. Beyond the locked and barred sliding glass door, the backyard was empty, save for fresh cat food in the bowls on the deck.

Where were they? Unease rippled through her. *It's fine.* Brett probably took Ty to school and returned to the base. His home. There was no reason he should spend all his time watching over her now that Joe had been caught. She rolled her shoulders back, wincing as sore muscles protested. *Pull yourself together, Em.*

The sound of tapping keystrokes broke the eerie silence. He *was* here! Grabbing a cup of coffee, she headed past the bathroom toward her office.

Dust motes swam in the bright sunlight streaming in from the two front windows.

"Hey," Brett said, turning from the computer screen. "How are you feeling?"

"Probably about as good as I look." She scanned the room. "Where's Ty? Did you take him to school?"

"Yes. He seemed happy to go, and he slept through all the activity last night, so I figured it was okay. I'll pick him up later, too. You shouldn't be driving."

She nodded. "That's probably a good idea." Her gaze fell to his scabbed knuckles. At least he'd changed out of the blood-spattered shirt. "And I'm glad you took him. After yesterday, I think maintaining the routine is probably the best thing. I just can't stop worrying about Joe, though. That he'll find a way to come after us."

Brett stood. "You don't need to worry about him anymore. Ever again."

She shrugged, lifting the mug to her lips. "I will, though. At least until—"

"No." Brett cut her off, his voice firm. "You don't need to worry about him anymore," he repeated, rubbing the knuckles of his right hand. "He's dead."

She sucked in a breath. "What?"

"One of the detectives from last night came by this morning. Detective Dawson. Joe died from his injuries around seven a.m."

"Oh my God." The coffee sloshed dangerously inside the shaking mug, and she wrapped her free hand around the ceramic to try to steady it. "I don't know what to say. Is it wrong to be glad?"

He shrugged. "I'm thrilled. I mean, what if he had somehow weaseled out of a conviction? And even if he *was* incarcerated, he would have been released eventually. So I can't say I'm upset about the way things turned out."

Her head bobbed in a repetitive move somewhere between a tremor and a nod.

He crossed the room and took the coffee cup from her trembling hands, setting it on a low bookshelf. "Are you okay? Sorry to spring it on you, I've had a few hours to digest the news."

She pressed a hand to her forehead, trailing her fingers over the tender lump. Joe was dead. Tyler was safe. Brett was safe. She was safe.

Gayle and Brandon were safe.

A wave of dizziness crashed over her, and she swayed drunkenly. Brett's hands shot out, catching her under her arms.

"Whoa. Let's get you sitting down." He turned her back toward the door and guided her into the kitchen, supporting her with a steely grip around her waist. He settled her into a chair and went back to the office to retrieve her coffee. As it heated in the microwave, he popped two pieces of bread into the ancient toaster oven.

"All right?" he asked, setting the butter dish and the steaming mug in front of her.

She nodded. "It's just…a lot to take in. Plus I just took my pills." She accepted the banana he handed her and ripped at the peel as if it were an Olympic event. God, she was ravenous. The last thing she'd eaten was a dry muffin at the police station. "Better," she said, swallowing. She cleared her throat. "And you're sure you're okay, too? I know I asked you already, but now he's…dead."

"Believe me, Em, I've seen much worse things." He didn't quite meet her eyes. "I'm fine."

Crap. She hadn't meant to remind him of the even more horrific events he'd witnessed while at war. Reaching for her coffee, she searched her medicated mind for a more lighthearted subject. "So, how did you get in to my computer, anyway? Are you a hacker now, too?"

"You shouldn't make the password our son's birthday." The corner of his mouth curled up as he sat across from her, sliding a plate of toast across the table.

She feigned annoyance, tearing off a corner of the toast without bothering to butter it. "Well, it's not like I have a bunch of state secrets to protect."

"Which is why I figured you wouldn't mind if I used it to catch up on work. I told them I had a family emergency, but I needed to answer a bunch of e-mails."

The word "family" pierced the haze swirling through her mind. Were the three of them a family? Could that ever be a reality? A sharp ache seared her chest, overpowering the fading pain of her injuries.

"It's fine," she said, gulping down more coffee. She inhaled the last of her toast and looked longingly at the loaf of bread on the counter.

"More?"

"Yes, please." The ring tone of her phone suddenly filled the kitchen. She jumped, snapping her head toward the docking station on the counter. *Tyler*. Before she even managed to start to get out of the chair, Brett had the phone in his hand. He glanced at the screen as he handed it to her.

"Claire Baron," he said, his brows pulling together.

"The medium?" She slid her thumb across the screen to answer. "Hello?"

"Hi, Emily. It's Claire. How are you?"

She touched the swelling on the side of her face. "I'm…okay." Did Claire somehow know what had happened? Or, wait…maybe this call wasn't even about *her*. Good Lord. Other people did have lives. "How are you? Did you have the baby?"

"I did," she said on a breathy laugh. "Max junior. He's beautiful. Six pounds, eleven ounces. He arrived on Friday afternoon."

"Oh, Claire...I'm so happy for you. Congratulations." Her heart melted as little newborn noises chirped in the background.

"Thank you. Hang on, I'm handing him off to Max." A mixture of whispers and rustling drifted over the phone line. "Okay, sorry about that. The reason I'm calling, actually, is because we think we may have uncovered something that might help your situation. I assume you're still having issues with Josiah?"

"Um...yes." She mouthed "thank you" as Brett set a glass of orange juice in front of her. "Do you mind if I put the phone on speaker? Brett's right here."

"Oh, no, that's fine."

Emily hit the correct buttons and placed her phone on the table, glancing up at Brett.

He nodded, moving behind her chair and settling his hands on her shoulders. His fingers kneaded the sore muscles of her upper back. "Hi, Claire. It would seem that congratulations are in order."

"Thank you. We're very excited. And exhausted. But we may have some good news for you. We've been trying to look at the information Josiah gave us from different angles. At one point last week, Max commented on how strange it was that both Josiah and his mother died the same year. At least that's what it seems like, since she virtually disappeared, not visiting her son in jail and never returning to her home.

"So we got to wondering if something unusual had

happened that year—1757. We both spent some time on our computers, searching, and then I found it. Barnstable was hit with a major smallpox outbreak in 1757. In those days, smallpox victims were ostracized. The disease was highly contagious and usually fatal. Townspeople tended to panic. If Abigail contracted smallpox, she certainly would not have been able—or allowed—to visit her son in jail. But since she was apparently a widow, it's just as likely no one even knew she was ill until her body was discovered."

Emily twisted her head back to look at Brett, momentarily forgetting about the damage done to her neck yesterday. *Ow.* She turned back to the phone. "That makes sense. A young boy locked up in jail might never even hear about an outbreak, or even understand the significance if he did."

"Exactly," Claire continued. "For all we know, they could have died only a few days apart. But here's the thing: they didn't bury smallpox victims in the church graveyards. People were too afraid of contamination. The bodies were buried away from the town, in little smallpox cemeteries, often in mass graves or without headstones."

"Oh my God," she breathed as Brett's fingers tightened on her shoulders.

"So then Max found an article from 1980, reporting the discovery of a probable smallpox cemetery marked with numbered stones, deep in the woods of the Old Jail Lane Conservation Area. In Barnstable. Emily, that has to be it!"

"Yes! Oh, thank you, thank you!" The chair creaked as she bounced with excitement.

"I think you need to go there. With both Tyler and

Josiah, somehow. I'd offer to go, but…"

"Oh, no, Claire, we'd never ask you to come along. You just had a baby!"

"I don't think it would help, anyway. The spirits who communicate with me haven't crossed over yet—they've failed to move on because of some unfinished business. But I think the mother—Abigail—would have been able to connect with her son if she were also stuck. If my theory is right, she knew she was sick, knew she was dying, and she passed on without a fight. But if you can get Josiah to that cemetery, he might be able to connect with her if her remains are actually buried there. He's in between—one foot in this world, one in the other. I won't pretend to know exactly how these things work, but I think it's your best bet."

Emily nodded at the phone on the table. "It's definitely worth a shot. And Tyler got Josiah to come here, to our house, with him. I'm sure he can convince Josiah to take another trip if he might find his mother."

"Okay, good. I'll e-mail you the links to the articles. Just keep me posted, all right?"

"Definitely. Thanks again, Claire. And tell Max thank you as well." As they all said their goodbyes, Brett came back around to sit beside her at the table.

Her heart raced as she leaned toward him. "Once we pick up Tyler, we can grab a quick lunch, then—"

"No." His voice was edged with steel.

What? "But, Brett, we have to find it."

"Not today, we don't. I can't believe you're even suggesting it. I could *feel* how tight your muscles are. Yesterday, you were thrown to the ground, knocked around, punched in the face, and nearly strangled." His hands curled into fists on the tabletop, exposing taut ropes of tendons along his forearms. "You spent the entire day in the hospital. Then you were awakened in the middle of the night, driven to a police station, and questioned extensively. You are *not* going for a hike in the woods today."

"But, he helped save my life. We have to help him."

"I know that. But he's been lost for hundreds of years. One more day won't kill him." Brett paused, dragging his palm over the short bristles of his hair. "Sorry, poor choice of words. You know what I mean."

"I do," she said, frowning at him. "Doesn't mean I have to like it." But exhaustion *was* creeping back into her bones as the pain pills worked their magic. Just climbing the stairs back to her bedroom suddenly seemed like too arduous a journey.

"But you get it, right? Your body needs to heal. Do you want some more breakfast?"

She sighed. This last hour had really been too much, physically and emotionally. "No. I think I'd better get back in bed, actually, before I collapse."

He stood, pulling her chair back with one hand as he hooked his other arm around her waist. "That's what I thought. Let's go. I'll pick up Tyler and get him lunch."

"Maybe we can go tomorrow, then?" she asked hopefully as they shuffled through the living room.

He shook his head in exasperation, towing her up the stairs. "I'll have to look at my schedule. Maybe I can get away early and we can go before it gets dark. But more importantly, we'll have to see how you're feeling."

"I'll be fine tomorrow."

"Sure you will," he agreed, his tone suggesting no real belief in her prediction. He gave her a stern look as he helped her into the bed. "Em, don't even think about going without me. Understand?"

She nodded, pulling the hair tie from her knot of curls. A yawn escaped as she dropped the tie onto her bedside table.

"Promise me."

She rolled her eyes. "Jeez, where is the trust?" she murmured, feigning annoyance. "I promise." She clutched at the covers, pulling the comforter up to her chin.

"Okay. Get some rest." He bent forward, pressing a kiss above the lump on her forehead. "I'll hold down the fort."

Chapter 34

Water clanked through the old pipes around two in the afternoon, pulling his focus from the manual he was reading online. Saving him, really. The revised version of "Multiservice Procedures for Explosive Ordnance Disposal in a Joint Environment" was fairly dry reading. He forced himself to finish the chapter, then leaned back in his chair and scrubbed his face.

Emily padded into the office a few minutes later, freshly showered and smelling of something citrusy. Her hair was combed back from her flushed face, and a red polka dotted robe was knotted around her waist. "Well, that felt good."

"I bet." He couldn't stop his gaze from traveling down to her bare legs. *Christ*. She walked around in less on a daily basis…it was just something about the complete nakedness of her body beneath the robe. One tug of the sash, and—

"Did I miss anything?"

He snapped his attention back to reality. "Oh, ah, not really. I picked up Ty at noon. The cabinets behaved suspiciously while I was gone, but I didn't open fire. I questioned them, closed them gently, and then made Ty a peanut butter and jelly for lunch and a few slices of pear. He seemed a little tired, so I put him down for a nap. I assume he's still asleep, unless you heard him."

The corners of her mouth lifted as she shook her head. "His door's shut."

"And how was your nap?"

"Okay, I guess," she said, the small smile vanishing. "I had a nightmare."

He flinched, his muscles tightening. *God, no*. He did not want to imagine her caught in the same hellish cycle that tortured him nightly. And yet, what could he do to stop it? Pushing himself to standing, he gestured toward the chair. "Why don't you sit down?"

She glanced at the chair. "I'm fine. I need to go get dressed. I just wanted to check in, and see if you needed to go home, or to work, or whatever. You probably have things to do."

Something twisted inside him. "You want me to leave?"

"No...I just wanted you to know that you *can* leave, if you need to. I mean, did you even sleep at all last night?"

"A little," he lied. Even after they'd returned home from the station, he'd been too full of adrenaline to even consider sleeping. As the predawn light had filtered through the windows, he'd grown drowsy, but the fear of waking in a screaming rage had kept him from succumbing.

So, yeah...he could use some sleep. And a workout. But the idea of leaving her still didn't feel right, even if the threat was gone.

"Maybe I'll go take care of a few things, and grab a nap. I'll come back after."

Her expression hardened, her mouth pressing into a thin line.

He'd overstepped—he had no claim to this house.

A thread of despair coiled in his chest. Would she shut him out again? "That way, I'd be here to put Ty to bed in case you're too tired," he added. "I could stay the night, too, if it would make you feel better."

Her green eyes sparked with challenge. She crossed her arms. "If you sleep here tonight, will it be upstairs, with me?"

He cut his gaze past her, over her shoulder and into the hallway. "No."

"Then no thanks. We're fine."

He tensed. "Em, it's not what you think—"

"Then why don't you tell me what I should think? Because if you're deliberately trying to mess with my head, you're doing a great job!"

What could he say? He knew he'd been giving her mixed signals for weeks now. This was his fault. He'd *known* he shouldn't get too close to her. And yet he'd been unable to stop himself. It was not only selfish, it was cruel.

He clenched his jaw, searching for the right words. He could never have a normal life, or be a normal husband or father. But to have to tell her that now, after everything she'd been through this weekend…it wasn't fair. It wasn't the right time.

"I see," she snapped, planting her hands on her hips. "I'm good enough to have sex with, but not to sleep next to afterward, is that it? I suppose that's crossing a line, right? I might start to get ideas." She stared at him, waiting.

"I just can't, Emily."

"Really? That's your excuse? Give me a break. Joe's dead. Tyler knows you're his father. I don't think you're worried about giving him false expectations, since you were here when he woke up this morning. So I'd love to know more about why you *can't*. You're playing games with me, and I don't like it!" Her voice trembled, rising in pitch with each accusation.

Anger rolled off of her in thick, blistering waves. It was all coming to the surface—the primal terror and devastating vulnerability she'd been made to feel yesterday. She had every right to be furious, and he was hardly an innocent target.

He had to fix this. Cupping the back of his neck, he blew out a breath. "I'm not playing games with you, Em. I wouldn't do that. It's just...I don't sleep well."

She looked away for a beat, dragging her fingers through her damp curls. "You don't sleep well?" she repeated, her eyes narrowing. "I'm going to need more than that."

Hell. Panic pulsed through his veins as he weighed his options. It wasn't only about pride; it was about protecting the fragile wall that held the memories back. He didn't want to give those images even the slightest edge in the eternal battle he waged with the past—but he would, for her.

He would risk the precarious hold he had on his sanity to tell her the truth—but with the truth would come the revelation that he could never give her the kind of relationship she deserved. Maybe he was fooling himself to think she'd even want that with him. Maybe the news wouldn't upset her at all.

Either way, she could handle it. She was strong. The deeper truth was that he didn't want to give her up. He was now faced with an agonizing choice—he could stop her pain and doubt right now, but only at the expense of this brief interlude of happiness he'd found.

Once she knew how damaged he was, how dangerous he might be, she'd move on. He'd still be able to see Tyler on his visitation days, but he'd lose her forever, and he didn't know if he could handle that. *He loved her*. The realization shook him to his core.

"I have nightmares," he said finally. "Very vivid nightmares about things that happened when I was in country."

Her arm dropped to her side, her fingers curling into the bright terry cloth of her robe. "And you think I'd be disturbed by these nightmares?"

"I *know* you would be. And Tyler." He sighed. "I wake up screaming, Em."

She frowned. "What about sleeping pills?"

"God, no. They rarely help, and it only makes it harder for me to come to my senses. I would never risk it around you two."

"I don't understand."

He grabbed the back of the chair, digging his fingers into the vinyl as though it were a life raft. "I get...violent. At least I have, in the past. When I was in the Naval Hospital, I attacked a nurse. I messed him up pretty badly before I came to. And that was a man. God knows what I could do to you if I couldn't wake up."

"That was months ago, Brett. Right after the blast that sent you home, right? Of course you'd be confused and agitated. From what I read in the paper, you had a pretty serious head injury. A concussion, it said."

"That's basically a less terrifying word for a mild traumatic brain injury. But it doesn't matter what you call it. What matters is how I behave now—and the answer is...dangerously."

"One time, Brett."

"I'm not interested in trying for a second."

The monotonous ticks of the desk clock filled the room as she blinked, trying to fight off tears. She pressed her knuckle to her mouth. "So the nightmares...they're about the blast?"

"Most of the time. Not always. There's no limit to the number of horrible memories stuck in my brain."

She paced a small section of the floor, rubbing her temple. "Tell me about the dreams," she said, lifting her eyes to his. "I need to know."

"No. I don't want to put those images into your head."

A crimson flush rose on her cheeks. "You don't get to say that to me. You have pried *every single thing* I wanted to keep buried out of me. And you know what? You were right to do it. Even if it was painful to discuss, I felt better once it was out. We both seem programmed to use avoidance and denial as coping mechanisms, but so far it hasn't worked all that great for us. So tell me."

He ground his teeth together as he stared out the window into the side of her yard. She had a point. Exhaling, he turned back to her. "Sometimes, they're about the right hands."

Her forehead creased. "The right hands?"

"At some of the blast scenes we'd investigate, it was difficult to tell how many victims there were. Too many...body parts. So we were forced to count the number of right hands." He squeezed his eyes shut as the smell of burning flesh and fresh blood filled his nostrils. "You get used to that kind of thing," he continued, his voice growing distant. "Which is both good and bad. Human organs—just lying in the street.

Shoes with feet still inside them. People wailing. And the whole time, you're wondering when the next IED might detonate, or when the waiting enemy sniper might take his shot. That's the daily horror you come to expect. But none of that compared to seeing…" His throat tightened, and he left the words hanging in the still air.

"What? Whatever happened in the blast? Someone died, right?"

"Our Team Leader, Mac. My friend. My mentor. I watched him explode, or maybe my mind has manufactured the details. Either way, he was blown to bits right before our tour was almost up. In my dreams, I see something in the dirt, right before it happens, and I think I can prevent it. But I never get the warning out."

"Oh, God." Her eyes were enormous green pools of anguish. "But could you really have prevented it?"

"I don't think so. It was a pressure-plate IED. Pretty much an indiscriminate killer. It could have killed me, or Brady, our other team member, or an Afghani kid playing. But it killed Mac.

"It was just waiting for us…a trap. The more ways we find to detect their devices, the more ways they find to get around our methods. There were no signs, at least that any of us could see. Brady agreed. But it doesn't change the guilt."

"I'm so sorry. I should have asked you more about what happened over there."

He shook his head. "I didn't want to talk about it. Especially with you. Being around you and Ty makes me feel normal. I can avoid the memories. But at night…" He leaned forward, bracing his weight on the back of the chair as he focused on pulling air into his lungs.

She crossed the room, coming to his side and slipping her arms around his waist. "It's okay," she murmured repeatedly, laying her head on his shoulder.

It would be over soon, once she put all the pieces together and examined the messy result in relation to her future. But for now, he would take comfort where he could get it.

He pushed the chair away, rotating his body to face hers. Inhaling her scent, he wrapped his arms around her as she moved into the embrace. "I couldn't save him," he whispered, burying his face in her damp curls. "I almost didn't save you."

"But you did. I'm right here." She slipped her hands beneath his T-shirt and kneaded the taut muscles of his lower back.

"Em, I'm messed up. I may never be right in the head." His voice broke as the admission came out.

"Yes, you will. We'll make it right. Together. We'll make it right, okay?"

He nodded into her shoulder, a sob rattling in his chest. "Okay," he repeated, crushing her to him.

Her heart thudded in time with his as they clung to each other. The bark of a dog outside pierced the silence briefly, and then it was quiet again, with just the sounds of their breathing and the ticking of the clock filling the room. She slowly moved her hands lower, beneath the waistband of his loose shorts. Her mouth sought his neck, her tongue leaving a trail of flames as she nipped at his skin.

He groaned. The heat shot through him, and his arousal was instant and demanding. But she was still healing. "Emily, we can't. Your body isn't ready."

"I think you'd be surprised what my body's ready for." Her fingers worked at the button of his shorts. "We're alive. We're all safe. And right now I just need to feel you inside me. Nothing but us." She pulled down the zipper.

He tilted her face up, kissing her tenderly to avoid the swelling on her jaw. "This is probably not a good idea," he insisted, even as her hands encircled his rigid flesh. He closed his eyes, drawing in a hitched breath.

"I disagree. I think it's an excellent idea." She glanced meaningfully toward the thick rug between the desk and the front windows. "Just be gentle," she added as she lifted her mouth back to his.

He couldn't fight this. Didn't want to. But first things first—their son was still upstairs. He walked her backward slowly as they kissed, kicking the door to the office shut with his foot. Then he tugged at the sash of her robe.

Chapter 35

The sun slipped in and out of the heavy clouds, making shadows dance through the trees like the ghosts they were seeking. It wasn't a great day for a hike through the woods, but it was time. Brett had convinced her to wait a few more days before attempting their excursion to the smallpox cemetery, so by the time Thursday afternoon had finally rolled around, she'd been adamant. They were going, rain or shine. Luckily, the rain seemed to be holding off, for now.

A light breeze rattled through the pitch pines and scrub oaks along their path. While miles of marked trails wound through the 180 acres of The Old Jail Lane Conservation Area, eventually they were going to have to forge their own route, guided by the GPS coordinates plugged into Brett's phone. According to the article Claire had sent her, the ten small unmarked graves in the desolate burial plot were hidden in the dense foliage and difficult to find. It was going to turn into an arduous trek for a three-year-old, but Brett had borrowed a sturdy framed backpack carrier that could hold Tyler's weight.

At the moment, the carrier rode empty on Brett's back as Ty trotted ahead of them on the trail. He paused to pick up a stick, turning and speaking to an invisible companion. Emily shivered at the exchange, pushing her hands into the pockets of her gray cotton jacket.

Initially she'd almost felt guilty, making preparations to send the lonely child ghost on his way. After all, he'd helped save her life. But then another sleepwalking incident had her searching for Tyler in the middle of the night—this time he'd been tugging on the handle of the back door. Her resolve had hardened as she carried him back to bed. Hopefully the abandoned cemetery would be the solution that ended this haunting.

Yesterday, they'd sat Ty at the table and told him he needed to instruct Josiah to listen to what they had to say. Brett hovered in the background silently as Emily explained smallpox to their three-year-old son and his twelve-year-old invisible friend. Using simple sentences, she laid out the plan: they'd all get in the car, they'd all go on a long walk in the woods, and they'd hopefully find Josiah's mother at the end of their journey. Then she'd stressed to Tyler how important it was for him to convince Josiah he needed to come with them. All last night, she'd tossed and turned, listening for some kind of rebellious disturbance. Nothing happened.

She'd questioned Ty gently as she buckled him into his car seat today, and Ty had assured her Josiah was with them. The swirl of icy air that accompanied his words seemed like confirmation, although it could have simply been her body's reaction to the creepiness of it all. They took her car, based on the theory Josiah had traveled in it once before. Anything to make this work.

Something scurried in the leaves on the edge of the trail, and she jumped. *Jeez*. Was it always so spooky in these woods, or was it the overcast sky combined with their bizarre mission? She slid a glance in Brett's direction.

The laughter shone in his eyes, even though his lips pressed together in a valiant attempt to keep it inside. "Attack chipmunk?" he suggested.

She gave in to the humor. "Those things can be rabid, I've heard." A moment of lightheartedness to break the tension would benefit them both.

"I'll protect you." He reached for her hand, lacing their fingers together with a reassuring squeeze. The statement hung between them, a promise beyond the playful banter. "I called today about going back for more PTSD counseling."

"I'm so glad, Brett." She tightened her own grip in a show of solidarity while she also marveled at the simple physical connection they were sharing. Holding hands, just like any normal couple might do. Just like they used to during those two weeks of blissful infatuation all those years ago.

Were they a couple now? No lengthy discussion had taken place to define their relationship as of yet…but she thought she knew where they stood. She certainly knew where she stood—in love with this man who was not only the father of her child, but undeniably her soul mate. "Why did you drop out, before?" she asked, pitching her voice low. Tyler was still ahead of them, fueled by both the excitement of the trip and post-nap energy.

He shrugged. "I didn't feel like it was working. If anything, talking about it made things worse."

Her heart throbbed, aching for him. "It will probably get worse again, before it gets better. But I think it's something you have to do."

"I'll do it. For you."

"For us." She stared at the ground as their footsteps fell softly on the bed of pine needles and dirt. The dark canopy of trees surrounding them made her feel like they'd slipped into a magical world, populated by only the three of them and the birds flitting through the branches above. "You forgave me, and that allowed me to lay down all the guilt I'd been carrying. Now you have to forgive yourself, even though there was nothing you could do. No one saw any evidence of that bomb. Not you, not Mac, not Brady. It wasn't your fault."

"Even if I can accept that, I'm still not sure I'll ever feel safe sleeping beside you. It's a risk."

"One I'm willing to take. We have to try. You deserve a normal life. Look…Mac died for our freedom. My brother died for our freedom. I think maybe we owe it to them to live the best lives possible. I know we owe it to our son. We've both been living in fear for too long. Is that what we want to teach Tyler?"

"I don't want to scare him, Em. Or you. Or hurt either one of you in some semi-conscious fit of rage." A root crunched beneath his boot like an ominous warning.

She shook her head. "You can't live your life in fear," she repeated. Up ahead, Ty leaned over an enormous fallen log, investigating the decaying wood. "It's what I did all those years. Trying not to love anyone. Putting you out of my mind so it wouldn't hurt if you died."

He stopped abruptly, glancing at Tyler as he pulled her to face him. "And now? Would you be able to love me?"

She met his steady blue gaze. "Turns out I don't

have any choice in the matter. I just do. I love you."

The column of muscles in his throat rippled as he swallowed. "I love you, too, Em."

He lowered his head, capturing her mouth in a deeply sensual kiss full of emotion and hints of things to come. He tugged at her lower lip with his teeth, groaning as he reluctantly pulled away to check on Ty. Tilting his chin, he gestured to continue their walk. "I'd do anything for you two," he said as they approached the toppled tree. His voice dipped lower. "But you do know I can't promise nothing will ever happen to me."

She gave him a solemn nod. "I do." Drawing in a breath, she pressed herself closer into his side as his arm tightened around her shoulder. The air smelled of damp moss and sharp pine. "The thing is…like you said before, no one can ever promise that—no matter what line of work they're in. I guess we just have to do our best to cherish each moment."

"That I *can* do." He bent his head for another kiss before turning to Ty. "What did you find, buddy?"

Tyler crouched on the opposite side of the massive trunk, studying the activity in the rotting wood. "We finded bugs," he announced proudly.

She cringed at his use of the word "we," even as a pang of sorrow tugged at her heart. If all went as planned today, Tyler would lose a friend who'd managed to share his life in some intimate and mysterious way. How would he handle the loss?

Climbing over the log, she picked her way through the brambles clawing at her jeans and lowered herself down to Tyler's height, her bad knee sending up a warning flare and an audible pop. Black beetles and gray potato bugs swarmed for cover as Ty pried another layer of soft bark from the tree. She wrinkled her nose. *Yuck.* "Neat," she said aloud.

Brett glanced between the screen of his cell phone and the endless expanse of trees in the distance. "Okay. Up ahead is where we'll need to veer off this trail." He shrugged the backpack off and pulled bottles of water from the storage compartments. Twisting off the cap, he took a swig and motioned for Emily to prepare Ty for the restraint of the carrier.

She nodded, rubbing her kneecap as she stood. "Ty, it's time for you to ride on your dad's shoulders, okay? We all have to go deeper into the woods now. *All* of us," she added in a commanding tone, searching the area for some sign their ghostly companion had heard.

A chill enveloped her, piercing the denim of her old jeans. She suppressed a shudder. There was her answer. Lifting Tyler, she carried him back toward the trail and passed him over the fallen tree into Brett's strong arms.

****

The stone posts rose in a circle from the forest floor, slanted and broken. The carved remains of a solitary identifying number could still be seen on a few of the markers. But the rest revealed nothing, their lone engraving having either worn away over hundreds of years of exposure or vanished entirely as the tops of the stones crumbled and returned to the earth.

This was it. An icy finger tiptoed up her spine. Was Abigail Matthews one of these forgotten outcasts, dumped in this isolated spot as an epidemic swept through a panicked town?

Brett hung back with Tyler in the carrier as she examined the stones. She was afraid to allow Ty to come closer to this circle of death. What if another lingering spirit tried to contact him? Her stomach twisted in a queasy knot.

Claire had tried to reassure her. In one of their subsequent conversations, she'd reminded Emily that, like Abigail Matthews, most of the people buried here had probably accepted their death and moved on long ago. It was unlikely Ty would encounter any more lost souls.

Still, it felt like a risk. But it was a risk they had to take to try to end this. Turning back to Brett, she nodded. "Okay." Her voice faltered, changing from a firm declaration to a croaking whisper as the word left her mouth.

Brett crouched down and unshouldered the backpack. Once Ty was free, he kissed the top of his blond head and leaned back on his heels, watching Tyler race around to stretch his legs. He tossed a bottle of water to Emily as she joined them.

She twisted the plastic cap with shaking hands. Streams of water dripped down her face as she took a swig, and she wiped her mouth with the sleeve of her hoodie. It was time. "Tyler, can you come here?" She dropped the bottle into the dead leaves and extended her hand.

He approached her cautiously, as though he understood the seriousness of the reunion they were about to attempt. Peering up at her with huge eyes, he slipped his hand into hers.

Here we go. She led him back toward the markers, holding her breath as they stepped together into the circle. The ground here dipped in a slight depression. According to the article Claire had sent her, the arrangement of the stones suggested a rudimentary pest house may have once stood in the center of the ring of graves.

"It's sad here," he said softly.

"I know." She squeezed her eyes shut. *Breathe.* "Remember what we talked about yesterday? How a long time ago, they didn't always have the right medicine to treat some people when they got sick? That is sad. Some of the people died. And I think if Josiah's mother got sick, he might be able to find her here."

Beads of perspiration gathered beneath her low ponytail. "Is Josiah here, with us?" she asked, trying to keep her voice from wavering.

He looked over to the right side of the circle and nodded.

Oh, God. Her muscles screamed at her to scoop him up and run from this place. She forced the words out before fear could take over. "Okay. Good. Tell him to call to her. Tell Josiah to call to his mommy," she repeated a little louder, aiming her instructions toward the spot Tyler had focused on. Her pulse thudded in her ears as she waited.

Mamma?

The whispered sigh filled her head, vibrating in her bones. She gasped. Was her imagination playing cruel tricks on her? *No.* Something strange was happening. The air grew thick with tension, like the heavy stillness that preceded an electrical storm. Even the birds overhead ceased their trills and whistles. The world around them fell utterly silent.

Tyler tugged his hand from her sweaty grip and wandered over to a stone engraved with the number four. Cocking his head, he reached out and touched the carved lines.

She swallowed the dust in her throat. "Do you think Josiah's mamma can hear him?"

"Yes. He's talking to her now."

She was here! Emily glanced back at Brett, and he gave her an encouraging nod. *Okay.* "Ty, honey…it's time for us to say goodbye so Josiah can go with his mamma."

"No," Ty said, not turning around.

Panic seized her. She strode over to him and sank to her knees, barely registering the throbbing pain beneath her kneecap or the burning ache in her leg muscles. "Yes, baby. His mommy hasn't seen him in a long, long time. If I didn't see you in a long time, I would miss you so much." Her heart broke into jagged pieces at the thought. "So we're going to say bye-bye now, so he can go visit his mom, okay?"

A hint of defiance crossed his features before his face crumpled. "Okay," he agreed sadly.

She exhaled in a ragged burst and pulled him into a fierce hug. "Okay." Her legs wobbled as she pushed herself up. "Um…I'll go first." Twisting her fingers, she gathered her courage. "Josiah? We all want to thank you for helping to save me from the bad man. That was very brave. And now you need to be brave again, because saying goodbye is hard. And leaving what you know is hard. But your mamma is waiting for you." She couldn't quite bring herself to say she would miss him, so she just repeated herself. "Bye, Josiah, and thank you."

"Now it's your turn," she murmured, touching Tyler's shoulder. "Tell Josiah bye-bye, and then you need to tell him to go to his mamma."

She took a few steps back from the stone marker. Somehow, it seemed right to give the two boys privacy, even though she knew Tyler could communicate with Josiah in his mind. This was a solemn and mysterious moment, and she wanted to respect that.

Brett appeared at her side, looping an arm around her. She leaned into his warmth as they watched their son's eerie conversation with an invisible boy from another century.

When Tyler moved away from the marker, she darted forward and scooped him into her arms. The air around the stone wavered like a ripple of heat rising from a desert highway. She clutched her son to her body as she stared in disbelief. The image disappeared almost immediately, as though the tear in the veil between worlds had suddenly repaired itself.

The expression on Brett's face told her she had not imagined the vision. Wind sighed in the trees overhead, yet no breeze touched her skin. Her heart hammered in her throat as she stood in shock, rooted to the ground.

The drill of a woodpecker in the distance broke the heavy silence. Then a squirrel chattered from the top of a nearby pine as he leapt from branch to branch. *Was it over?* She shifted Tyler onto one hip, smoothing his hair. "Is he gone?"

Ty didn't speak, but the fat tears welling in his blue eyes served as an answer. His mouth puckered as his lower lip trembled.

She squeezed him into her chest once more before transferring him into Brett's waiting arms. Her own arms were leaden weights. How was she going to manage the hike back? She suddenly envisioned Brett carrying her in the pack as well, and a hysterical giggle bubbled in her lungs. She was losing it. "We have to start back to the car now. We have a long walk, and it's going to be time for dinner soon."

"Will he come back?" Tyler asked.

She glanced at the marker. "I don't know, honey." *I hope not.* Clasping her hands together, she offered up a silent prayer. *Rest in peace now, Josiah. You're home.*

Following Brett out of the circle, she forced a cheerful tone. "You know who you will see tomorrow, though? Brandon." He was due to return to school on Friday, now that the news of Joe's death had reached Gayle at the shelter. Gayle and Brandon were back at home, and she'd finally been able to speak to her friend on the phone yesterday. "We're going to go to the playground together after naptime."

"'Kay," he murmured, yawning. He dropped his head onto Brett's shoulder.

They shared a look—he must be exhausted. Together they maneuvered his limp body into the carrier and hoisted it onto Brett's shoulders. She eyed the backpack enviously.

Brett picked up on her meaning immediately. "Sorry, Em...it's a one person ride." His lips quirked into a grin as he checked the GPS coordinates on his phone.

She frowned, feigning annoyance. "Whatever. I may just collapse here and have you come back and get me tomorrow."

He lifted an eyebrow. "You're going to sleep in these woods?"

She shuddered dramatically. "On second thought, I'll stick with you guys. Lead the way."

Chapter 36

She awoke slowly, rising through each layer of sleep to a new level of awareness. *What was that noise?* Oh, yes…the new air conditioning unit Brett had installed in the window. It hummed furiously, struggling to keep up with the August heat. *Wait, what day was it?* Saturday. Good. Brett wouldn't have to leave for work. She wriggled toward Brett's side of the bed, searching for his solid warmth.

Brett! Her eyes snapped open.

He was there…propped on his elbow, head resting in his hand, his eyes trained on her face. His mouth curved into a triumphant smile. "Good morning, beautiful."

Her gaze darted to the window. Yes, it was morning—bars of strong summer sunlight filtered through the blinds. "You made it?" She searched her groggy brain, but she couldn't remember a single disturbance during the night. "Did you make it?"

"I made it." His grin grew wider.

"Dino didn't even have to wake you up?"

"Nope. Dino got the night off."

At the mention of his name, Brett's new service dog scrambled from the floor in a series of jangling tags and clicking toenails. He hooked his front paws onto the edge of the bed, peering at them with his large, expectant eyes.

Terence hissed at the dog from his spot at Emily's feet. The two animals were still working on their relationship. "Stop that," Emily commanded, craning her neck up to give the cat a stern look. "He didn't do anything to you." She used her foot to poke at Terence from beneath the covers, and he rose and arched his back in a stretch. Stalking across the comforter, he gave a haughty flick of his tail before he leapt to the floor and disappeared beneath the bed.

Dino, a rescued German shepherd mix, had come to Brett about two months ago through a program pairing service dogs with soldiers in need. He was trained to sense the initial signs of a nightmare and wake Brett up immediately. For Brett, Dino's presence made all the difference in the world. Now, even if the dreams began, they could not escalate to their horrifying conclusion. And something about being woken by a dog jolted Brett right out of the combat zone in his mind and into the present.

Brett rubbed the top of Dino's tawny head. "It's not that he doesn't like you, buddy. He just doesn't know you."

Dino's floppy ears pricked at the words, as if he understood the explanation. Dark rings circled his intelligent brown eyes, and the inky markings flowed down to converge with the solid black fur of his muzzle.

"Poor Terence," Brett added, turning back toward her. "We got rid of the ghost, only to bring in a dog."

Emily stretched, her fingers catching in the curls spread across her pillow. "Well, he did have a nice, peaceful two-month break in between." Brett had only recently decided he'd made enough progress to try sleeping over, so Dino's presence in the house was a new thing. "It's only been a little over a week. They'll get used to each other."

"I hope so. I realize Terence was here first, but I've decided I really like waking up next to you." He slipped his finger beneath the lacey lavender strap of her nightgown, pulling it down her shoulder.

"Yes, well, I like it too—but just so you know, you shouldn't stare at people while they're sleeping. It's creepy."

His blue eyes darkened. "But you look sexy while you're sleeping."

She arched a brow. "So you're delusional as well."

"You also look like you taste delicious." The tip of his nose grazed her neck as he brought his lips to her ear. "Let's find out." His teeth closed around her earlobe.

Shivers rocked her body as he sucked and nipped. She moaned, her muscles tensing.

His tongue trailed a line of fire beneath her jaw. "Turns out I was right." He kissed his way down her neck, his mouth tugging at the sensitive skin as his hand cupped her breast.

She tipped her chin back, squirming as each nerve in her body came to life. *Oh, God. A girl could get used to this.* Heat gathered between her thighs, heavy and demanding. Still, she couldn't resist playing with him. "If you're that hungry, I'd better get downstairs and get started on breakfast." She lifted her shoulder, pretending to get up.

"Oh, no, you don't." He rolled on top of her in one fluid motion, pinning her wrists above her head.

She sank into the mattress, trapped by his solid

weight. His erection pressed against her, and her hips rocked in an effort to slake her desperate need. But he denied her, levering himself up and pulling his lower body away, still anchoring her in place with his iron grip. He dipped his head, dragging her nightgown down below her breast with his teeth. She shuddered with pleasure as his rough stubble scraped her taut nipple.

He bared her other breast, tracing the tender raised flesh with his tongue. Exquisite torture. She arched her back, struggling to free her hands. "Please, Brett."

He pulled his mouth from her nipple with a slow, agonizing tug. His face returned to her field of vision, a small grin curving his wicked lips. "Please what?" He hovered above her, waiting.

She strained, trying to close the distance between their bodies. No use—he was too strong. *And oh...how he did love to make her beg.* Damn if it didn't turn her on as well. Not that she ever needed any help in that area when it came to this man.

"Please...I want you inside me. Now." Her breath was jagged, her voice pleading. "Please."

He released her, and she clamped her hands around his back, digging her nails into the shifting muscles of his back as he further teased her with his fingers. She writhed beneath his touch, moaning. Her legs shook as the tension built, and she whimpered another soft plea. He plunged into her at last, filling her, making her whole even as he shattered her to pieces. Violent spasms wracked her body, and she fought to muffle her cries. His last few strokes were brutal pleasure against her sensitive skin, until he came inside her with one final deep thrust.

He held himself above her on one elbow, his other

hand smoothing her damp hair away from her forehead. "Okay?"

"Mmm. I'll let you know when I remember how to think."

Chuckling, he dropped a kiss on her lips. "Take your time." He rolled off her, settling her head into the crook of his shoulder as he curled an arm around her. "I've got to say, having a full night of uninterrupted sleep has me waking up feeling pretty damn good."

"It has me feeling pretty good too." She snuggled closer to him, sliding her hand across his flat stomach. "Although I'm worried about my long-term survival once you start getting a solid eight hours every single night."

His chest rumbled with laughter. "We'll come up with a safe word."

She stretched luxuriously as she moved her hand lower to play with the trail of hair leading down from his navel. "You know I'd never use it," she murmured seductively. Then she dropped the lighthearted tone from her voice. "Seriously, Brett, I'll never get enough of you. Not ever."

"It's probably obvious I feel the same." He tightened his hold on her, kissing the top of her head. "I love you, Em."

Her heart stumbled. She could never get enough of those words, either, as terrifying as they were. But she'd meant what she'd said that day in the woods. Going through life trying to guard her heart against loss was no way to live. Besides, her feelings for Brett were beyond her control. Her love for him simply existed, with or without her permission. "I love you, too."

More words from that day in the woods echoed in

her mind. *Cherish every moment*. She lifted her head. "Hey, we should celebrate."

"Again?"

She slapped him playfully. "No...like go out tonight to celebrate the no nightmares thing. It's a big deal."

"I can get behind more celebrating. In fact, there's someplace I've wanted to take you. Let's see if we can get a sitter." He paused. "A real sitter."

She knew what he meant. His parents were always eager to come over and watch Tyler, even until late at night. They couldn't get enough of their new grandson. But although they were polite to Emily, the resentment was still there, hanging in the air like a gritty fog. She didn't blame them, but it did dampen her mood to be around them. Hopefully, as time passed, they could forgive her too.

"Maybe Olivia's free."

He toyed with one of her curls. "Make sure her dad comes in when he drops her off. I want to say hi."

She slapped at his chest again, suppressing a giggle. "Stop! You are so bad."

"Am I?" He captured her hand, sliding it down beneath the sheets.

"Oh no, you don't." She snatched her hand away. "*You* may not be worn out, but I need sustenance. And Ty will be up soon."

Outside, the low growl of a lawnmower could just be heard above the rattle of the air conditioner in their window.

Laughing, he eased his arm from beneath her head. "Stay put. Read your book. I'll bring you something." He rolled out of bed and crossed to the corner of the room, where his duffle bag was stashed on a chair.

Her brows lifted. "Really?" She tugged her nightgown back up where it belonged. "What did I do to deserve that?"

"We're celebrating, remember? It's an all-day affair. I'm guessing you'll do something today deserving of breakfast in bed. Maybe during nap time, for example." He grinned as he pulled on gray boxer briefs.

She shook her head, rolling her eyes. What she needed to do was clear out some space so he could at least have a drawer around here. *Maybe after some breakfast.* Reaching for her novel, she settled back into the pillows.

"I'll be back, beautiful." He picked up his cell phone and slipped it into the pocket of his cargo shorts. "Come on, Dino," he called, and in an instant, the dog was up, tail wagging, following him from the room.

Chapter 37

Once they'd left the marina in Mashpee, it only took about twenty minutes to cross the bay to reach the Popponesset Spit. Brett had filled her in on the area as he navigated the borrowed boat toward their destination. The first part of the beach's name, Popponesset, was most likely derived from the similar name belonging to a Native American chief, Poppononett. And "spit" apparently referred to a long bar of sand formed by drifts and currents off of a coast.

It looked to her like a simple peninsula, separating the bay from the Atlantic Ocean, pristine and isolated. Dune grass and wild flowering bushes covered the highest parts of the landform, and sandy slopes rolled down from the vegetation on either side to meet the water. All types of boats, from kayaks to powerboats like the one they were on, dotted the shore along the bay side.

The sun had begun its descent, coloring the sky to the west as it dropped behind the trees of the mainland. A trio of seagulls wheeled overhead. Brett slowed the boat as they entered the No Wake zone, and Emily pulled strands of loose curls back into her hair tie.

"What spot looks good to you?"

He steered the boat parallel to the shore, following the channel markers. Beachgoers had claimed various spots along the beach—individual campsites that varied from large circles of chairs grouped around a fire pit to a lone figure curled up on a towel with a book. Near the very tip of the spit, people waded in the shallow water with metal rakes and buckets, searching for clams.

She shrugged, leaning back in the captain's chair. "I'm hardly an expert. It's all beautiful here. How do you know about this place?"

"I worked for two years at a marina before joining the Air Force. You tend to learn all the spots."

"And how to drive boats, I guess." Her gaze wandered over all the switches and gauges lining the instrument panel.

"Yes. When I came up with the idea to bring you here, I called one of the guys I used to work with to see if he could hook me up with a boat. It was actually really good to talk to him. He mentioned getting together sometime."

"You should."

"Yeah. I think I will. It's hard, sometimes, to transition back into old friendships once you've seen the things I've seen. But I think it would be good for me."

"I do, too. As long as you don't spend *too* much time away from us."

"Never." He leaned over and kissed her. "How about there?" He pointed to a stretch of unoccupied sand farther down the beach.

She nodded, standing to get a better view. "Looks good to me. Nice and private."

He glanced at her, feigning shock as he lifted his eyebrows. "What did *you* have in mind?"

Warmth flooded her cheeks. How did he always do that? She crossed her arms and nodded toward the pile of supplies he'd packed. "Well, *you're* the one who brought blankets."

He shook his head as he guided the boat toward the beach. "Yes, for our picnic dinner. Jeez, Em, there are kids here."

She tried to pull off an exasperated sigh, but it ended in laughter. He was too much. "There *are* a lot of kids here, actually, even this late." They'd passed a brother and sister digging for sand crabs near the water line, and a group of older children pitching beanbags into an angled wooden platform. "Maybe we should have brought Tyler."

He cut the engine, crossing to the stern to set the anchor. "Another time. We're going to build a little fire," he nodded toward a few pieces of wood stacked on the deck, "and have dinner and relax. Somehow, I didn't see the 'relax' part happening if we mixed water, fire, and a three-year-old."

They quickly transferred the blankets, cooler, and wood to the beach, and Brett got the fire started as Emily spread out blankets and opened the cooler. A bottle of champagne and two plastic glasses lay nestled among the sandwiches and salads Brett had packed.

"Wow, we really are celebrating," she said, holding up the bottle.

The wood in the sand pit crackled as the flames gathered strength.

"Well, that was the plan, right?" He smiled, dusting his hands against his shorts. Taking the bottle from her, he pulled off the foil and wires and tucked them into a plastic bag they'd weighed down with a rock. "We have a lot to celebrate," he added, turning away from her to pop the cork. A wisp of gauzy vapor drifted into the air, joining the rising smoke.

She held the glasses as he filled them. "We do. Most importantly, your first nightmare-free night. But also Kay's news. I'm so happy for her." Two weeks ago, Kaitlyn's pregnancy test had come up positive. It was early, so aside from Michael and the Winslows, only she and Brett knew. "We'll have a drink for her, since she can't."

He frowned. "I feel like there's something else we're celebrating. Hang on." He took both glasses out of her hands, setting them on the cooler's lid.

"Hey," she complained, staring at her empty hand. Then she suddenly realized he was down on one knee in the sand, looking up at her. *Oh, God.*

He opened a small black box and held it up. "Marry me, Em."

A glittering diamond ring sparkled inside a bed of midnight velvet. *Was this really happening?* Her hands flew to her mouth as she gaped at the ring.

"Um, Emily? I've never done this before, but I'm pretty sure a yes or no answer is required."

She nodded vigorously until she found her voice. "Yes. Yes. A thousand times, yes. I just can't believe this."

He took the ring from its slot and tucked the box back into a deep pocket in his shorts. Reaching for her hand, he slipped it onto her trembling finger.

"It fits perfectly." Her heart pounded as she stared at it, dazed. A large round diamond rose from the center of a bright platinum band set with side baguettes.

His lips curved as he stood back up. "I had it sized to one of your other rings." A flicker of guilt crossed his face, chasing away the smile. "I've actually had it for a few weeks now…I just wanted to wait, you know…" He shrugged, glancing at the fire as the words trailed off.

Her chest tightened. "Until you made it through a night without the dreams. I get it. But even if you woke me up a dozen times every night, I still would've said yes. I love you, Brett."

"And I love you." He bent down, retrieving the glasses and handing one to her. "To finding our way back to each other."

The plastic glasses produced a hollow tap as they touched the rims together.

She tipped her glass back, savoring the sweet bubbles. *Had the love of her life really just asked her to marry him?* Extending her hand, she stared at the engagement ring. Yes, it was there—capturing the flickering golden light of their fire in its brilliant depths.

He clasped her hand, running his thumb across her knuckles as he pulled her closer.

"I can't believe this is real." She moved into his embrace, her feet sinking into the damp sand. His head lowered, and she rose on her toes and lifted her face to his.

His lips brushed against hers with tender restraint, sending a series of tremors rippling through her. Then he deepened the kiss, claiming her with his mouth and tongue until her insides threatened to ignite.

Her knees wobbled as they parted. "You are literally sweeping me off my feet, Staff Sergeant Leeds."

He chuckled, catching her around the waist with one arm. "We'd better sit down, then. I have another surprise for you." Gesturing toward the blanket, he smiled over the rim of his glass as he swallowed some champagne.

"What?" She held her own glass steady as she lowered herself onto the blanket. "You can't be serious."

Flashing her a secretive grin, he refilled their champagne glasses. Then he dug around in the cooler and pulled out wrapped sandwiches and plastic tubs.

"Are these lobster rolls?" She drummed the balls of her feet into the sand in an excited stationary dance as she peeled off the wrapper.

"Yes, they are," he confirmed, setting plates and utensils on the blanket.

She bit her lip as he handed her a fork. "Oops. Putting out the food was supposed to be my job. I guess getting engaged distracted me a bit."

He laughed, sinking onto the blanket beside her and opening his own sandwich. "I'd have been concerned if it didn't. Any good?"

She speared a giant chunk of lobster from the overstuffed roll, popping it into her mouth. *Oh, wow.* "Yes, it's fantastic. You really went all out. Another wonderful surprise." She dug around for another piece as he piled coleslaw onto their plates.

"Well, I can't exactly take credit for the food. I mean, I did procure the stuff for dessert, but that's pretty much make-your-own s'mores. Everything else I ordered from Rose's. But this isn't the other surprise." He dragged the bag with extra blankets across the sand and pulled out a small package wrapped in red tissue paper.

She flushed. Another gift? This was all too much. "Brett, you've already given me the perfect night, not to mention a diamond ring." But she set her plate down to accept the little present. Inside the tissue, a silvery rectangle gleamed in the firelight. A business card holder. Inscribed with the name "Dr. Emily Leeds."

"For when you become a vet," he explained.

She nodded, wiping at the tears gathering in the corners of her eyes. Down near the water's edge, a pair of tiny shorebirds searched the tide's offerings for food. She watched them forage, struggling to compose herself. "Thank you." Her voice was a thready whisper. Clearing her throat, she tried again. "This means a lot to me."

He rubbed the back of her neck. "It will happen someday, Em. We'll figure it out. I'm willing to separate from the Air Force, if that's what seems best for us. Having an EOD background makes me highly employable outside the military as well." Dropping his hand, he motioned for her to eat. "Hey, this is still a celebration, remember?"

Nodding, she gave him a shaky smile. "I'm just overwhelmed. I didn't realize I could be this happy." She struck away the last of the tears and picked up her plate. "So, would you still get to play with bombs if you got a new job?"

He grinned, lifting his lobster roll. "Oh, probably. But much less so than if I was overseas. I'm good at my job, though," he added, biting into his sandwich.

She scooped up some coleslaw. "I believe you. You definitely proved how calm you can stay in a dangerous situation during the Joe ordeal. That couldn't have been easy."

His jaw tightened. "It was hard not going after him right away, especially after seeing…" His voice trailed off as he stared into the fire. "But staying with you and Ty after the attack was what I needed to do to keep my family safe at that moment. I'm just glad I had the opportunity to get him later." He turned toward her, tucking an escaped curl behind her ear. "I'll always do what has to be done to keep my family safe."

The word "family" sent a thrill of happiness surging through her veins. She glanced down at her ring again. *Still there.* "Wow. We're truly going to be a family, now." A smile twitched at her lips as she took a sip of champagne. "What do you think about expanding that family, someday?"

He lifted his brows, his eyes shining in the falling shadows. "Another baby? Nothing would make me happier." His hand crept beneath her sweatshirt and settled on her waist as a roguish grin spread across his features. "In fact, let's start working on that tonight."

She laughed. "We should probably wait until we're actually married. Do things in the right order, for once."

"I think we've done okay, all things considered. We had a lot of obstacles in our way." He drew her closer, turning her chin toward him with the tips of his fingers. The fire warmed her cheek as he captured her lips in a series of lingering kisses.

Breathe. "We did." She studied his face in the firelight, running her thumb along the stubble of his jaw. The last of the sun's rays had vanished, leaving a chill in the air. She shivered.

"Cold?" Brett pulled another blanket from the bag and draped it over her shoulders. Leaning forward, he stowed their trash and the leftover food and poked at the fire with a stick. Sparks spiraled into the darkness as the burning wood popped and crackled.

She scooted closer to the flames, holding out her hands to catch the shimmering heat. "That's better."

He wrapped his arms around her, falling backward and dragging her with him. "How about this?" he asked as he settled the other blanket over their bodies.

"Even better." She curled into his warm embrace with a contented sigh. A half-moon hung in the sky, framed by a few wispy clouds.

He threaded his fingers into her hair. "Don't forget we have some marshmallows to roast, too. And lots more champagne to drink."

"That sounds good. Although lying here and watching the stars come out sounds good, too." She tipped her head back, reaching for his hand as the first few pinpricks of light pierced the endless black canvas overhead.

"We can do both. We have all night." He pulled her closer. "In fact, we have forever."

A word about the author...

Kathryn Knight spends a great deal of time in her fictional world, where mundane chores don't exist and daily life involves steamy romance, dangerous secrets, and spooky suspense.

Kathryn writes contemporary romance spiked with mysterious hauntings as well as YA paranormal romance filled with forbidden love. Her novels are award-winning #1 Kindle bestsellers and RomCon Reader Rated picks.

When she's not reading or writing, Kathryn spends her time catching up on those mundane chores, driving kids around, and teaching writing classes. She lives on beautiful Cape Cod with her husband, their two sons, and a number of rescued pets. Please visit her at
www.kathrynknightbooks.blogspot.com

Other Kathryn Knight titles available from The Wild Rose Press include *Gull Harbor* and *Silver Lake*.